T0274113

MORTAL QUEENS

Books by Victoria McCombs

The Storyteller's Series
The Storyteller's Daughter
Woods of Silver and Light
The Winter Charlatan
Heir of Roses

The Royal Rose Chronicles
Oathbound
Silver Bounty
Savage Bred

The Fae Dynasty
Mortal Queens

MORTAL QUEENS

VICTORIA McCOMBS

To Dad—
Thank you for my love of stories.

POWER STRUCTURE
IN THE FAE REALM

MORTAL QUEENS

SEVEN FAE KINGS

THREE HOUSES
(Delvers, Low, Berns)

THIRTEEN LORDS

THREE HOUSE
REPRESENTATIVES

MY LIFE HAS BEEN DEFINED BY
bells. The first time, I got whipped in the square for stealing while
the old brass bells tolled like laughter. The bells were on their final
note the morning I found my mother gone. And when Desmond
kissed me by the celestine fountain, the bells kept count.

They rang now, reminding me I was late. Already, the trumpets
sang from the heart of the island, their low sound reaching the fish
market at the docks. I tripped over cobblestones in my rush to get
home before the ceremony began.

Splinters from the wooden ladder dug into my hands as I
struggled to keep a few squashes tucked under my arms while I
scaled the walls of close-knit homes. Rampant weeds clawed at the
stone and scratched my cheeks, sending sharp bolts of pain with
each movement and tugging at my grip. Some of the squashes fell,
landing with a thud on the ground. I stared down. I hadn't the time
to go back for them. Daven would see it and know I'd been thieving
from his gardens again.

I clutched the remaining vegetables and sprinted across the roof,
flinging myself over the other side. Discomfort rippled through my
heels as they collided with stone on the next roof, but I bit my

lip and hurdled again. Twice more I did this, until I reached the familiar grey-speckled slab of my home.

I stole a peek behind me toward the heart of the sandy island, where caravans of camels packed the outlying streets with their noses pointed inward like they knew what greatness would descend upon us today. For one day a year, one beautiful hour, the magnificent fae appeared. The ache inside me to turn and find them sank deep, and my betraying feet angled in the direction of the governor's house where they would be. Had the three fae ambassadors arrived already? I looked up to the pluming clouds like pillars of sand in the sky, thick enough that I couldn't see through.

The skies could have been clear and it wouldn't matter. No one ever saw the fae ambassadors arrive until they stood at the grand balcony of the center square, overlooking the mortals. I ought to be there already.

It took all my focus to quench my thirst for the sight of the fae for a little while longer, but the Queen's Day Choosing Ceremony was the only event Daven might leave his gardens for. That man's diligence to his crops might have been strong enough to cloud his love for the fae. I leapt over the final roof with what vegetables remained in my grasp.

Thoughts of Daven and his pitchfork fled my mind as soon as I climbed down the iron trellis and pushed through the door. Cal stood in the foyer with his arms crossed and his mouth set firm.

"I'm going to kill you."

I arranged the squashes on the ground and spread my arms wide like a prized treasure, but Cal only gave them a passing glance.

"You could have left without me," I said as I dusted myself off.

Sweet little Malcom stood by the door holding a wraparound dress for me. He wore one shining, emerald earring in his left ear, while Cal wore the other. That left the nose ring for me. It sat in Malcom's tiny palm, waiting for me to put it on.

Cal tapped his foot, sneaking peeks outside. "Next time I will."

"Next year I won't be eligible for selection, and I won't care."

It was a lie, and Cal knew that, but he was kind enough not to say so. I'd always care about the fae. I'd always want a glimpse of them, even if this was the last year I was eligible to be chosen as their new high queen. The desire to be connected to them ran so deep, it might as well have been in my blood.

I shivered with nerves. I'd see them in a minute. My fingers fumbled to slip the ring in my nose and tie the garment over my clothes, hiding my faded purple tunic beneath the fiery silk. Both my brothers wore shades of orange, too, Cal with his stiff blazer and Malcom with his pointed shoes and ruffled top. We'd show up to the ceremony late looking like a scorching fire.

Cal's foot-tapping accelerated. "You act like you don't care now." He nudged my sandals closer with an impatient kick. "I can just see it—you're going to be selected as the next Mortal Queen from the five islands, and you'll be forced to stand in front of the fae with wild hair that more closely resembles a wolf than a girl."

"A very pretty wolf," Malcom said. Our little peacemaker. His large brown eyes were filled with none of Cal's worry.

I straightened Malcom's collar. "I could be a wolf. Makes me sound dangerous." But I raked my fingers through my hair all the same, and tried brushing smut from my hand before realizing it was paint from this morning.

"Thea." Cal held the door open and inched out. Our father's figure appeared from farther down the hall, tall and narrow, unlike a gnarled tree but with a morality just as crooked. Cal mumbled something about us being the only family still in our home followed by something that sounded suspiciously like, "I'm the only one with good sense."

Father took in the sight of us.

"You're late." Father's voice was warm as fresh tartlets and smooth as the gown beneath my fingers. But his eyes, pale slits, were his downfall, pools of ice that refused to hold warmth. He leaned his body against the far wall with one foot crossed in front of the other.

I tugged on the straps of my golden sandals and coiled them up my calf before tying a knot. The slit in my dress allowed the shoes to peek out. "I know, it's my—"

The sound of silvers clinking together froze my tongue.

Father grinned. He held a burlap sack, swelling at the edges, and dropped it atop my squash. Coins trickled out and rolled across the floor. "We'll eat well tonight." Father's voice seeped triumph.

The silk trickled to my toes as I stood and stared at the money. Even on this island, where everyone had wealth overflowing their purses, that was a lot. And for us, seemingly the only ones struggling for funds, that would last years. For a moment—fleeting, no doubt—we were rich.

Whatever bet he'd made, he'd won this time.

"A hoard such as this makes whatever Passions would earn look weak," Father stated, biting on a coin. I braced myself for what always followed his off-handed remarks about Passioning.

Sure enough, sweet Malcom tugged on my hand. The pang that shot through my heart was the same as always as I looked at him. "Can you not Passion?"

The words were stones cutting through my insides. "I have to." *I want to*, I'd never say. But the thought rested near the surface, and someday he'd see it. Choosing my Passion tomorrow and studying painting would be the first time life allowed me a chance to sculpt my own path through the five islands, and one day Malcom could follow.

We were bound to the island we were born on until we turned seventeen and could Passion, unless we were one of the few lucky girls chosen by the fae first. Tomorrow, my chances of being chosen would be gone, and Cal and I could Passion. As soon as the sun rose, we'd dedicate ourselves to three years as apprentices to our chosen Passion—painting for me and academics for him.

"Everyone has to Passion," Cal said with only a hint of steel to his words, directed at our father, who was inspecting the silver. I knew it was only our father's extensive battle training that kept either of us from his neck. "Just as everyone is meant to attend the Queen's Day Ceremony."

Father's eye twitched as he watched us, as if he'd set a trap and now waited for the bait to work.

I had plans of my own, and his money would help that. Tonight, I'd steal some of his recent loot and stash it below the boards with the rest of the pile I was saving for Malcom to survive on after Cal and I chose our Passions tomorrow. Next week, Father could place another bet and lose it all—but he'd always go back, drunk on his game of luck and foolish wishes. When I followed my Passion, I needed to know Malcom would be cared for.

The thought of leaving him here on the center island, built for battle and betting, made my stomach tighten. It was a rich city, but a ruthless one, and our father's determination to have one of his children Passion as a soldier would multiply when only Malcom was left. Our little brother would be in the arenas before the sun came up every morning with a blade in his hand.

Cal and I survived the merciless training, and Malcom would too. I wouldn't Passion as a soldier and remain here. I felt as if I'd been fighting my entire life. I wanted to stop.

Trumpets sounded.

Cal tugged my arm. "We need to leave if we want a decent spot. Are you coming?"

Father plucked a fistful of coins and let them drop one by one with elaborate deliberation. "Go. I'll see you when you return."

Cal tucked Malcom's hand into his and stepped into the dusty courtyard to make way for the street. I paused at the door. "Are you certain you don't wish to come? This is my last year eligible."

Never mind that all the other girls had every relative surrounding them like a flock to cheer them on. That every other girl had been doted on all week to exemplify her beauty in preparation for today.

I didn't need a flock. My mother couldn't cheer from the grave, and my father was not cold-hearted enough to wish his daughter not to be chosen. Though, to stand by my side wasn't why I asked. I wanted to unravel the mystery of why he was the only one in the five islands not drawn to the presence of the fae.

I studied him as his eyes fixed on the glint of silver between his fingers. He'd given the same answer as every year, and this year it carried more enmity than usual. "I won't go. I don't care for them."

"But why?"

I'd hardly said the words when his head snapped up to lock eyes on me. "Thea. Stop. I will not."

I will not speak on it.

I will not explain.

I will not see the fae.

It was all I'd ever get. His sharp words sliced the air with hints of stories untold. Before I could pull the door shut behind me, Father added a new string to his usual answer. "Although, I'm very invested in this year." A coy smile played on his lips, and it gave me an uneasy feeling. The way he said "invested" didn't rest well.

"You made a bet on Queen's Day."

There was a gleam in his eye. "The best kind there is. I bet you'd win."

The breath was knocked from my lungs. Out of all the girls on the center island, my odds of being selected were miniscule. One girl was chosen as the fae's new high queen. One girl, her name plucked from a large bowl. There was no way to guarantee the outcome when there were *thousands* of names to choose from.

I couldn't win. The odds were too low.

But those same odds made betting on the new queen-to-be this island's favorite gamble, as well as the most foolish. As often as my father bet, he'd never been this reckless. I clenched my teeth to bite down the anger. "How much?" I steadied myself for his answer.

"Everything."

"You fool!" I spat. "You absolute fool. I won't be chosen." Angry tears heated my lids, but they were only a sliver of the fury writhing inside.

Trumpets called again. I couldn't wait any longer, even if I wanted to. The fae were here, and the desire to see them couldn't be dimmed. I turned away, taking my fuming malice with me.

Father's voice came. "Goodbye, my child. When I see you again, you'll be a queen."

I turned back and saw him stare toward the sound of the trumpets, while his pale eyes filled with a clarity I hadn't seen on him in years. He let out a long breath. Then he closed the door between us.

I hurried on, hoping my pace could strip his words off me. He'd been like this for half my life, making bets and collecting winnings. Losing everything the next month. Providing us with the finest clothes one day while hardly buying food the next. We would go from being the richest in all the five islands to hardly scraping by, and while Father claimed it built character, it bred resentment much faster.

Dust licked my sandals and filled my mouth with its dry texture. The sandy roads felt smaller than usual, almost choking me between polished stone gates. Ahead, Malcom laughed atop Cal's shoulders. I debated telling them about Father's recklessness for only a moment. Today was special, decked in free sweets and a glimpse of the fae. It shouldn't be ruined by foolish fathers.

Life would change for someone today.

The fae ambassadors came once a year to select their new high queen, a mortal girl to rule in their realm. She'd be swept into a world so beautiful, it made the stars weep, or so the stories went. We'd see her at next year's Queen's Day Choosing Ceremony, then never again. She'd be lost to us, but she'd be royalty among the fae.

It was a life I'd always dreamed of, even grander than that of a painter's apprentice. *But you won't win.* I was reminding myself of that now, burying the words between the hopeful beats of my heart, the way I always had to on this day of the year. *You won't win.*

I passed under the golden sparrow-tailed banners that swept from pillar to marble pillar, and the growing roar of the crowd drowned out the hissing wind. Cal finally paused to let me catch up, then we melded into the throng.

The excitement of the day wafted from everyone around us. Cal said something in my ear, and Malcom's smile dimpled his cheeks.

"I knew we wouldn't be late." But Cal didn't act like he'd heard me.

We were lucky we lived so close to the governor's house. The rest of the island traveled across the desert from outer cities to bring their daughters here today. Though they were luckier than those living on one of the other four islands. The fae only selected a queen from here.

"It's because you are stronger," my mother had said. "The center island grows strong girls." She was gone before I was old enough to be chosen, and she never got to see if I was strong enough or not.

She'd been right, though—the girls here were strong. And loud today. The courtyard outside the governor's house was packed, fig trees shaking as bodies pushed in around them from all sides. Our backs squeezed against the wall.

Rows upon rows of raised seats stretched as far back as my eyes could see, all filled with eager girls and their promise-giving families. Four aisles paved the way to a mounted balcony under the shade of the governor's building, where the three beings stood in all their untouchable glory.

Everyone adorned themselves in their finest, but none could outshine the fae.

Three fae poised on the balcony—tall, young, and painfully beautiful. One with dark hair that curled at his shoulders, skin pale, and cheekbones high. Eyes that said he had a secret worth dying for. Another had layers of silver fabric hugging her curves, chiseled by a generous hand. Her white hair shimmered as if it had captured the essence of the moon. And the third, he was the most intriguing. A strong jaw, thick brows, black jacket, and a stance that said he owned us all.

How could a mere mortal hope to rule over people such as this? I shivered.

Then there was the peculiar detail the fae never failed to appear with—the masks. Each wore one. It moved as if one with their skin, covering most of the forehead and partway down their cheeks, leaving openings for their eyes and their mouths fully exposed. They'd never been seen without them. If anything, the masks magnified their beauty, tempting us with what might lie underneath.

I reached to squeeze Malcom's hand, needing an action to let out the excitement bubbling inside me. Wind flittered through the crowd, carrying harsh sand with it, but nothing touched the fae. Not even one hair trembled.

Behind them stood Gaia, the captain's daughter who was selected last year. She'd changed in such a short time, her skin now glowing and the muddy hair that once struggled to reach her collar now rippling down her chest. She wore a mask, too, one of pure white. Hands folded in front of her as she stared straight ahead, even while her family called her name from below.

Musicians dressed in purple robes played lyres for the fae, who watched politely. They'd practiced all year for this one performance. Tomorrow, they'd begin work again, preparing their piece for next year. Only the best for the fae.

I'd hear them practice on my next island. Their Passion was one of the arts trained on Ruen, along with painters like myself. Perhaps we'd sail across the sea together tomorrow after I Passioned.

When the last flute lowered, the silver fae stepped forward to let her sweet voice captivate us. "The fae realm is honored to visit the five islands once more. You are such a humble land filled with quaint delights, and the girls you offer as our new queens bring us such joy. Our High Queens are most loved in our realm." She glanced at Gaia, as did the other two fae. I saw the adoration in their eyes. How cold their gazes appeared when placed on us, but how they softened at the sight of their queen beside them, and that one look stilled me.

Imagine, to be adored by the fae.

Long ago, when the five islands were connected by bridges, a general loved the fae so much, they visited him to honor his devotion, and he was able to forge a deal. He himself couldn't go to their realm, but they needed a queen, and thus the ritual of selecting one lucky girl each year began, starting with that general's daughter. With the close friendship came the exclusivity that the girl came from our island, and the bridges between the lands were torn down.

"Jealousy burns quicker than fire," my father would say. "And it burns much hotter."

The silver fae continued. "We thank you for your previous queen, our marvelous Gaia, who will now be joined by another."

The history tale always left one thing out—the mysterious reason the fae could hold a mere mortal in such a position of honor above them. And they must have many countries, to need a new queen every year.

The energy in the crowd shifted as she spoke. The fae's voice, though it had nothing to project it, settled over us with power. "The next Mortal Queen will come to the fae realm to live as one of us in our splendor. Her family will be sent a pension as a sign of our deep gratitude."

The island was rich. It needed no pension. But Cal caught my eye, and I knew we thought the same thing. Malcom could live on that pension. If I could live among the fae while simultaneously ensuring Malcom's security . . .

You won't be chosen. Still your wishful heart.

But my father's confidence picked at my resolve not to hope. He'd sounded so certain.

Cal gazed past me, and it was easy to guess whom he searched for. Eliza stood several meters away with red-painted lips, rubies glued to her forehead, and delicate diamonds coating her eyelashes in a way that looked angelic. She flashed Cal a hopeful smile.

She was a year younger than us. One more year of eligibility. If she won, that'd be good for her family of many brothers and sisters, who would be well sought after. Siblings of the selected were like royalty in the five islands, the closest we could get to being related to the fae. If I were selected, my brothers would have good prospects.

The dust itself settled to hear the ambassador's next words. I found Cal's hand and held it tight. *"Tritshu un kuy,"* he whispered. He spoke in the language our mother created. *May he favor you.* I repeated the saying to him.

An ornate bowl sat before the ambassadors. The silver fae's

billowing sleeve collected at her elbow as she dipped her fingers in. She didn't dally with shuffling. She picked a slip of parchment from the very top and held it close.

Her voice trilled over the still crowd. "The fae have selected their next Mortal Queen. Althea Celeste Brenheda, will you rule over us?"

I tried to breathe but I couldn't. My vision blurred. The land buzzed around me while all I could see were the smiles of the three fae as their eyes swept over the crowds. Searching for *me*. I might never move again. I'd live right here, forever immobilized by the way the silver fae's lips had formed my name.

The explosive cheers of the center finally dragged me to reality. Malcom screamed loudest of all. Cal hugged my shoulders, and that hug was the only thing anchoring me to the ground.

Father had been right. I was chosen.

Cal nudged me and somehow my feet moved. The crowd separated to make an aisle. Remembering Cal's words, I pulled my hands through my hair as quickly as I could to tame the mess.

The walk to the balcony took eons. I passed thousands of girls, all who'd spent hours getting ready, with their polite smiles masking disappointment as I tripped by. All the while, the fae stared down at me. I'd never felt so small.

Gaia stepped forward to take my name from the fae's hand, as was customary. She was to place a kiss on the paper to bless me as I joined her in the realm, but the fae slid the paper into her pocket instead. Gaia hesitated and her hand shook before she stepped back into her statue-like position.

Next year that would be me, standing like a copper behind gold.

I made it to the stairs and ascended without falling. The fae ambassadors were even more magnificent up close. Not a blemish on their skin. They regarded me from behind crisp masks, and I tried to hold my chin up so the first look they got of their new queen was one of strength. It was all I could do to keep from trembling.

"Althea Celeste Brenheda," the silver fae repeated. A diamond crown with three thin, sharp points rested in her hands. She lifted it above my head. "Will you rule us?"

I pulled my shoulders back, hoping my mother's old dress did me half the justice it had her. "I will."

The center cheered again, but I hardly heard it. There was one sound that rose above it all. As they placed the crown on my head, the bells tolled.

2

THE WORLD MOVED FASTER THEN,
as if it had been holding its breath for that very moment.

The silver fae gripped my hand in her cold and rigid fingers, raising it above my head. All I could focus on was the weight of the crown paired with the weight of my disbelief. I looked at Gaia. She remained void of expression.

The silk of the silver fae's dress brushed my arm as she said something in my ear.

"What?" My voice was hardly audible.

"Your home?" she pressed over the victory music. I guessed I wouldn't be hearing them practice for next year's ceremony after all. The next time I would hear them, they'd be playing for me when I returned.

"My home?"

The silver fae exchanged a look with the dark-haired fae. The third remained a statue beside them, looking more like a king than an ambassador. "We need to return to your home to get some things in order before we take you to our realm. Do you have a home?" I didn't miss how she took in my unkept hair.

"I do." I pushed confidence into my voice. "I can lead you."

That was always the extent of the ceremony. The fae appeared, we worshipped the fleeting sight of them, then they took a new girl. Officers would hold us in the square for several minutes, then let us loose into the streets where we'd talk about how majestic the fae looked, this year's selected, and what the fae realm must be like. But this time, the fae didn't disappear from my sight. They followed me into the governor's hall to the front door.

"I don't live far," I said.

They gave no reply. The trio walked in a line behind me along the streets, where the sun beat down on hanging sheets that cast shadows over our path. Gaia kept her head low and hands crossed over her silky, pink dress.

The silence allowed my thoughts to run untamed. In a matter of hours, I'd become a part of the fae world. I'd sit on a throne of gold or silver, I'd eat food so delicious I could cry, and I'd be revered by beings who held more power in their finger than I did in my entire body. I'd be a queen.

We had no queens in the five islands. That honor was reserved for the fae. Reserved for the select few—a group I now belonged to. I'd be welcomed into a sisterhood of Mortal Queens.

I tried to remember the girls from the previous years. Portia, Tris, Ivory. Years of muttering their names served me when my memory did not, until I'd dredged up twenty queens of years gone by. Soon we'd be reunited.

Fig trees bent at the will of the wind, almost bowing to us as we passed. The ambassadors trailed their eyes over our island with the faintest of frowns. The center island was the richest of the five islands, and even that wasn't enough to impress ambassadors from the fae realm where they say jewels run like rivers through the sky. And soon I'd see the realm I'd only heard of in stories.

Gaia was nearly at my side.

"What is it like?" I whispered.

She twisted a ring around her finger as we walked. Her white mask hid many of her features, but it didn't cover a tattoo of a crown like bleeding gems on her forehead, right under her hairline. Her blank eyes kept on the streets as our feet kicked up dust. She breathed the words, "It's like owning a beautiful world you can never be a part of."

We'd always said the fae realm was beautiful, but this was the first time someone from there had confirmed it. But Gaia's words carried a shroud of pain spooled so tightly, I wasn't certain where to pull to start unraveling. So I withdrew.

"I live just over here." We passed Daven's home, where the stolen squash still rested beneath the ladder. That moment felt so far away now. I pushed back the iron gate to our small courtyard where Cal's and Malcom's sandals were kicked off at the doorway. They must have run ahead.

Tears formed as a new realization bit me. Being queen meant losing them. The privilege came at a steep price, but the reward was Malcom's security and a life with the fae. It was a painfully joyous trade, one I'd forever celebrate and eternally mourn.

It was with that hallow thought that I entered my home.

"Thea!" Malcom jumped on me and the crown wobbled on my head. Malcom's hair tickled my cheeks, and his breath warmed my neck as it had many times before. I held tight, closing my eyes against the world for a moment.

Cal stood more composed at the end of the hall, where whisps of light caught in his curls and gleamed from the earring in his ear. His sweetheart, Eliza, stood at his side with her hand woven around his arm. I didn't know why, but I guessed she was holding him up. Without her, he'd crumble.

Losing my twin brother was the steepest price I'd pay for a taste of the fae realm, but the painful part was knowing it would hurt him more. I'd be fine. I'd be with the fae.

My woven bag sat at their feet, already full. My paintbrushes poked through the top. I carried Malcom down the hall as the fae assembled behind me. "You packed for me?"

Cal shook his head. "Father."

My brow wrinkled. He'd truly known. I searched for him, but the arched stone halls of our home were empty. I'd find him before I left and demand an explanation.

Cal rubbed a hand under his glossy eyes. "I'll go fetch him. Saints know where he's wandered to." Eliza let him go, sending me a soft ghost of a smile. I promised myself I'd find time to speak with her privately before I left, to be certain she held things together in my absence.

The air stilled, and we all turned as, one by one, the ambassadors' presence filled the entryway, their steps quiet and their backs tall.

The silver fae came first, her steady gaze sweeping the hall, landing on none of us. The dark fae came next, and his eyes did find us, soaking in each face with an expression of such composure and ease, that for a moment I thought we were in his house and not my own. The third came last, stiff and straight, planting himself close to the door and setting his jaw firm.

His gaze never left mine.

I blinked at the sight of them *in my home.* I'd painted the fae many times in many places, but this was one place I'd never envisioned them. Gaia stood like a meek cat at their side, rolling her ring between her fingers.

"We need to discuss some things before you become our queen," the silver fae said. "First, your mask."

I lifted a hand to my cheek. "Do I have to wear one?"

The masks were beautiful, much like something we'd wear for the yearly masquerade. Each one different in its design, and each equally striking. The way it moved with their expressions was curious, like it shared a mind. The masks left generous room around the eyes, but that wasn't what unnerved me. If I put one on, I'd look like one of them, instead of like myself. A new realm awaited me and a new life. Now a new face.

I wanted something familiar.

The dark fae produced a satchel I hadn't seen before. I wasn't entirely certain he hadn't pulled it out of the air.

"Always," he replied. My chest fell, but he didn't appear to take note as he opened the bag. "Guard it with your life. It is a powerful thing to know one's true face. Never reveal it if you don't have to."

The odd wisdom hung in the air, waiting for me to absorb it.

"You three have seen my face."

He paused, gazing at me as if seeing me for the first time. His eyes were so dark, I might get lost if I looked too long. "We are remedying that now. In our realm, this mask will be your shield. Select a color."

I kept a hand in Malcom's as the fae held out his. Five masks sat in his grasp. One more golden than the sun. One as dark as his eyes. One pure white. One blood red. And one striking silver.

My hand led me to the second one. "That one."

His jaw twitched. "You're certain?"

I nodded. It had been my mother's favorite color. "Black."

He pinched the corners of his mouth but set the other masks back in his satchel. "As you wish." His hands grazed my hair as he lifted the mask to my face. It felt very much like putting on a shield. Like this was my weapon, my guard against the world, yet I was so vulnerable beneath. It had no strings to tie but sat on the bridge of my nose lightly without falling off. When he let go, it molded to my features perfectly.

Then it heated slightly and felt curiously like it was settling into my skin.

My hand flew to my face, but the edges of the mask were still there. "Can I take it off?"

"If you desire. It will feel as natural as if it were your own skin, but you can remove it whenever you wish. Again," he said with emphasis, "you should *never* remove your mask in the presence of anyone."

The dark fae kept his voice low and trailed his attention over the curves of my mask. "How interesting." His words were a whisper filled with curiosity. Now that the mask was on, he studied me freely, but it was the mask he was looking at and not me. "Black is an odd choice."

I didn't care to unveil that I'd chosen it solely because it was my lost mother's color. "Does it matter which I picked?"

The silver fae was ferociously scribbling on unfurled parchment. Now I knew they were pulling items from somewhere unseen.

"Each color reveals a trait of its wearer. White speaks of inner beauty. Silver"—he indicated his own mask—"of knowledge. Red is for reckless bravery. Gold for vanity. All virtues common for a queen. But black? Black is for mischief. I've been making the masks for Mortal Queens for hundreds of years, and you are the first to select black."

He tipped his head. "It also means fear. I wonder which one you are."

Afraid. Very afraid. It was a healthy fear, the type that realized these creatures were unlike anything I knew and I'd be counted as weak against them. Among the anticipation and desire for a taste of their world, that fear kept me grounded.

"She's strong," Malcom's young voice chimed in. He looked up proudly. "My sister will be a great queen."

I smiled, but there were tears in my eyes.

"Her earrings," the silver fae pressed. "We must go."

The dark fae almost seemed apologetic as he fetched something new from his satchel. "You might want to let go of the boy's hand, lest you crush it."

My eyes widened in understanding. I let go, but Malcom held on. "I'm strong too," he whispered.

The fae held an earring to my ear. I clenched my free hand at the sharp pain as he pressed the needle through the soft flesh. The gold-crusted earring hung from my ear with a small chain at the bottom, only three links long. Pain throbbed at the spot.

Then he pulled another earring from the bag. I was beginning to hate that satchel. At my expression, he pressed his lips together. "You must wear seven," he said. "To show your status."

He wore five in his own ear. I'd outrank him by two earrings. That meant nothing to me. The pain came again as he inserted the second. He punctured my ear four more times, until inserting the final ring into the hole already punched through my lobe. Malcom squeezed my hand tighter with each stab. By the time all seven were in, tears freely fell down my cheeks and marks were left in my palm from my nails. I exhaled. "Is that all?"

"Yes, my Queen."

The title was enough to make me forget the pain. *Queen.*

"You will receive a proper tattooed crown at the coronation. One that will never fall nor fade," the silver fae said. I looked at Gaia's tattoo. Her eyes fell to the floor once more. What did that white mask stand for? Inner beauty? It certainly wasn't bravery.

"The last thing." The silver fae brought the parchment to me and handed over a quill with a feather as black as the ink. She pointed a thin finger to the line at the bottom. I scanned the document as well as I could, but the swirly writing was not easily read. "It's directions for the pension. You must sign it to someone here on the island."

Her words gave me pause. "Do they have to be on the center island?"

She nodded. "We only deal with the center island."

I lowered the quill. "Can I sign it to a child? Or to someone born on the island but pursuing a Passion?"

"No. An adult, living on this island alone."

My fingers trembled with the decision. I couldn't give it directly to Malcom. Eliza wasn't of age yet. My father would bet it all away. Cal was pursuing his Passion on one of the other five islands tomorrow.

The decision was impossible, and I prayed my brother wouldn't hate me for the one I made. I wrote a name and signed my own below it.

She glanced over it. "Very well. Are we ready?" Each of the ambassadors looked at me expectantly. Malcom's hand tightened harder than it had when my ears were pierced. His lip quivered.

We all knew the honor of being selected as the next Mortal Queen. Thrill seeped into our voices whenever we spoke of the fae realm and how lavish it must be. We all fantasized over the fae every time they visited. To be chosen—this was as good of a fate as I could ask for.

But no one spoke of this. Of leaving behind your family.

"No," I told the fae. "I will say goodbye first."

"Of course, my Queen." She inclined her head. Her silky

hair swept over her shoulder. "We will be outside waiting for further orders."

Just like that, I'd given my first order.

My father appeared down the hall with Cal leading the way. He paused to look me over. While Cal kept himself as rigid as ever, Father's stance caught me by surprise. He smiled oddly and sucked in a breath. He let it out slowly. "You look like a queen already."

3

I WAITED FOR GAIA AND THE ambassadors to step outside before turning to Father. "How did you know?"

"If I'd known, then my bet wouldn't have been legal." There was a glint in his eye and a steadiness in his hand as he flipped his favorite gold coin through the air. It was a motion of confidence, but I knew better. He did that when he was nervous. I eyed the fae outside, whom Father had not looked at directly, perhaps the only beings capable of making my father uncomfortable. Now that they were gone, his collected demeanor returned. "We can afford to eat lobster every day of the week now. But you, my lucky daughter, will be dining on food much finer."

"Father made a bet that I'd win. A lofty one," I explained to Cal.

His eyes narrowed. "That's a foolish bet."

"I told him that."

Father didn't appear wounded by our lack of confidence. "I won."

"But how?" I repeated. I motioned to my bag. "You knew."

He wore his crossed arms like a shield. But the playfulness fell from his voice. "Be careful. You are not ready for a realm such as theirs."

"No," I said. "I don't need another lesson." I'd grown up on his lessons, mornings of fighting and evenings of puzzles. Little sayings he'd recite with no apparent meaning. He was good with calculations, which was why he usually succeeded when betting, but giving straight answers? Never. "You wouldn't take those odds without knowing something."

"I'm serious, Althea." Father stepped to me, the thin grey tunic making his eyes look like a storm that settled on me. His toes touched my bag with how close he stood. "You must be strong like I taught. Being High Queen will challenge you, but if you can be smart, you'll rule well."

"That's not an answer."

"I can't let you go if you aren't ready."

The thought of him keeping me from the fae realm sent a jolt through me. Even though he had no choice now. I planted my feet and raised my chin. "I'm ready."

He stared at me a long while. "You look just like your mother." Just before his hand brushed mine, he pulled himself away, ducked under the doorway, and left. My desire for him to return caught in my throat, as my stubborn pride said to let him go. I'd never learn how he knew it'd be my name in the bowl, but he'd never hear me beg for an answer.

Malcom filled in the space he left, and I clung to his curls, staring at the place where my father had gone, realizing he never said goodbye.

When Mother went missing a few years ago and Father had been unable to find her after months of searching, he'd fallen into a silence that lasted four months. When the silence broke, the betting began. He said it made him feel close to her, which I could never understand. Mother was so different from the man he'd become.

Malcom stilled a moment. "I'll be back." He released my hand and fled the room.

I had a final chance to speak with Cal alone as the clock on the wall seemed to tick louder. My moments with them were fleeting. "Cal, they are giving our family a pension when I leave."

"They always do. Are you excited? Ruling the fae is all you've spoken of since you were a girl and mother fed you all those stories. Remember how disappointed I was when I found out only girls could be selected?" His rough hand reached to my ear to touch the gems. My ear was like fire against my head, and I could only imagine how swollen it was. "She hadn't mentioned this though." "Is it painful?" Eliza peeked over Cal's shoulder. She could hardly look at the tender skin.

"I'll survive." I gave her a little smile, then turned back to Cal. Seeing him—bronzed skin and copper eyes that shone with our promising futures—I could hardly bear to tell him what I'd done. "Mother didn't mention the details of the pension, either. It can't go to Malcom. It can only go to an adult who remains on this island."

It took a moment for the information to register and he tensed. His eyes dropped to the floor. It wasn't fair that my triumph should come at his loss.

"Can you really not trust your father to watch him?" Eliza asked.

My father could lead legions in battle if he was called upon. My father could out swindle the smartest man. My father could likely walk across the desert barefoot and not be burned if he put his mind to it.

He thought his children were the same way.

He forgot we were small and fragile. He forgot we needed care. Cal and I didn't need a father anymore. But Malcom did.

Cal swallowed before speaking. "I'm uncomfortable leaving him for too long. I'll stay."

I exhaled. "Good." I smiled gratefully and admitted, "I already said you would. I'm really sorry."

"I'm an adult next year—I'll stay with Malcom then," Eliza offered. "You can sign the pension to me while you study mathematics."

"One year." Cal nodded. "I can handle that."

That would leave Malcom with Eliza for three years while Cal studied. And put a great deal of faith in their relationship enduring. Beyond that, academics weren't like painters—they were sent to whichever island needed them. I wouldn't know where they'd end up after Cal finished his apprenticeship. I wouldn't know how any of their stories ended. This moment in time, this was all I'd get. Whatever happened to me, whatever happened to them, our tales were no longer intertwined.

I struggled to speak. "You take care of them," I told Eliza. "Malcom is sensitive and innocent, and Cal can get so wrapped up in work that he forgets to eat. Please take care of their gentle souls."

She squared her shoulders. "I will."

The patter of Malcom's feet silenced us. He flung himself around the corner with a toy in hand and held it out like an offering for me. One of his soldier men—the typical toy for a child on the center island where strength was valued above all else. Its left arm was broken from when Malcom was younger.

"Your favorite soldier?"

"Antonio will be your guard when you feel scared." He rolled it from his palm and into mine. The cool metal of the tiny soldier pressed against my fingers and I closed them around it.

"It's perfect. He and I will have quite the adventure together."

Malcom grinned, but his eyes glossed over. I picked him up in my arms. "Don't be sad. I'll see you again." Outside, the fae bumped against the door. "I'll come back each year, especially for you."

"We only see last year's selection," Malcom said though a pouted lip.

"Well," I said as Mother used to, "that's because the other girls are so in love with the fae realm, ruling with a handsome fae king and living lavishly. They no longer have taste for our world. But that won't be me. I'll always love the five islands. I'll be back, little one." I put as much confidence into my voice as possible.

"*Uhnepa te,*" he said. *I love you.*

"*Uhnepa te,*" I repeated. Cal wrapped his arms around us until we were a ring of affection squished so tight, my mask pushed against my cheeks. From the side, Eliza tried my mother's language on her tongue as well. We'd taught her for a few years, but she couldn't get the dialect right. I'd thought Mother was silly for creating a language no one would know aside from us, but it became a token of affection to speak it, even more so when she was gone.

She'd be delighted if she were here today. This was what she spoke of more than anything, and she'd always been so that determined I'd be chosen. While the rest of us were battling tears, she'd be the one singing through the halls and reminding us what an honor this is. Telling tales of the fae realm as if she'd been there, while her late parents could attest to the fact she had not.

I let some of that excitement seep into me, if only to feel her once more. It wasn't hard to summon. The world that had been closed off from us would now be mine, and I'd soon see if the tales were true.

I tried to show none of my eagerness as my brothers stepped back, only the bits that would fiercely miss them. Each of their eyes were brimmed in red. Cal found his voice first. "Go ahead. Go be queen of the fae."

The soldier toy, Antonio, clinked against my paint brushes as he fell into the bag before I picked it up, and the rest of the house sat quiet as it watched the spectacle. I almost couldn't move.

You are leaving them with a generous pension and great marriage prospects, I reminded myself. *This is the kindest thing I can do for them.* Still, my feet were heavy as they led me to the door.

I stole one last look. "Take care of them." Eliza nodded and, satisfied, I twisted the brass handle and stepped back into the warmth of day.

The ambassadors waited in an arch. Gaia stood in the center with a slight tremor in her leg and scanned the courtyard with the first real sign of life today. The dark fae placed a hand on her shoulder to steady her.

The third fae, the silent one, took it all in with an unblinking eye.

"With your permission, my Queens," the silver fae said. She reached for me with fingers adorned with ruby rings. Each ruby was larger than anything we had on the five islands, and they belonged to someone ranking two earrings below me. I could only imagine the glamor of the life I was about to enter. "The fae realm eagerly awaits its new Mortal Queen."

4

"TAKE A LAST LOOK AT YOUR WORLD.
You won't be seeing it again," the silver fae said before we left.
She raised her hand. I opened my mouth to counter that I'd be
back next year until I realized she'd been speaking to Gaia. Gaia's
breathing quickened beside me, but she said nothing.

The fae might not have meant me, but I soaked in another
glimpse of my realm: the hunched fig tree in the middle of the
courtyard and stone walls like a cage around us. Bits of dust
collected between my toes to join me on the adventure and remind
me of the home I left behind.

My heart raced faster than the wind.

With a downward strike of the fae's hand, a chariot encompassed
in light appeared beneath our feet. My fingers curled around a
golden crossbar, and solid gold surrounded us. The yoke wasn't
attached to any animal, but rather a sliver of sparkling wind that
twisted through the air with a jittery energy.

Without prompting, the chariot rose into the sky.

I braced myself for the change in motion but remained as steady
as if planted on the ground. The treetops fell away, and when I
looked down, the entire brown island sat below.

My stomach lurched. Gaia's hand touched mine.

"You'll get used to it," she promised. Then she pulled her hand back and swept that blank expression on once more.

The sky stretched out in a sheet of turquoise and white.

"Welcome to our realm," the dark fae said as we reached the clouds. My brow furrowed. There was nothing here.

At that exact moment, the world exploded. My land peeled away, and the sun extinguished. All that remained was darkness and inexplicable beauty.

My world had been one of heat, sand, and sunshine. Even if it hadn't been, no land could have prepared me for the fae realm. All I could think was how the stories didn't come close. I had no control over my awed expression or the sudden lump in the back of my throat.

It was the most glorious night there ever was.

No moon hung in the sky, but white stars clung to black that blanketed as far as I could see. They had islands here, too, but these didn't sit on the ground as one might think they should. Instead, floating masses of land spread throughout the sky, packed with vibrant buildings and lush growth. I'd never seen so much color in one place.

A shimmer caught my eye. "The river of gold," I breathed. It ran off the edge of one island, gushing into the darkness below. I leaned over the side of the chariot. The gold water ought to fall onto our land, but our land was nowhere to be seen. I'd spent hours staring at the sky and never expected to witness such splendor just beyond our clouds.

Chariots much like ours soared through the skies as if the stars themselves were roads. Hundreds of these chariots lit the distance between the lands.

"Does a different Mortal Queen rule each island?" I asked Gaia. What I could see of her cheeks paled.

"Do you hear the cheers, my Queen?" The dark fae pointed over the crossbar to the island we headed for—one as large as the home I left behind and bursting with narrow, pointed buildings constructed from marble and lit with lanterns. It was a beacon of light against the night. The buildings opened in the middle, where a castle encompassed a grand courtyard with trees thicker than any fig tree and swollen with fruit. Before our chariot soared near, the chants reached our ears. "They cheer for you."

Their voices were melodic, and intertwined with each other like a song. I caught only one word repeated over and over among the others. *Queens.*

The air around the island was coated in chariots, all facing the courtyard. All waiting for us.

The wisp of wind guiding us floated in circles around the chariots from afar, teasing them before drawing near. We descended as the roar grew louder. A stone circle paved the center of the courtyard with an image of a crown identical in design to the one on my head painted inside, while the fae kept to the grass, leaving the stone open for us to land upon.

Before we did, the three fae ambassadors positioned themselves in a tight circle around me. They blocked my sight, but I suspected the intention was to block me from the other fae's sight.

The sparkling wisp directed us down, and the chariot met the stone.

Through the slit between the silver fae and the quiet one, I watched Gaia straighten and raise a hand to the crowd. They cheered for their queen. She stepped off the chariot and stood on the stone.

The silent fae lifted his voice for the first time. "Are you ready to meet your next Mortal Queen?"

Cheers thundered.

"I present to you, High Queen Althea Brenheda."

They split in unison like a veil, thrusting me into full sight of the world.

I straightened my neck until the skin was taut, hoping I looked regal and not wolf-like, as Cal had teased. The gold beneath my feet gave way to the stone pavement, and a crisp wind caressed my arms. The fae before me came in many sizes and were bedecked in all colors, but one thing remained true for each—they were as stunning as the ambassadors. Smooth skin, striking eyes behind half masks, and smiles as lethal as they were charming. Even if my dark hair grew as lush as Gaia's had, or my lashes thicker over my caramel eyes, I'd only be an ounce as magnificent as them. They looked stunning for being hundreds of years old.

The fae lifted goblets of deep red wine in approval. Without any cues, I stepped next to Gaia.

Across the courtyard near the castle sat a dais with six figures atop it, so still I thought they were statues at first instead of six men, each with broad shoulders and narrow bands circling their foreheads. They wore gold masks and sat on elaborate thrones.

"Who are they?" I whispered to Gaia.

"The six fae kings," she answered quietly. "We outrank them, but never think they aren't as deadly as they are beautiful."

I tried to remember what the ambassador told me about gold masks. Gold meant vanity. Did they have faces to be vain over, even among a world of fae such as these? The urge to peel back their masks and see for myself grew so strong in that moment, I could think of nothing else.

I tore my eyes away with difficulty. *Deadly as they are beautiful.*

I looked behind me, expecting to see a mirroring dais with the other Mortal Queens. There was nothing but the expanse of bodies and marble walls of the pristine castle.

"Where are the Mortal Queens?" I asked. I'd pictured them greeting us in their fold or dining at a banquet with them later. But Gaia only shook her head.

The silver fae approached with a torch in hand. The scent of burning oil wafted by as she passed it to Gaia. Gaia took the torch and crossed to the side of the stone circle, where a pole was set with cloth wrapped around the tip.

She posed by the torch. Her silver heels peeked from her dress to reveal rings on her toes that reflected the red flame. "I am honored to be your chosen Mortal Queen," she declared. "And am delighted to share the throne with another. Together we will rule you well." As the fae clapped, she lit the lantern.

Then she passed the torch to me with a nod over my shoulder. A second torch, unlit, stood at the opposite end. I took the flame there while its heat licked my skin.

The crowd hushed, and I panicked in search for words. "Thank you for choosing me to be your new Mortal Queen," I said. That didn't feel like enough, so I added, "I will devote my life to being worthy of the role." I glanced to Gaia for her approval. If they wanted me to do or say a certain thing, they might have offered me a warning before throwing me at the mercy of the fae. If I had to scramble for more words, there was no telling what might come out, and I didn't want to accidentally declare a war or whatever else Mortal Queens might have the authority to do.

It must have been enough. They cheered as I held the flame to the cloth until it burned in brilliant oranges. The silver fae retrieved the torch. "Well done. That is all the fae need from you right now."

A figure broke from the crowd to hold her hands out for us. Three earrings, I noted without knowing why. A cream dress hugged her thin body, and her mask was white. If any others wore a black mask, I hadn't seen them.

Gaia followed her, and I trailed behind through the crowd, which split for us then and turned away.

"That's all the fae are permitted to see of you for now," Gaia explained. "They only get one sip, but tonight they'll feast their gazes upon you at your coronation."

My last look at the ambassadors was of the silver fae approaching one of the torches and taking a slip of paper from her pocket. She threw it into the flames and guarded the post until the parchment was fully burned. She caught me staring and held my gaze for a moment. I swore there was a warning in her eyes.

The dark-haired one still watched me like he was waiting to see what I may do. The girl who chose the black mask.

I couldn't ponder on their strange actions because in the next step we broke from the crowd and came directly under the dais with the six fae kings. Each masked gaze bored into me as they sat. A couple of the statuesque fae were fair-skinned and polished with chiseled jaws and icy eyes. Others were darker and cloaked in intrigue. I lowered my face before getting a satisfactory look and held my breath when passing them. At the end of the platform, a seventh throne sat empty. It was built of black iron with twisted ivory up the back, sharp spokes on the top, and curled legs designed into snakes. Lanterns cast shadows over the vacant seat.

As soon as we were far enough away, I risked speech again and leaned in to Gaia. "Where is the seventh king?"

She peeked back to the haunting throne. "He's been missing since before I first arrived."

The arched doorway opened and the castle welcomed us with the scent of citrus. The floors and walls were an unblemished white, but the ceiling was an array of diamonds that sparkled despite there being no sun to bring them to life.

The area split into two, with a river running through the center.

"The east and the west," Gaia said. "I rule in the east, and you will rule the west." At my frown, she added, "It means nothing other than which side of the palace we are on."

"Where do the other Mortal Queens rule?"

She cleared her throat. "Carlene will take you from here." Her shoes tapped against the floor as she withdrew to the east, leaving me with the certainty that something was amiss. As soon as the echo of her steps died, I faced Carlene.

The girl who stood before me had green eyes behind a red mask. "Are you ready for your room, my Queen? You are to be kept until your coronation tonight."

"Where are the other Mortal Queens?"

"I'm not to say."

Gaia had avoided the question too many times for my liking. No one ducked a question three times unless there was something worth hiding. I tightened my grip on my bag and pushed authority into my voice. "Can I order you to answer?" Unease stirred inside at pulling rank already, and the girl set her jaw. She spun on her heel, and her hair whipped behind her. Apparently, being five earrings above her in rank didn't qualify me to receive answers.

She strode over the bridge of the river, forcing me to follow. The trickle of water sounded loud against the stillness of the castle. As we crossed the room, the walls widened, and the roof opened to a chandelier above. Behind us, the courtyard began to empty, the fae climbing aboard their chariots and gliding through the sky, while the stars winked like they held secrets.

Perhaps they held Gaia's secrets and knew where the other Mortal Queens were.

We came to a wide stairway with banisters of ruby and emerald. At the top, Carlene paused with a huff, as if she spoke against her better judgment. "You cannot ask anyone questions. Information comes at a price, and no one will give it willingly. The only free wisdom I give you is this—the next time you ask something, be certain you are willing to trade for the answer. And be certain you know what you are trading away, my Queen."

Unprompted, my father's warning came to mind. *You are not ready for the fae realm.* Mother coated it as rich and fulfilling, but Father's lip would curl up at each story, and he never daydreamed over it with us. Suddenly, I wished I'd paid more attention to his grumblings than Mother's stories.

What a day. Becoming a Mortal Queen and wishing I'd listened to Father. Both equally surprising.

My mouth opened to ask another question, but I quickly closed it when Carlene raised a brow over the tip of her mask. Not trusting myself to speak, I nodded.

Cal would love this. He loved puzzles. So far, this realm had offered me a few.

The stairs led to a hallway longer than my eye could see. Thankfully, we stopped at the first door. Carlene pushed it in. "This is where you'll stay."

Mother's stories of the rooms were some of the best. Entire chambers for baths with fountains in the center. Sleeping in beds of feathers and silk under the stars. Walls of fire that kept occupants at the perfect temperature, whether they needed to burn hot or cold. My personal favorite included platters of chocolate-coated berries.

Carlene stepped aside and I blinked.

There was no fire. There were no berries. There was nothing aside from three men clad in emerald-buttoned long coats, standing in an empty room.

"What is this?" I asked before realizing that was a question. Carlene sent me a look.

"Choose one." She kept by the doorway while I stepped farther in to survey the scene. The walls were lined with lanterns, but that was all. There wasn't even a single window. I eyed the door for a lock. This was closer to a cell than a bedchamber.

I stared at her, then at the men. The situation was beyond my understanding, and no matter how I placed my words in my head, I couldn't form anything but questions.

"My name is Thea," I began, hoping to get them to speak. "It's a pleasure to meet you."

The one on the left nodded, and a twist of tightly coiled red hair toppled across his forehead. "Thomas of the House of Berns. Friends to all, and enemies to none."

At this point, I wasn't certain they were speaking the same language as me, because nothing they said made sense. The middle one cleared his throat. "Caedmon of the House of Low. We are known as warriors and academics alike."

I wished I could give the proper reaction, but my mouth hung slightly open as I sifted through everything I'd heard of the fae realm. What was going on?

The third straightened and tilted his head back. His chin came to a little point between wide jawbones and sat beneath sharp cheeks. His hair matched the shade of cotton, far from resembling mine, but his eyelids rounded at the top just like Cal's and, for a second, I'd found a hint of home.

"Talen," he said. "From the House of Delvers. We are the richest of the Houses and have been aligned with King Arden's bloodline for centuries."

"Thieves," Caedmon whispered.

"*Rich* thieves." Talen wore a ghost of a smirk.

Then they looked at me, and the pit in my stomach grew. "I don't know what I'm to do with that information." It wasn't a question, but my tone begged for answers.

Carlene delivered. "You enter our realm as our queen, but you come with nothing." She ignored my packed bag in my hand as I glanced toward it. "Alliances are everything. This will be your first one, and unlike future alliances, this one is binding. Whoever you choose, they and their House will be aligned with you. They will gather things for your room, connect you with other alliances, steal secrets for you, whatever you need."

She said it so simply, as if that made perfect sense. The three waited for my answer with polite smiles.

"I'll take whoever can get me a bed," I said. They all chuckled.

I sighed. The first said his House had lots of friends and no enemies. I'd need friends here. But having no enemies spoke of weakness. Only powerful people incurred enemies. As queen, I didn't want to set myself up as weak. My eyes glided over him to the next.

Warriors and academics. I'd had enough of warriors while growing up on the center island. But rich thieves . . . my attention went to the third. Something in that sounded promising. Plus, his resemblance to my brother soothed me, and that alone made the choice worth it.

"Talen."

Thomas drew his lips into a dangerously thin line, and I hoped I hadn't earned him his first enemy. Caedmon took the decision better with a polite bow. "My Queen." He stepped from the room.

The doorway was massive, yet Thomas practically pushed against me as he passed. "Be careful with that one," he muttered. Then he was gone.

Carlene was bowing. "Very well, my Queen. May your alliance serve you well."

She left me with Talen, who stood stiffly until the door closed.

Then his entire demeanor relaxed, and he clapped. "Let's get you that bed, shall we?"

My next breath came easier. "Yes, please."

He tapped a long finger against his pointed chin. "I say we put the bath through that wall, and a sweeping balcony over here, with roses sculpted into the balustrade. Should we open the ceiling for you? I can hardly breathe in here."

I dropped my bag by the door as he knocked on solid walls. The room wasn't tiny, yet he measured the marble with his hands as if preparing to plow through it. "Can you do that?" I asked. "Make rooms where there are only walls?"

He gave me a quirked smile. "Not me, but then again, I'm very rich. I can make it happen."

"Right, rich thieves."

"I will answer to that, if you forget my name." His energy filled the room. "And don't worry if you forget how rich I am. I love reminding people." His fingers went to his light hair, and he tugged on a piece as if in thought. Four black earrings hung from his ear.

With a start, I realized he was the first person I'd seen with a black mask like mine.

He clicked his tongue. "If there's anything particular you want, you should tell me now."

A fire wall sounded ludicrous, so I abandoned Mother's stories. My own room back home was nothing but a bed and a chest for my art supplies. The tips of my brushes still poked through my bag. "I'd love some canvases and paints."

He stroked his chin. "It will take a day, but consider it done. Anything for my queen. Is that all? You can ask for anything."

That word *ask* hung between us like a trap. My eyes narrowed. "Carlene told me never to ask anything."

His expression split into confusion before he made a little noise in the back of his throat. "That was slightly deceptive of her. You and I are aligned now, which bars me from tricking you into any deals or favors. But tonight you must be on your guard. Anyone wearing this lapel are now aligned with you." He tapped the blue pin at his collar of a snake wrapped through a dead tree. "The trust of others will be at your discretion."

"That sounds . . . exhausting."

"It gets worse. It's in your best interest to align yourself with others. Some nobles would be a good start. A king would be ideal. The more powerful the alliance, the more power you hold. Understand?"

I collected the information in my head. I knew being queen was more than fine wine and handsome suitors, but the seriousness in Talen's tone suggested alliances were far more important than I understood. "What exactly are my tasks as queen?"

He folded his arms. "Keep the kingdom alive. There is a power here that everything survives on, and in order to keep your kingdom alive, you must in turn be powerful. It seems simple, but it's not."

He was wrong. It did not seem simple.

Thankfully, he elaborated. "When you create alliances, solve riddles, or make strategic choices, the realm is pleased. In return, it grants your kingdom power. This keeps the soil healthy, buildings strong, and you in a good position. Too many alliances and you are seen as weak. Fall prey to trickery, and you lose power. Curate favors and you have the power back. It's a delicate game, but you mortal girls always play it well."

I thought of Gaia and her quiet demeanor. Was there more to her than I'd guessed? What games did she play?

Talen crossed to the doorway. "If your stream of questions has come to an end, allow me to prepare you and the room. The coronation is tonight, and I want to show off what an alliance between a Mortal Queen and the House of Delvers looks like."

5

MY SEVEN EARRINGS WERE REPLACED
with heavier ones, and my ear throbbed under the weight. Talen
acquired a healing balm to soothe the irritation, claiming it would
work in ten seconds. It took seven.

"Was that magic?" I wondered.

"Science," he replied, reclosing the lid on the jar. "If it's magic
you seek, you'll get it soon enough." Then he turned back to help
with the setup of the chamber.

I was certain I'd seen some magic already, as there could be no
other explanation for how he'd transformed the plain white room
into something so glorious. Talen instructed the fae behind us as
they converted the space. Sure enough, he found fae powerful
enough to move the walls to create a room where the floor gave way
to water to form the largest bath I'd ever seen. The sweet scent of
lavender floated through the archway. In the main area, rugs were
rolled over the floor, windows appeared in the walls, the ceiling
was lifted, and a canopy bed, coated in what Talen swore was the
finest spun silk in all the realm, was set in the middle. If I holed up
in the comfort of bed for months, he said he wouldn't blame me.

A girl with white hair and lustrous skin strolled into the room.

"She's to get you ready," Talen ordered me, hardly pausing his work long enough to look my way.

I sat still as her hands moved quickly, curling my hair for the first time until it lay in soft ringlets and not wild tangles, then pinning a crown atop my head. "The pins are here and here," she showed me. "You'll take them out at the coronation to trade this crown for your eternal one."

I winced. The tattoo of a crown imprinted on Gaia's forehead was stunning, but it was also very intricate, and I didn't love the idea of needles so close to my eyes dealing with delicate skin. "Will it hurt?" Crying in front of the fae would be a terrible start to my rule.

She brushed rouge on my cheeks. "Not in the slightest."

"There," Talen said from the side. He laid his hands on the new curtains that a slender fae had positioned over enormous, open windows, their midnight-blue color speckled with diamonds shimmering in the moonlight. He then flung the fabric upward until it billowed out like a river, the diamonds letting loose some sparkles until my room appeared caught in the night sky. "Perfect," he pronounced. "It's perfect."

"A queen hasn't chosen to align with the House of Delvers in ages," the girl whispered, eyeing Talen as he slipped through an open partition to another room, where dresses had been appearing by some unseen will. "He's excited."

"Did I make a good choice?" I asked. Talen had been nothing but helpful so far, but I couldn't ignore the surprise on his face when I'd chosen him, or Thomas's warning.

She shrugged. "It was an interesting choice, but everything about you has been interesting." She dabbed gold powder on my eyelids. "Just a bit more, then you are ready."

I pulled my head away. "What do you mean it's been 'interesting'?"

She pursed her lips as she clasped golden bands around my arms. I'd been put in a dark red dress with a low back and high collar, and in tall shoes that would make walking difficult, but all my focus right now was on her answer.

"Please," I pressed. "I feel like I'm drowning in confusion in this realm."

She relented. "The circumstances surrounding your selection were unusual, that's all I know." Her gaze roamed over me. "Perfection. Fairest queen we've had in ages."

Ages could mean a few years to me. *I haven't had a pastry this good in ages. I told you to sweep the courtyard ages ago.* I suspected it meant hundreds to a fae.

She bowed. "She's ready," she declared to Talen before leaving.

Except for dressing, he'd watched me get ready, but I appreciated how he pretended to be seeing me for the first time. "You are stunning. You'll attract the attention of the kings for certain."

A ceiling-high mirror rested on the wall nearby, and I caught my full look. Three rings in my nose, bands on my arms, crown on my head, and gorgeous red dress. I'd looked over myself many times at home pretending I were the Mortal Queen, but this was real.

I could only hope to be worthy of this role I'd acquired—somehow. "Talen, how did I get selected?"

He pretended to pluck a name from a bowl. "Thea, please be our queen. We desperately need you."

I shook my head. "No, the girl said the circumstances were unusual."

Talen's hand dropped and he put on a thoughtful expression. Once again, I was struck by how similar he looked to Cal, and the pang of missing my brother throbbed again. "That's all I know," Talen promised. "There have been rumors, but I don't know more than she does. What I do know"—he flashed a grin— "is that we are going to be the talk of the realm tonight."

He'd dressed in a gold tunic with the emblem of a crown that was impossible to miss, his honey complexion complemented by the firelight as he leaned near the hearth. If he'd told me he was nobility, as opposed to a rich thief, I'd have believed him. He looked as much like a king as I did a queen. He held out his hand to me while his eyes gleamed. "Are you ready to meet the realm?"

I raised my head high. "Ready." He opened the door.

The hall outside my rooms was empty, but not quiet. Melodies from a lyre drifted through the crisp air in a tune that made mortal instruments sound flat. I pitied the musicians who trained for a year for their one piece. Only three seconds of hearing this song and I knew my homeland music could never compare to this.

Laughter echoed up the staircase from below where the realm waited. A great, black curtain was strung atop the stairwell for me and Talen to stand behind. He straightened his jacket more often than I fidgeted. "Tonight will be perfect," he whispered and winked.

I faced forward. A fae with dark locks stood at the cusp of the stairwell, and as soon as we were in position, he lifted his hand and the lyre paused. The room hushed to such a silence, and I feared they'd all vanished and abandoned their new queen.

But then a voice boomed.

"For centuries we have depended on our Mortal Queens to rule us." I wondered if the other Mortal Queens would be here as well, and I'd finally meet them. Or if I'd finally learn why the fae agreed to let a mortal rule them in the first place. "Tonight we welcome a new queen into our fold." He gave a dramatic pause. Talen adjusted his jacket once more.

"Welcome, High Queen Thea."

The sheet was pulled back with such force that wisps of hair danced across my face. The room erupted into cheers. Just as earlier, they were dressed in satin attire, heavy jewelry, and joyfully shouted my name. Talen's sturdy hand lifted beneath my trembling one to guide me down the long marble stairs.

I wished Cal and Malcom were here to see this.

At the far end of the room, the river met at two thrones, Gaia's and mine. High Queen of the East and High Queen of the West. The seats were ten times as elaborate as the fae king's thrones. These stretched almost to the ceiling and demanded all to worship whoever sat atop them. I'd look like a child in such a thing—small and insignificant. Gaia sat in hers already with a stiff back and tight lip contrasting the bored expression in her eyes.

I did a quick sweep for the other queens but found only a sea of

MORTAL QUEENS   41

fae spreading throughout the throne room and into the courtyard. I thought I spotted the band of a fae king but couldn't be certain. If the kings were here, they weren't given a seat.

At my feet, a red rug ran along the west side of the river for me to follow. A woman with silver braided hair waited at the end of it. By some mercy I didn't trip in my shoes and made it to the front safely. Talen bowed and took one step back until he was at the front of the crowd, where he held his head proudly.

"My Queen," the elderly fae woman said.

For a fae to look as old as she did, she must have been around since the start of the Mortal Queens. The corners of her eyes wrinkled with pleasure. "We are delighted to honor you tonight."

I bent to my knees.

They didn't require much from me. I removed my crown and held my head steady. She drew the new crown on my skin in black ink with a silver pen in swift movements that left no more than a tingling sensation. The dark tattoo would match my mask well. Now I'd have a band around my forehead, with dainty detailing like a tiara imprinted forever upon my skin, so all would know that from this point onward, I was a queen.

Her soft hand cupped my chin, lifting my face to hers. A slow smile came to her lips. "You may sit."

My knees straightened. The throne towered behind her shoulder, summoning me. I hesitated.

This morning I was a girl stealing vegetables from a garden. This moment didn't feel real. It was a dream I'd soon wake from.

But the touch from the old woman was very real as her hand pressed against my back. "It is yours, my Queen," she murmured. "Take it."

My footsteps echoed in the large hall as I took one, two, three steps to the threshold of my throne. I gathered my long dress in hand and swept it to the side before lowering myself onto the seat.

The cold of the stone armrests against my sweaty palms felt unnatural. I kept to the front of the throne so my feet could touch the ground, leaving a chill to travel down my back, matched by a shiver of excitement. Or perhaps a shiver of nerves. The two were becoming impossible to differentiate. My first breath was shallow, and the second was almost impossible to take.

You have dreamed of this since you were born, Cal's voice reminded me in my head. *You can do this.*

Just like that, my third breath came deeper, and the dizziness in my head cleared.

At my feet, the crowd roared. It was enough to make any girl feel adored, but all I could wonder was why creatures such as these, capable of moving walls and creating rooms with a click of their fingers, said to have built the stars themselves, would ever need a Mortal Queen. I may be their ruler, but I wouldn't forget for one second that every creature in this room was stronger than I was. Except perhaps Gaia.

The elderly fae took great effort to bow. With her next line, my position was sealed. "Let a new reign begin."

The music restarted. Talen drew near to the side of my throne and stood tall. "Stay here for a few minutes," he said quietly. "Let them get a proper look at your beauty before you form strong alliances tonight." He folded his hands in front of him and stared down his nose at the others.

"How important is it that I make friends?"

"Your reign depends on it." He placed a hand over mine. "But not at this moment. Take a few minutes to breathe first. Then dive in."

I tried to look in control on a throne so large I could hardly reach both sides.

"Who did Gaia align with?" I asked under my breath.

"Initially? The House of Berns. You remember Thomas, right? Pleasant chap. You are much better off with me. They try to keep her quiet and hidden. Me, however? I intend to show you off."

Gaia had been quiet when I met her. It didn't occur to me it might not be by choice.

She might be quiet, but the rest of the room was not. The party extended beyond the grand hall and into the courtyard where chariots still danced through the sky that had yet to show anything other than brilliant stars. "What time is it?"

"Evening," Talen replied.

"I never saw the sun."

"We have no use for such crassness. It steals all the beauty of night."

I tried to fathom such a thing. "Well, you might not need one, but it's practical. How do you tell time?"

I didn't care for the bemused way he looked at me. "Clocks."

"Oh."

The room was a chorus of faces turning to me then looking away, the throne room surrounding us yet keeping the two thrones in their own bubble of space. I desperately wished to know what they spoke behind their hands. While the realm was a flurry of activity, this was the first moment since being selected that I rested, and the day caught up with me. My thoughts that had been at bay now seeped in, reminding me how unprepared I was for this role.

"Can you get me something to drink?" My voice clawed from my throat.

Talen bowed. "I'll fetch you the finest spiced wine."

He melted into the sea of fae, leaving me exposed on the throne. Gaia continued to keep so still she might not be breathing. I watched as her head tilted slightly toward my throne then moved back.

I slid to my feet. I didn't care to look anything like she did right now. A statue set apart from the realm.

My feet hitting the floor was like an invitation to swarm me, and bodies pressed to mine. The first to reach me was a button-nosed gentleman with sleeves rolled at his elbows and five earrings collected on his left ear. He offered a soft hand for me to descend the stairs. "You are truly the most beautiful queen we've ever had."

He spoke loud enough that Gaia must have heard.

I lifted my skirts away from the river right by us where bright fish circled. "Thank you."

He stepped with me. "How are your rooms? I possess the finest wools and would be honored to offer one in an exchange for my friendship." At my look, he held up his hands. "Just a wool, nothing too grand. A soft wool for my beautiful queen to adorn her room with."

Before this, Malcom and Mother were the only ones to call me beautiful. That number had doubled already, and it still sounded odd when directed at me. *Pretty words are used to cover pretty lies,* my father would say. He was often right. "Just a wool?"

"It's only a wool." His mustache twitched.

I wanted to say no. I wanted to turn away from the person whose presence reminded me of my father, but my father was powerful, and his friendship was often sought after among the generals of the five islands.

Your reign depends on it.

"Alright," I said. "I accept the offer of friendship."

He broke into a broad grin. "Splendid. I'll have a wool sent to your room." He backed away just in time for Talen to appear at my side.

"Wine." He handed me a goblet. "I see you're braving the realm."

"Trying to. I'm here to make friends, right?"

"Alliances," he corrected. "Friends are far less useful."

I took a sip of wine. The deepest, lushest, earthiest flavor swept over my tongue, and I let it sit for a moment before it slid down my throat. I immediately took another. It held a rich, fruity aroma in each drop. My reflection stared at me through the copper ring of the goblet. A wine this fine would cost more than my life back home.

As my goblet lowered, a woman appeared before me, lifting her draping skirts in her slender hand, a lithe smile on her face. Talen waved her off. "No, Ginny. We don't want your kind. Go away." Her mouth opened, but he shooed her off again. She dropped her hand and sulked away. Talen glanced at me, a twinkle in his eye. "You're welcome. You have no idea what I saved you from."

I took another sip of the glorious wine. That was all I trusted myself to do at this point.

Two tall fae were watching, but their eyes met Talen's and they slipped away. "I think they are scared of you," I said.

"Good." But he eyed me. "It won't do if no one approaches you. Can I trust you on your own for a bit? I'll go put in some good words for you, secure friendships that can lead to alliances."

I caught his sleeve before he could leave, ignoring the looks we invited at the touch. I turned my back to the other fae to whisper to Talen over the brim of my glass. "What will an alliance do for me? I don't understand."

He leaned close. "Sometimes very little. But a good one? That will ensure you power. People are waiting to decide how strong you will be, and that all depends on whom you align with."

"But why? Are we at war?"

His grin was sly. "Not with armies. Think of it more like an elaborate game of chess that never ends. Your goal is to be the one with the most power."

The queens held the most power in chess, yet I felt more like a pawn that was sacrificed with the first move.

Talen placed a hand on my shoulder. "Trust your instincts, and never forget you have more to offer them by your title." He said it so simply, but I couldn't quite grasp the importance of these alliances. As if he saw that, he added, "You'll find your time here to be lonely without those bonds. Can you manage this?"

I didn't want to appear weak. I nodded. "I can."

He exhaled. "Alright. Remember, don't do anything rash."

That covered a broad subject of things, but I would do my best.

I filled my lungs with a breath of confidence to face the fae on my own. I noticed Gaia now observed me from her throne. If I were to struggle tonight, I didn't want her to witness it. My feet sank into the thick red rug as I headed outside before someone could speak to me, and I swallowed another deep breath. I followed it with a gulp of wine for good measure. My arms brushed many fae, but most watched me silently with looks I couldn't discern.

A cheerful smile stretched beneath one of the fae's red masks. "Is our wine to your liking, my Queen?" he asked in a kind tone.

I'd been holding my goblet like armor in front of me and I relaxed a bit. "It's strong," I said. Most of the wine I'd tasted came from Mother's old cellar when Cal and I used to sneak in at night to steal a sip and talk.

"That it is." He laughed, then turned to continue walking with me, keeping a polite distance and an eye on those around us. "I have wine finer than this at my home." A silver cloak hung from his broad shoulders, and grey stubble adorned his cheeks. "I live on an island where water falls from all edges, and the streets are built of rivers. All the Mortal Queens have visited."

Unprompted, my father's voice in my head warned me. The strap of my shoe dug into my ankle as I inched away.

"I'd love to paint you," the red-masked gentleman continued. "I've been painting my entire life, but the Mortal Queens are my favorite subjects."

His tone was kind, but something about him scared me.

Talen's advice to make friends combatted his advice to be on guard. There may be a way to tell if this man sought friendship or trickery. I tested him. "I adore painting as well. Perhaps we could paint together in the courtyard sometime."

He spun a finger on the rim of his own cup. "It'll be much more enjoyable at my home."

The voice to be on guard won. I narrowed my eyes at his insistence. "What happens if I say yes? It's a trick, no? What mischief are you up to?"

His chest fell. "A clever queen. Had you said yes and allowed me to paint you, a piece of you would have been trapped in my painting."

My eyes bulged.

He shrugged. "You are welcome to come visit whenever you like, and I won't paint you."

All I could do was gape at him as he trotted away. The lyre music picked up as if congratulating me for not falling for the trick, but my shock was stronger than my pride.

"I need you," I whispered to Cal, though he was in another realm now. "You'd excel here." Father would too with his cunning mind. But Malcom . . . I'd be forever grateful that boys could never be chosen to reign.

My stomach rumbled and my attention traveled past the large doors and into the courtyard until it found a vast array of tables, platters of dishes centered around a skewered boar larger than myself.

"These blasted shoes." I sent a silent apology to my tender feet. If anyone asked for a dance tonight, I'd have to decline. As long as my feet carried me to the food, I'd be content.

I almost stumbled, but a swift hand caught me. "Headed for the glazed cakes?" A gentleman slid his arm beneath mine. "A girl after my own heart."

His grip relieved some of the stabbing pain in my feet, so I resisted the strong urge to recoil. "I've heard wonderous things about the cuisine here," I said politely. "I'm excited to try it for myself."

The man had golden hair to match his mask and a towering height that I dwarfed beneath. His steps shortened at my words, and those bronze eyes landed on me. "How is it that you heard things before you came here?"

I chided myself. Admitting my fascination with these beings wasn't how I'd wanted to present myself. "We spoke of the fae realm sometimes. It was all speculation, of course, but the stories had been told enough that they were accepted as true."

"Ah, I see." He took a few quiet steps. A soothing feeling radiated off him like a hint of fresh air. The only time he touched me was loosely at my waist to slip behind me as we slid past another couple who watched us with hungry eyes. I gave them a little nod, and the fae removed his hand. "And how do we compare to the stories?"

I searched his collar for the pin of which House he belonged to but found none. Perhaps he served a king, instead. I treaded carefully. "Beyond what I'd hoped. If this food is good, then I'll die happy."

I pondered his grin. If he had motives, he'd yet to reveal them. But no one was without motives. My father's words again. "So, you like food and you're beautiful. Tell me more about my new queen."

I sought something innocent to give him and tilted my head toward the sky. "I find I'm rather fond of the chariots here."

He brightened. "I own the fastest chariot there is. Ride with me."

We reached the nearest table, and I paused with my fingers on the tablecloth to inspect him, hoping instinct would tell me whether to trust him. A dash of freckles spread over his cheeks before disappearing under the silver mask. His eyes were pieces of a daytime sky, and his suit was like the beach outside my home, tan and smooth.

The offer hung in the air.

"What is the cost?"

A brow rose from under the mask, but his voice was light. "I didn't think you'd ask. See how quickly our realm turns innocent girls into untrusting queens? The cost is simple—a visit to my home. Walk the streets with me, have dinner, spend a day there. I have a business deal coming, and it'd be good to be seen with the Mortal Queen."

An uneasy feeling curled down my spine, though it was impossible to discern if that came from him or worries over making a bad deal. His gaze intensified, and I stepped back. Unwelcome images of being trapped in a painting made my heart skip a beat.

"Not yet," I said. It was a gentle answer. "I'm not confident enough to make deals." As soon as I said that, I regretted admitting any lack of confidence.

"Very well. I'll be here if you change your mind."

He didn't leave a name before walking off. I sorted through the crowd for Talen, catching sight of fae with hair pinned like horns to their heads, eyes peering over goblets, and men in sweeping coats, but not the gold tunic of my one ally.

This is exhausting. The worst part was, I couldn't know if I'd made the right decision this time. Perhaps an alliance with the bronze-eyed man would have been exactly what I needed, and now I'd lost that. I'd never know.

He wasn't far off. I could change my mind and offer an alliance to oblige Talen in the one thing he requested of me. If I could even trust Talen.

I pressed my hand to my forehead. One day here and my mind was whirling. Whom could I trust, whom could I befriend? What games did they play behind their delicate masks?

You are not prepared for the fae realm.

The strength of the wine tipped down my throat again. At this rate, I'd end the night with no alliances and the inability to trust anyone.

I turned and bumped into someone behind me, facing gold buttons on a black jacket. This new gentleman had lavish dark eyes that bore into me. His mask was as gold as his buttons and so polished that it reflected the stars in the sky above me. But he didn't need his entire face to be seen to show its beauty.

It all rested in those eyes.

I thought I'd seen beautiful humans on the center island, but the fae were like sculptures of perfection I couldn't get enough of. I stared longer than I intended.

The man straightened his cravat with a little frown. "I want to align," he said.

I blinked myself from the daze. "Excuse me?"

"I," he began more slowly, "want to align. Please." His arms rested still at his side, and I tried not to notice how nice his brown skin looked against the black suit.

I fought against saying yes right away. "That's it? Others have offered chariot rides and paintings."

His brow lifted. "Do you know who I am?"

"No."

He peered over my head into the mass of fae. "Your poor choice of an alliance with the Delvers is failing you already. He should have told you."

I made a mental note to find time to go over faces and names with Talen later. The gentleman studied me with such intensity that I looked away for a moment. "This is usually the part in the conversation where you offer me your name," I said.

Dark lashes coated his eyelids. "No," he said with a crooked smile. "This will be more interesting."

Then he was gone like a swift wind, the colors of night blending into the tapestry of the crowd, leaving me longing for one last taste. The second man to leave me without a name, but with a string of curiosity.

The familiar pin of the House of Delvers flashed on a collar, and I grabbed the girl's wrist. "Do you know anything about the man who was just here?"

Auburn hair fell over her shoulders as she looked around, almost spilling wine on her cream dress. "Who?"

"I'm hoping you can tell me. He had a gold mask and was, er, beautiful . . ." I felt like an idiot and released her.

But she nodded knowingly. "Black suit and gold cravat?"

That would have been a better way to describe him. I nodded.

She wore an impressed smile. "That would be King Bastian himself."

"A king?" Suddenly I didn't feel foolish for being enamored by his beauty. *Deadly as they are beautiful.* "I've been warned about him."

Her tone was low. "Let me offer you your second warning. Many have fallen for him with dire consequences. Do not be one of them. His heart has never been cracked."

I drew my brows in. "I don't know what that means."

She sighed. "Mortal girls. It means he's incapable of love. And don't think you'll be the first to crack him."

I stared through the crowd, already searching for him again. Just one last look. Her hand caught mine. The yellow flecks in her irises blazed with caution.

"This isn't a challenge, my Queen. This is a warning. A serious one. Stay away from King Bastian."

6

THE MAN FROM LAST NIGHT HAD
been right—his wool was extraordinary. I searched for the tag on
the corner to find his name. Lord Winster. I sent him a silent thanks
while curling the wool closer. The heat of the fire licked my toes.

Someone knocked on the door. "Come in."

Talen poked his head in. He'd changed into silver cuffs with his
crisp suit the shade of berries that complimented the cool shades of
his white hair. I'd discarded the gown for a relaxed outfit from the
collection he'd brought yesterday and thrown those dreadful shoes
in the back of the wardrobe.

Talen eyed the bed. "Did you just get up?"

I gestured to the window. "It's still dark. It's always dark. I don't
know if it's sleeping time or awake time."

He tapped on a clock that hung on the wall, one made of
wrought iron with bone-white spools. "Awake time, but that's your
call." He pulled back the sheer curtains over the windows. If I'd
paid attention, I would have noticed there were more chariots
riding through the sky than there had been earlier, but I'd been too
distracted by the comfort of the wool and fire.

"Did you make friends?"

I collected my wild hair away from my face to prepare myself for the day. "I thought you said I wasn't supposed to make friends."

"That was a test. You passed. Did you make alliances?"

"No."

He blinked. "No? You didn't make a single alliance?"

I stroked the wool. "I have the start of one, though. Lord Winster kindly offered me this luxurious wool."

Talen inspected it from a distance. "In return for?"

I thought back. "Just friendship, I think."

Talen sat in a high-back armchair and propped his legs up on the footrest, his hand aimlessly searching through the stack of gift baskets I'd been sent the day before, the sheer number of them too many to count. "Think hard. What were his exact words?"

"'It's a token of my friendship.'"

Within a heartbeat, Talen's feet hit the floor and he leaned forward until his elbows rested on his knees. "I've known Lord Winster for a long time, and he always says either 'gift' or 'exchange.' Think again. Did he say 'token'?"

I sifted through the memories until my chest fell. "No, he said 'exchange.'"

Talen ripped the wool from my arms and hurled it into the fire. It crackled with pleasure. "Thea, you beautifully naive creature."

"Talen, you cruel human. That wool was like a cloud." My gorgeous wool turned charred as it burned.

"I am not human."

My gaze sliced to him. "You didn't combat the 'cruel' part."

He shrugged. "We are what we are. Give me your arm." He grabbed my hand and ran his fingers over my skin, holding it close to his face. He turned it over to inspect both sides, then pressed the back of his hand to my forehead. "How are you feeling? More mortal than usual? Like you're about to die?"

My heart sped up. Lord Winster was the only person I hadn't turned away yesterday, and it might have been a mistake. "I feel fine."

"You're burning. Feel." He pushed my hand to my forehead

where it met with fire. I cursed. "He's done this to you. Stay here while I go see what he wants to fix it, and pray to the stars you don't die before I return." He spun on his heel and stormed away.

"Talen." He poked his head back through the doorway. "Thank you for helping," I said. "But if you throw any more of my things into the fire, I'm asking for Thomas instead."

"Thomas was probably the one who gave Lord Winster the idea," Talen grumbled. "To get back at me." Then he left.

Whatever ailed me, it came in full force within the next few minutes. My head felt so thick, I buried it into the pillows and prayed for sleep to steal me away from this pain. I found no relief. When Talen returned, I rolled from the bed with a moan. Talen dropped something with a thud. A second wool, larger than the first, rested at his feet.

"I stole it for you," he said with a satisfied grin.

"Thief," I recalled.

"Rich thief," he corrected.

"Splendid. I shall die, but at least I'll be comfortable as I do it."

"Feeling worse?" Talen asked and I sent him a glare. Whatever was infused into that wool was working fast. Already the effort of standing took all I had, and even then, the floor swayed.

This realm was supposed to be paradise.

I was nothing but a seventeen-year-old girl thrown into a place she knew nothing about, who had clearly been overwhelmed last night. Winster took advantage of my naivete to poison me and even dared to speak of friendship while doing so.

I should feel like a fool, but if my father taught me one thing, it was this—never cry when you can act. I tightened my fist with what energy remained. My voice was dry and only half coated with humor. "My first order to you is simple. Go kill Winster."

Talen's brows shot up, and he grabbed his satchel from the desk. With a brisk nod, he sprang away.

"Wait," I called after him, lurching forward. Talen paused. My humor must not have come through because he seemed quite serious. "You were really about to do it, weren't you?"

He lowered his satchel, noticeably disappointed. "I'd kill anyone you ask me to. This doesn't seem a good enough reason for it, but your orders will always be followed."

I sank back to the bed as my head got thick again. His loyalty was comforting. "Poisoning a queen isn't enough reason? Is this a common thing here?"

He came to put a hand on my forehead. "Do your leaders not do such things? What a polite home you must have had."

I gave an empty laugh. "I grew up on the center island. Polite was not the word to describe those trained for war. But we drew the line at poisoning each other." I heaved a breath. "Am I going to die?"

Just like that, my time as a Mortal Queen would come to an end. I'd forever be remembered as the girl who couldn't even survive her own coronation.

"No. You will not die. As soon as you agree to your first dinner with Lord Winster, you will be healed."

I groaned. "This feels like a second trap."

He sat on the bed beside me. "In a way. Your first dinner is important as queen. It symbolizes who you wish to form a strong alliance with, and now Lord Winster has tricked you into granting that privilege to him. He's a sneaky man. I always knew there was something about him I liked. All you need to say is that you agree, and you'll be healed."

"Or else?"

"You die."

I frowned. "Just speak it?"

He nodded.

"Fine. I agree."

Instantly the dizziness lifted and my head cleared. I buried my face in my hands. "I accomplished nothing last night aside from almost dying."

"True." Talen patted my shoulder. "But luckily you have me. I created many soft alliances with nobles who are interested. Couldn't land a king, but all in good time." He began to poke around my other things as if one of them might poison me as well.

He shuffled through my desk until he found Antonio and studied the little soldier boy. I jumped to take it back.

"That's harmless," I said.

"As you say."

I rubbed Antonio's broken arm. "If we did have a king interested, who would be best to align with?"

"Vern is powerful." Talen now poked at the fire. "As is Brock. We should aim for one of them first."

I set Antonio down beside my paintbrushes. "What of Bastian?"

He froze. "Who told you that name?"

"Bastian himself asked for an alliance last night," I said.

Talen turned slowly, putting down the poker. "His father never aligned with a Mortal Queen. I don't know why he would. And given his reputation, I'm not certain it's wise."

I tried not to look too interested. "Reputation?"

"His heart isn't cracked."

That was the second time the odd phrase was used for him.

"Let's go after the other kings first," Talen said. "Bastian is a wild card I don't trust. He's best left alone." He fetched his top hat and straightened his maroon jacket. "I need to go see about getting your paint supplies. If I were you, I'd walk around the city and meet people before your dinner tonight. This time, try not to get poisoned, will you?"

I held up my hand. "I will do my very best."

"That's all I ask."

He left, and while I should have focused on how I'd get through the night without being tricked again, all I could think of was the fae king whose heart couldn't be cracked.

7

THE CHARIOT CHARTED A CIRCLE
through the sky to offer me a proper look at Lord Winster's
home. This island was smaller with one manor featured near the
edge where cliffs climbed and seas trickled over, disappearing
somewhere below like a river of diamonds. Someday, I'd follow
them to see where they went. Perhaps they'd lead me back home.

The chariot drifted closer. Iron lanterns hung on posts around
the perimeter, lighting the stone pathways through a hedge maze
in the back of the manor. Inside, hundreds of bodies mingled in
seamless fashion. That man must have invited every island in
the realm.

"I wish I could stay up here all night." I ran a finger along the
smooth end of the crossbar, dreading the descent.

The chariot stooped lower in reply. "Traitor," I muttered.

Though I'd been tricked into this evening, I held my head high
as I descended. I wore a cream gown fastened with delicate pink-
and-gold daisies trailing from the shoulders to the hemline, and I'd
traded the high-heeled shoes for slightly lower ones that came to a
point at the toe. These I could walk in. All my mental energy would
go toward steering clear of any foul deals tonight.

Lord Winster stood in the elaborate pillared entrance. His smile stretched wide. "Welcome, Your Highness."

My heels clicked on the stone. His courtyard was not decorated with flowers but with gems that caught the starlight in tiny splinters. A curtain of sapphires hung like a sheet outside his home, making sweet music as the wind played between them.

"I'm delighted to come," I lied. His grin told me he knew.

He opened the double oak doors to lead me into the parlor with amethyst curtains, heavy wools on the floor, and the scent of dry wine soaked into the air. The room easily held a hundred people, all who bowed at the sight of me.

They mostly mingled about a table with brightly colored fruits and dark meat as Lord Winster beckoned, "Eat, please. We wish to welcome you to our realm with the finest things. By the end of the night, I'm certain we can sort out an alliance."

At least he was direct about it this time. He sought an alliance with the Mortal Queen.

"What does an alliance with me give you?" I asked. My finger trailed the skin of a purple apple.

"My family has been aligned with a Mortal Queen for as long as Mortal Queens have ruled." Lord Winster glanced at his guests. "It'd be an embarrassment not to be aligned now." Those around us nodded in agreement. A lady with golden hair circling her forehead laced her arm in his.

I inspected the fruit. The smooth skin showed no impurities or scars, seemingly perfect just as the fae appeared. "And is this always how you forge alliances? With poison and lies?"

I spoke loud enough for anyone to hear. Let him be embarrassed by how he'd tricked me into attending tonight, and let his guests know what sort of a man he was. But Lord Winster only puffed up his chest and beamed as if I'd offered a grand compliment.

"I'm a man who knows how to get what I want."

I held back a shiver. What he'd done to me wasn't a sin—it was a triumph among the fae. He'd tell the tale of how he conned the Mortal Queen into giving away her first dinner with only a few words. The lady beside him tightened her hold on his arm with a lithe smile.

The sweetness of the apple trickled over my teeth with my first bite. I would not be a queen so easily manipulated again.

"What would be in the alliance for me?"

"Land."

Though I tried to keep a straight face, I was certain my bewilderment showed.

Lord Winster plucked a white grape. "As of now, your reach doesn't extend past the Queen's Palace. Even your alliance with the Delvers can't give you more than that. But I can. I own almost as many of these islands as one of the fae kings, and I would give some to you."

I studied my apple, hiding my confusion while pretending to consider the offer.

"The more land you own, the more respect you are given," the woman at his side said. "Land is a good thing."

After she spoke, Lord Winter stepped back to present her. "Queen Althea, this is lady Calliandra, my beautiful wife. And she makes a good point."

They watched me as if expecting an answer now. I should have made Talen come with me, but he'd said something about me only learning the ways of the realm if I went alone, so here I was.

"You won't get this offer from someone else," Lord Winster pressed. "You would have to win your way into land without me."

I drew in my lips. The only downside to the deal was being connected to a man who made my skin crawl and being reminded of how he'd all but fooled me into such an alliance. Would the fae see me as powerful for gaining land or would they respect me for turning down a deal? It was impossible to guess which way their opinions would sway.

"Your Highness?" A girl's gentle hand landed on my elbow. "I brought you a goblet of the finest wine you've ever tasted."

I eyed the white liquid. It was clear enough to be water and filled almost to the brim. Small bubbles drifted from the bottom to gather on the surface.

Lord Winster sighed. "Think on it."

He waved a hand and musical instruments picked themselves off the wall and played for us, a harp plucking its own chords and a flute dancing in the open night's air. My mouth dropped open as Lord Winster and his lady mingled with the crowd. The girl held the goblet while gazing after the lord of the house.

She looked my age, whatever that meant in fae years, and had a button nose over full lips. While my dress carried ribbons of flowers, hers held ripples of leaves, almost as if we'd coordinated the outfits like friends might, but I had no friends here.

"What happens if I drink the wine?" I asked.

The corner of her brow lifted above her red mask. "I wonder, were you always such a skeptic, or have we done that to you already?" Her voice was as sweet as berries, and her smile just as captivating. "It will bring you no harm. I promise."

Did the word *promise* bar someone from deceit? I couldn't remember. "Is it a trick of some sort?"

She let some of the wine trickle down her own throat. Then she held out the goblet again.

"It's just the best wine I've ever had," she smiled impishly. "I stole it from Lord Winster's cellar."

My reflection stared back at me when I took the cup.

"It isn't a trap," she said. She flipped over her wrist. The mark of the House of Delvers was drawn into her skin, a snake coiled in a dead tree. She hid it quickly. "I'm Odette, a friend of Talen's, and he sent me to accompany you."

I relaxed. "To spy on me, you mean."

Odette shrugged as she tossed a lock of her long hair over her shoulder. The gold band coiled around her arm flashed. "He can only do so much damage control. My task is to keep you alive and preferably talk you into an alliance with Lord Winster."

My stomach twisted in knots. Talen thought me to be far more forgiving than I was.

"There's something about that man I don't like," I said. "I can't put my finger on it. It could be those narrow eyes or his curly mustache. Maybe it's how he tried to kill me. Just something inside me wants to say no."

"I get it. But you'll need alliances, and you probably should have garnered some last night. You're our first queen to finish her coronation without one, while others have walked away with as many as seven. You'll be seen as weak without them, and if you finish your first week with only the House of Delvers, the realm will wonder why no one else will align themselves with you."

I looked at Lord Winster. He laughed and tossed another grape into his mouth, fully capturing the attention of his wide audience. If I'd just walked into the room, I'd have guessed he owned it within a few minutes from the way he commanded the eyes of those around him and held his chin high.

He reminded me of my father, back when he was a general in the war. Then the war ended, and Mother was gone. This man was more like my father than my father was now.

I had no interest in being aligned with someone like that, either version of him.

"You might think me weak for turning him down, but I'd think myself weak for saying yes." I took a drink of wine. "I'm not aligning with Lord Winster."

Odette's red lips pressed into a line. "You're being difficult."

I turned my back to Lord Winster. "What if I promised to think about it?"

"Then you'd be lying." The faintest smile touched her lips. "Do things your way. I'd expect no less from a girl who chose a black mask."

I scanned the room for another wearing a black mask, but there was no one. I already stood out in that regard, and now I'd be a Mortal Queen with only one alliance.

"As long as you're just here for the food . . ." Odette nodded toward the sitting room off to the right. A large chandelier lit up the oval area where a grand piano sat in the middle. Leaning against the piano was a large cream canvas with clay jars beside it. I sucked in my breath. "Talen got the art supplies and wanted them delivered here first. You can show off your talent to the realm."

"Talen has no idea if I'm any good," I said. But my chest welled with gratitude.

Odette took the goblet back. "Try not to let him down. With any luck, your painting skills can acquire you respect, which can be as powerful as an alliance."

I looked at her. "My painting skill can carry as much weight as an alliance with Lord Winster?"

"No," she admitted. "But it can lead to new ones. If anything, you can give the painting to Lord Winster as a gift of friendship to soothe the blow of not aligning."

The last gift of friendship almost killed me. But I nodded. "May I?"

Odette pulled her skirt out of the way. "Go ahead. Entertain us."

Wind from the open windows tossed my hair from my face as I strode into the sitting room, letting the dainty music outside lull me into happier thoughts. Masked faces turned to watch me as I ran my hand over the canvas. It was larger than any I could afford back home and was as thick as a hide. Nine clay jars held paints, the oils already mixed for me. Talen had found long brushes with clean bristles as white as sand, but he'd sent my old brushes as well. I chose one of those to have something familiar between my fingers and sat in the provided chair.

I glanced over my shoulder for Odette. She stood with the fae gathered outside the sitting room door, Lord Winster in their midst, all watching me intently.

Entertain us.

I dipped the brush and began.

My fingers itched to paint some of the wonders I'd seen in this world, like the curtain of delicate sapphires outside Lord Winster's home or the golden chariots in the sky or the islands with rivers of gold flowing off them, but none of those things would impress the fae. Instead, I painted something of my world they hadn't seen.

I painted a boy—calculating and thoughtful—and his sister—reckless and naive—trapped in a world of sand and heat. A stone wall surrounded them, while the sand whipped around their feet and a storm brewed in the clouds. Their father pushed dull blades into their hands to force them to spar once more, though they both bled. Their eyes were fixed on each other, but I knew a moment before this image, the boy had stared over the marble wall to the university while the girl looked up in search of a realm she only dreamed of.

Smooth paint glided over the canvas. If I hadn't been selected, I'd be on Ruen studying art right now. I'd have paint on my cheek instead of gold flecks in my hair and an apron around my waist instead of seven earrings in my ear. Teachers would watch me instead of fae.

They didn't make a noise, and twice I checked to be certain I held their attention. Odette gave a nod of approval.

"It's my brother and me back home," I explained while giving more attention to Cal's features. "We trained under my father to fight, even though there was no battle that needed soldiers. But my brother always wanted to study academics, not fight in a war."

My brush hovered over his face. The eyes weren't quite right, but I'd captured the ruffle of his hair and the curve of his head as he looked down his blade at me.

I'd nailed my father's eyes. Strong and demanding.

I'd drawn the last day all three of us fought. Cal and I planned to tell Father the next morning we didn't want to train further. We wanted to Passion as an artist and an academic. Cal had scripted the exact words we'd say so we didn't disappoint Father too terribly, and he was smart enough to suggest we first tell Mother so she could calm Father when we told him. He'd given it much more thought than I had. All I knew was I didn't want to fight anymore.

Mother disappeared that night. We'd been in a shaky peace, but enemies from the mountains in the west who were unhappy with how the war had ended stormed upon the five islands. When the dust settled back into the sea, our mother was nowhere to be found. Those enemies never attacked again, but they'd already taken everything from me.

We never got the chance to tell Father about our Passions. He never asked us to train again.

That wasn't true. Two months ago, Father had taken me alone to the training brig. He'd worked me relentlessly all day.

Why? I had asked him through the sweat on my face. *It's pointless. I don't need to know how to fight.*

You do, he'd insisted. *You need it more than you know.*

I had humored him for one last memory with my father before I left for Ruen. But now his cryptic words settled over me like an unsolved mystery. Had he known back then I'd be chosen?

"If there was no war, then why learn to fight?"

I glanced up but couldn't figure out who had spoken.

"To fit in," I said. "The center island was built for fighting, and we had to fit in."

I dipped my brush in the brown paint and pulled back on the bristles to release them slowly. They sent specks dancing across the canvas to make the sand more lifelike, and the crowd hummed with admiration.

I stood and surveyed my work. It was a simple picture with not much more than the marble gates, swords in our hands, and three figures, but it was all I could hope to paint in one night. The fae drew closer to peer at it, the jadeite bracelets and taaffeite rings beat together as the fae applauded. I bowed.

"Our Mortal Queen," Lord Winster said as he came near and drew a finger along the top of the canvas. "Who knew she was so talented."

Although art was to be my Passion, I'd never thought myself to be exceptionally talented, but the painting wasn't terrible. It wouldn't bring me much more than a few compliments though. This one painting couldn't grant me any power as queen, not in the way an alliance could.

"It's yours," I said to Lord Winster before I could change my mind. I took another look at the picture. I'd been so young, so lost in the world and trying to figure out who I would be. My next move I made for that girl who never envisioned she would be here.

I'd prove to her that she could be stronger than any blade, and she didn't need to wield a sword to find power.

If Lord Winster could give me that, then I could swallow my damaged pride.

"This is a token of my gratitude for the dinner, and I hope you'll accept it along with my alliance."

His eyes widened before a satisfied smile spread across his face.

"With the promise of land included," I added, to be sure I announced his end of the alliance.

"Deal," he said promptly, before I could ask for more. "It's a pleasure to be aligned with you, my Queen." He raised a glass to the room. "Let the music play once more! An alliance has been forged."

8

I MADE A BIG SHOW OF ENTERING
the palace of the Mortal Queens, sweeping my arms out and
holding my head high. The entryway was as empty as ever with
only the silver fish weaving along in the river to witness my grand
entrance. I repeated the gesture as I came up the stairs and once
more when opening the door to my room to be sure Talen saw.

He sat by the fire with his top hat crooked and a thick maroon
book in hands. I cleared my throat.

The book snapped shut. "How did it go?"

"I created an alliance and now own land." I took a bow.

"Land?" His brows shot up. "He actually gave you land?"

I kicked my shoes off. "That he did. You are looking at the
proud owner of Dunfall and Eclipse, wherever those are."

He sank back into the seat. "Oh. Those are tiny."

My shoulders fell. "Why would you say that? Don't do that.
Celebrate with me!" A tall pitcher of cider sat on the bedside
table, and I poured two glasses. "I think I'm getting the hang of
this realm."

Talen rose and joined me, rolling his sleeves carelessly around
his elbows. "One successful night and you think you own the realm."

I shrugged and took a sip.

"I'm a bit surprised, to be honest," Talen said. He went to adjust the fire. The stars outside pulled back on their light, my one sign that true night had begun. It only made the few chariots burn brighter. "I hadn't thought you'd align with him."

I set the glass on the wardrobe beside my bag of things from home, still unpacked. It was clearly out of place among the fine silks and vivid colors of the rugs and curtains and the polished wood of the wardrobe. Antonio sat on the desk, dutifully watching over the room. I picked him up.

"I wasn't going to align with that horrid man after he tricked me," I confessed. "But then I got a better idea." I put down the soldier toy. "I'm going to trick him back."

Talen laughed. "Let me know when I can be of service."

I was determined to deceive Lord Winster the way he'd tricked me and somehow obtain more of his land by doing so. Talen said earlier that an alliance prohibited me from tricking him, so I'd have to find a way around that. In the meantime, I'd use whatever status being aligned with the House of Delvers and Lord Winster would give me to create new alliances before breaking this one.

An intense hunger grew within me to thrive here. I'd do so in honor of my mother who loved this realm and to prove my father wrong. I'd do it for myself, to take hold of the future I desired.

For the first time since arriving, my head wasn't spinning from the intoxication of the realm. I wasn't struggling to sort myself out among the fae, who were more powerful than I could ever be. This realm, this lush realm, could be conquered.

All I had to do was not get lost in this game of alliances and lies.

"I knew when you first walked into this room you were a queen who'd be different," Talen remarked. He put his book away on a shelf over the fireplace. "We fae can't help loving our Mortal Queens, but you might be my favorite one yet."

His words ignited the question that pricked the back of my mind. The tiny thorn in this world of roses that I preferred to tuck away but could no longer afford to ignore. Not when the price for a mere wool could mean my life and a painting could steal a piece of my soul. Beneath the star-blinding exterior—perhaps because of it—these fae were dangerous.

Gaia avoided my questions. Carlene refused to answer. Time to see how deep the alliance between Talen and me ran. I asked slowly, "Did you meet the other Mortal Queens?"

"Each one for the past fifty years."

"Where do they rule?"

"High Queen Gaia is in the east." He straightened the books, unfazed.

"The others," I pressed.

Satisfied with the organized shelf, he faced me. "Dead. Anything else?"

My bliss shattered. "Dead?" I squeaked.

The ground fell from beneath my feet. Every memory I'd created in the past several hours now hid behind a veil of horror. We still sent up prayers to the Mortal Queens from the five islands and asked them to bless us, when they never had a chance to hear. They could do nothing for us. We could do nothing for them. I bit down bile that rose in my throat.

The girls we'd sent from home with fanfare, the ones we praised for being so lucky, the children whose mothers thought them married to a fae king and dining in luxury—*gone.*

"The most recent death occurred two days ago." Talen wore a placid expression, unblinking as he delivered the news. Gone were the visions of uniting with sisters from my realm, dining together, exchanging stories. All torn away with one simple word.

My knees felt weak. "How?"

"It's how it has always been," Talen replied. With two strides, he was by my side. His hand lifted to hover by my cheek, his knuckles brushing the mask. "Such a pretty thing," he said in the softest of tones. "We rely on Mortal Queens to rule us, and we fall in love with them, every time, no matter how hard we try not to. But the Mortal Queens are not ours to keep—and we seem to have a problem in losing you. However, while you are still ours, it is my duty to provide you with a lifetime of luxury."

His words soaked into my skin like poison I couldn't expel. *"I'm* to die."

"In exactly two years." For the first time, I detected pity in his voice. "Such is the fate of being a Mortal Queen."

9

I COULDN'T BREATHE. THE STARS outside the window drew near, suffocating me. Drowning me. The beauty no longer swept me away. *Deadly as they are beautiful.* I closed my fist around Antonio, but not even he could help me. "I want to leave. Now."

"There is no way out of this realm unless an ambassador leads you there. Calm down, you'll pass out if you keep huffing like that. Here, take a piece of chocolate." Talen removed a wrapped square from his pocket. Normally, I'd be delighted to be friends with anyone who constantly carried sweets on them, but even sweets couldn't calm me.

"I'm a prisoner here?" I eyed the door. It stood wide open, and he didn't move to block it. In fact, he spread out his hands.

"Quite the opposite. This is all yours." That might have been more enticing if we hadn't been standing in a mere room. "You own this realm. But only the three ambassadors can take you home, and that is something they will never do."

A knot formed in my stomach like a heavy stone. I tore the jewelry from my arms and let it clatter to the floor. "I can't stay to die."

Talen took my hands in his. His eyes no longer soothed me. "My

Queen, I hope this realm is anything but insufferable. So far, you are anything but ordinary, and I swear I will find a way to make it feel less like a prison for you." He bowed while taking small steps toward the door. "I promise. I'll make it a home you won't want to leave." He said it as if the beauty of the realm was the problem and solving it would make everything else okay.

"Who is killing the Mortal Queens?"

He placed a hand on his chest. "No fae would touch them. We love you all with a feeling so deep that nothing could hinder it, and it would be impossible for any of us to do such a thing. Your deaths are beyond even our power."

I shook my dizzy head. "This makes no sense." Queens don't just die. Someone must be killing them.

"Queen Thea, tell me what I can do for you. I can lift my hand and summon winds or stretch it out and calm any beast. Do you want a pet? A lion perhaps?"

I gawked at him. "I want to live."

His head tipped to the side, the black chains on his four earrings swaying with it. "You get to live. Until you don't. Same as us all."

Hot tears filled my eyes, and my breathing was choked. My dress suddenly clenched too tight, and the room squeezed smaller than before. I'd dreamed of this for my entire life. Every girl on my island prayed to be chosen. This was my secret desire above all else. But now? The desk rammed into my side when I clambered back. "I don't want this."

He was silent for a while, taking me in. "I'm sorry," he whispered. "The House Representatives have been tasked with delivering this news for centuries, and we've yet to find a good way to do so. You seemed like someone who would want it straightforward, but perhaps that was not the way I should have done it." Talen showed emotion for the first time as he wiped his eyes quickly and cleared his throat. "I'll do everything in my power to make this better."

There was no way to make this better. The fae realm was a beautiful death.

"Thea," Talen said kindly. "If there was anything I could do to save you, I'd do it in a heartbeat."

I clutched Antonio to my chest, and his sword drilled into my skin. I needed the pain to plant me back on the ground.

When Mother spoke of the wonder, she failed to predict the danger. That was why they needed queens so often. That was why we never saw more than last year's selected. That was why Gaia paled at the mention of girls before us. *The Mortal Queens are not ours to keep.* What did that mean? Who took them?

My promise to Malcom to return swelled in my throat. I had to fulfill that promise. Antonio weighed heavy in my hand with the memory of my brother and the idea that I'd never be reunited with him again. My sweet little brother. I pressed the metal figure against my lips. "I'll find a way to you." My eyes darted to Talen. "I have to live."

He removed his top hat and knelt on the ground before me. "My Queen, it can't be done. None have survived."

I clenched my teeth together and gritted out each word. "I . . . will . . . live."

He bowed his head. "And I will do all I can to try to save you. I make this vow to you."

"Go," I ordered, ignoring the hurt in his eyes. I turned away toward the window. "Let me have peace as I sort this."

His footsteps retreated, and the door closed. When I turned again, he'd left his hat on the handle.

I sank to the floor. Cal would excel in this situation and have it all solved before the night ended. I could paint it, but my brushes couldn't solve the dilemma.

A tear fell upon the little soldier's eye as if it cried with me. Malcom had held my hand so tight as they pierced my ears and reminded me how strong I was. I didn't feel strong. I felt hopeless. If I could draw some of Malcom's bravery and Cal's intellect, I would have a better chance of surviving. All I knew how to do was paint and hide from Father when he was in a nasty mood.

I lifted my head. I wasn't entirely alone. Another Mortal Queen still lived, and Gaia must know the fate that awaited us. She'd had a year here before me. That would be ample time to learn about the world and uncover a way out of the realm safely. I stood. There was no time to mourn when Gaia would have answers.

Poor Gaia only had one year left. She needed saving more than I did.

I took off without a second thought, hurrying through the empty hall and down the long stairway to the throne room with the river. I fled over the bridge to the east side, where identical features greeted me. The same long stairway in the hall, the same tall door at the start of the corridor.

Talen had rooms down the hall from mine, but the rest of my wing was empty. If Thomas stayed here with Gaia, I never saw him. The rest of our home was eerily large and quiet.

My heart thundered as I pounded against the door.

By the clocks, it was well into the night and neared morning. I pounded harder. A moment later, the door slid open.

Gaia peered out. "What in the fae's name are you doing?"

"Surviving." I pushed past her and into her room. A light pink carpet welcomed my bare toes as not one, but two fires burned on either side of the large room. I spun to face Gaia. "I'm going to help you live. We have to leave."

She shut the door slowly. "The Mortal Queens?"

I crossed my arms. "Dead. I appreciate the warning. You could have saved me before I came to this realm. Instead, you watched them pierce my ears and cover my face with a mask without saying a single word."

She pulled her shawl closer. Her silky blue nightdress flowed like wind around her body as she moved to the open doors leading out to a balcony. Her rooms sat on the exact edge of the island, so it looked as if the balcony was suspended into the night sky.

After an irritatingly long pause, she spoke. "There was nothing I could have said."

I gaped at her. "I can think of a few things."

"It is not for me to disrupt the ways of the fae."

"Are you truly so complicit that you'd roll over and perish willingly?" I stood beside her. "Did you not grow up on the same island I did, training in the same arena while preparing for battle? This, Gaia, this is our battle."

She looked up at the dark sky. "Fighting will get you nowhere." The calm in her voice splintered. "Ivory fought every day to find a way to survive, no matter how much I begged her not to. It did her nothing. The night fell on her second year, and she faded away." A tear rolled down Gaia's cheek.

My heart faltered. She'd been with Ivory for an entire year and lost her two days ago. Everyone had.

When they celebrated me upon my entrance to this realm, had they just finished mourning the queen who died? Did they mourn her still? Would they mourn me? "Talen told me they love us, but did they even cry for Ivory?"

Gaia twisted her hands together and stared at them with tight shoulders and a quivering chin. "They did. It's the only time I've seen them broken. But then we left to fetch you, and when I returned?" She gave a slight gesture. "They hid their sorrow well, but I could still see it."

Ivory must have slept in my same room. *The High Queen of the West, gone in the blink of an eye and replaced by another.* My skin prickled. "If you do nothing, you die."

"You don't know that," Gaia said. "This is how I hope to win. By appeasing the fae in all they ask. If I find enough favor in their eyes, perhaps I'll be spared."

"Spared from what? How did Ivory die?"

Gaia almost recoiled at the question. "It was horrible. The entire realm flocked to our palace to try to save her, but when the day ended . . ." She clenched her jaw. "She was here, then she was dead. Same as them all."

I swallowed. "How? How are we to die?"

"It's different each time," Gaia said. She shut her eyes. "No one knows. No one can stop it."

I ran a hand over my face. It was like another one of the fae's games, and that meant it could be won. There had to be a way.

I sat on her bed. "No Mortal Queen has survived?"

She opened her eyes and shook her head. "None."

My body settled, but each breath caught in my throat like I was hearing the news for the first time again. "Why?" I wanted to know. "Why do they need the Mortal Queens? Why not just leave us on the five islands?"

"That," she said somberly, "I'm afraid I haven't solved. It's clear they need us, and they don't enjoy us dying, but I don't understand why."

"Then maybe I start there. If we knew our purpose, perhaps fulfilling it would save us. Something tells me the story we were told about a general who convinced the fae to take queens is not true."

Gaia stood like an angel on the balcony, hands poised over the balustrade, thin dress floating in the breeze, stars over her head. The stars shone brighter, and eight chariots carried fae from one island to another other. It must be nearing morning now. She took a deep breath. "If I'm going to die, at least I'll get two years in this paradise first."

She straightened to her full height and squinted at me. "You lost your mother, right?"

I drew back. "What?"

"Your mother? She disappeared one night. No one knew where she went. Your father was a brilliant general, but he was aimless without her. You and your brothers barely got by." I didn't know how she knew that when I knew nothing about her. But with her next breath, she gave me something. "I had both my parents, and I had a decent life lined up. And yet?" She held her hand out for me to join her and I did. "Look at it all. We are *queens* here. We have everything we need, and anything we could want. Surely two years here is worth a lifetime on the five islands."

It was a sweet idea, but not mine.

"I want a lifetime."

She looked at me sorrowfully. "Let it go, Thea. Fighting it is not the key. It'll drive you to your death, just as it did with Ivory."

I stood tall. "We will see. I'll save us both."

10

MORNING DAWNED. WHICH MEANT little in this realm. Simply a continuation of the night. Torches lit themselves around the perimeter of islands and chariots took to the skies, and I watched them glow from outside the palace courtyard while summoning my courage.

I tightened my fist over Antonio, the little toy solider that made me feel connected to Malcom. "This will work," I told myself. "It will get me home."

I stared over the edge of the floating island at the vast darkness. When we arrived in the fae realm, we ascended through the clouds. So to get back, down had to be the answer. Down currently showed nothing other than endless black sky and a sea of stars. Eventually it had to give way to my realm.

If I jumped, I was bound to find my way back home.

My feet inched over the edge. Rocks broke from the cliff face to tumble below. They faded from sight. What would happen back home if I died here? Would they still send pensions to my family if I was gone?

Cool air sent goosebumps rippling over my skin. Or perhaps the goosebumps were already there. *Fear keeps you alive*, my father would say. *But it doesn't win the battle.*

Maybe bravery would come if I focused on the weight of Antonio in my hand instead of the drop at my toes. I tried, but fear still coiled around my fast-beating heart.

"You're going to jump," I ordered myself. "There's no honor in hesitating."

I took a few steps back. Then, with a short run, I flung myself into the open air.

The wind whipped at my face, tearing my hair across my cheeks as I screamed. I pressed my eyes shut and tried to steady myself while twisting in circles, struggling to discern which direction was up and which was down. The fae realm shot away as black blanketed everything, but somehow the blasted mask didn't waver from my face. The air rushed through my fingertips and over my arms as the dread of what I'd just done overtook me.

I clutched Antonio and gulped down my scream. With great difficulty, I pulled my knees into my chest and prayed to the fae that I'd land in trees. The fall was endless. Each second lasted a hundred minutes, each minute only a second. I searched for a light like my sun, something to guide me back home, but everything was distorted. Time, direction, my logic. I'd lost all three.

Fool. I was such a fool. A brave, dead fool.

Something grabbed my waist and yanked me upward. My back slammed into something hard, and the stars stopped spinning. I choked on air. The next moment, I shot up toward the faded lights of the fae islands, held in a chariot by someone's hand.

"No!" I screamed. "I have to leave."

My logic hadn't returned yet. I clawed to the edge of the chariot to throw myself down again. I had to get home.

A hand seized me. "I won't save you twice."

Bastian stood in the chariot behind me, his warm brown skin lit by the golden rails and his dark eyes inexpressible behind the sharp words. "If you care to die"—he released me—"jump."

I stilled. He held out his hand. "You don't want to try again?"

"I need to get home." My words sounded childish to my ears.

Bastian's mouth opened slightly. "You were trying to return to your realm?"

I nodded, leaning over the edge of the chariot to peer down in hopes of catching a glimpse of the five islands. As always, only stars greeted me.

Bastian held my arm, steadying me.

"I'm not going to jump." I sighed.

He motioned to the chariot with a flick of his wrist, and we drifted up toward the island of the Mortal Queens, to my beautiful prison.

The relief of survival was not as great as the sting of failure.

"There is one way out of our realm, my Queen." Bastian steered the chariot, while I tried not to notice the lovely way he said *my Queen*. His accent rolled the vowels and made the phrase sound endearing instead of dutiful. "And that is not it. You would have fallen for eternity. Long after you stopped breathing, your body would have continued tumbling through the stars until it was nothing but fire and ash."

I shivered. "That's not what I wanted."

"What did you think would happen?" He adjusted the thin gold band around his forehead and leaned against the rails. "Even had you been transported to your realm, you would have landed with such a force that you'd be nothing more than a hole in the ground."

I turned away. "It made sense at first."

"How?" Amusement plated his tone. "I truly want to know how you arrived at that conclusion."

"I'm to die anyway." I whirled back around to face him. "At least I tried to find a way home."

He held no pity for me. "I'm guessing there are a few other things you could have tried first."

We flew closer to the fae realm, and each moment broke my spirit a little bit more. "One way out of this realm," I pondered. "The ambassadors?"

"There are three ambassadors, so you may look at it as three ways out."

The six earrings in his ear were like golden orbs, reminding me he was a king. A great fae king who had to bow to a mortal girl. He could have let me die, then killed Gaia, and he'd bow to no one.

They needed us Mortal Queens for something. The fae were dependent upon us. But why?

I cared more about getting home than uncovering what purpose they had for mortals.

"You're a king," I said. "Why can't I put my knife to your back and order you to do it?" I carried no knife, only Antonio, but the little soldier could jab an eye out at least.

He threw back his head and laughed. "I could snap my fingers and break every bone in your mortal body, mortal." It was a far cry from *my Queen*. "Your dagger couldn't convince me to take you to your home. Ambassadors are the bridge to the mortal realm, and only they have the power to cross into it. If it pleases you, you can think of the rest of us as trapped here alongside you."

I pushed as much authority into my voice as my quivering body could muster. The insanity of falling through empty skies hadn't quite faded away. "Will you die in two years as well?"

The side of his mouth curved up. "I certainly hope not. I'm not much older than you are."

Oh. I thought he would be much older. It was hard to tell with these fae.

The first of the islands appeared in the distance, marble buildings creating a gate along the border where sand collected to spill grains over the edge. Mother told me of an island just as this. Of all the tales of the fae realm, hers had been the most accurate. It would have pleased her. But her story, just like all the others, missed one fatal detail.

"How can I be queen over all this, yet be so powerless?"

Bastian brought the chariot closer and a dozen more floating islands came into view. "You are not powerless. You hold more power over the fae than you know."

I gave him a sideways glance. "Yet I'm still to die."

"Even I can't stop that."

That was all anyone had said about it. They don't want the Mortal Queens to die, but they can't do anything to keep them alive. The knowledge that he wanted me to live didn't bring any comfort as it was yet another disheartening answer. I tightened my grip on Antonio.

"What's this?" Bastian noticed my fisted hand.

I held Antonio behind my back. "It's a token from home."

His expression was unreadable. His majestic blue cloak rippled off his broad shoulders as he nodded. "I see. You must love someone there very much to be willing to die for them."

"I didn't want to die," I mumbled. "But yes." Cal would laugh if he heard I thought hurling myself into the sky would somehow land me back on the center island.

Bastian stroked the chariot, and just as it neared my new home, it twisted to the side and carried us away from the palace. We passed each island I could see from my chamber window and ventured beyond. New islands appeared, larger than before. One was purely made of water, with falls running off each edge to land on four islands beneath, where lakes touched forests and stone cottages clustered around fires. Another held a string of mountains with caves carved among them.

Bastian watched me absorb it all.

"I can't take you home," he said quietly. The chariot swept low. "But I can bring you to mine." Before us sat the largest island yet with a grey palace towering over it all, built into a mountain against a valley. A sea so dark it was like gleaming ink at the foot of the palace.

"Welcome to Umbruin." A courtyard was chiseled into the side, and the chariot landed there near the face of magnificent glass doors opening into the mountain.

I stepped off the chariot. Solid stone chilled my bare feet. I still wore last night's dress, though the pink flowers had wilted, and many had torn from the fabric due to my jumping escapade.

"I own Umbruin and every other island as far as your eye can see." His navy boots clicked on the ground, and the doors opened at the sound. "If it's land you desire, I can grant that. If it's friendships, I can order anyone to be kind to you. If it's a star . . ." He held out his hand. A brilliant white light melted from the sky to reform in his hand. The star flicked light across his cheeks and brightened the gold mask. "I will give you a star."

Heat caressed my face, and I gazed at the orb in his hand. It danced at the will of his fingers.

"Why would you do something for me?" I spoke with an awed voice, still fixated on the star before me. All he did was hold out his hand and the skies bent to his will.

With a toss of his wrist, the star flew to retake its position above. "In exchange for an alliance."

My fascination gave way to suspicion. "Why? What would I do for you?"

"You can fix my reputation." He gestured to lead me inside, where the walls were glass and the ceiling was a rocky cove. "I've been king for only a short time and am still considered very young in fae years. An alliance with the Mortal Queen would give me the credibility I need to convince those faithful to my father that I'm worthy of ruling."

"Can't your father make a declaration on your behalf?"

His lips twitched. "That's unlikely, being as I recently stole the throne from him."

"Ah. I see."

He paused in the middle of the room. Just like in my palace, his throne sat at the far end of the first room, the spools of it stretching almost to the ceiling. I rather doubted he looked as foreign on his throne as I did on mine.

"I don't think you do. I need an alliance with a Mortal Queen to prove I'm not heartless. I need a tight alliance. Then the islands will let me lord them."

My eyes narrowed. "How tight?"

"Being seen often with a pretty queen would be beneficial. To show your bond with me, you'd need to make no further alliances. If you make many alliances, the value of each is diminished."

That made sense. One alliance showed a strong bond. Ten alliances would mean I was stretched out. But agreeing to give up my power to form new alliances put a lot of trust in this one to grant me enough prestige. With so many unanswered questions about how to survive, I'd need all available options. And I planned to break my alliance with Lord Winster, which would leave me solely with the House of Delvers and King Bastian.

"I save your rulership, close myself to all other alliances, and all I get is a star?"

"I can give you two." Though he joked, he didn't smile. "I need this. I'll grant you whatever you ask."

That promise hung between us, and I searched for what he could give me that could save my life.

"I give you two years of my allegiance, and on the final day, you take me home so I live."

He hung his head. "I can't grant that. It's forbidden."

"By whom?"

"The fabric of this realm. I'd die."

I turned away. "Then I don't want anything."

His hand caught mine, sending a tremor to my heart. "Please, Althea. I need this."

I startled at his use of my name and slid my hand out from his. He stood with desperation in his eyes as he waited for me to give an answer, but while my heart broke for him, he could be twisting my emotions to make me care. As a fae king, he was one of the most powerful beings in this realm. Refusing him could be unwise. The choice balanced before me.

The key to my freedom might rest with him—if I was clever enough to find it. "I would want the honest answers to two questions of my choosing," I decided.

"That's it?" He brightened.

"And three stars."

He clapped his hands with a boom louder than thunder. When his hands separated, three blazing stars rested within. "They are yours. I would have given you the galaxy." With a snap of his fingers, a glass globe formed around the stars, and they twinkled inside. My little stars. They had no value, but they were gorgeous.

The smooth glass rested weightlessly in my palms.

"Now your questions."

I only had one for now. "I want to know why you need Mortal Queens. What is our purpose?"

His brows shot up before settling back beneath his gold mask. I kept my own expression blank. If I knew the purpose of the Mortal Queens, I could fulfill it and be freed. I might never need to ask my second question.

Our alliance bound him to give me an honest answer, and that answer would lead me home.

Bastian swept his cloak away from his shoulders and tossed it back toward the door. "That is not a tale we fae give up lightly." In three strides he crossed to his throne, built of rock, and took his seat. Beside it sat an obsidian pedestal holding up something shaped like a cloche but covered with red cloth. Bastian's hands flickered in its direction as his eyes darted like he was making sure I couldn't see underneath.

I held my stars to my side. "What's in the cloche?"

"Is that your second question?"

"No." I eyed the thick drape. Its ends skirted over the stone floor with a hushed sound.

Bastian leaned forward and looked down over me. I'd been right—the large throne didn't dwarf him at all, it only exemplified his magnificence, and once more his beauty awed me. I could search the entire five islands and never find anyone quite like him. After a moment of my dumbed silence, he grinned. "Do you still want the answer to the first question?"

I set a hard look over my face. "I'm listening."

Instead of beginning, he focused on me with an intense gaze that was difficult not to squirm beneath. The stars beside me hummed to fill the silence, their vibration ringing in my ear. When Bastian finally spoke, it wasn't to give answers.

"I must know," he said slowly. "What do you hope comes from

this knowledge? How will the past change your fate?" He rested against one arm and cocked his head to the side.

His question quickened my fears that this wouldn't solve anything, but I shoved the doubt away. "I'm hoping the answer lies within," I said stiffly.

"You're about to be greatly disappointed. Nothing will save you." With that somber declaration, my heart sank. "The tale of the Mortal Queens dates back thousands of years, when my grandfather was still a young lad." I brushed past the oddity of that sentence. "A fae king fell in love with a mortal girl and made her his queen. She was our first Mortal Queen, and she was adored."

Already a million questions swarmed, starting with how that didn't align with the story I knew of a man from the five islands forging the relationship between the mortals and the fae. How did a fae king meet a mortal woman when our realms were separated? What was her reign like? Was she closed off to her home realm just as I was?

I bit my tongue to keep from speaking and ruining my second question as Bastian's tale continued.

"Their relationship was greatly esteemed, and though a mortal, that queen's beauty surpassed all. But it is difficult to hold the attention of a king, and exactly two years after making her a queen, her reckless husband betrayed her with another. In her sadness, our beloved queen threw herself off the land and died."

He watched me knowingly, and my blood turned to ice. She'd died the exact same way I'd just tried to return home. Both of us sought freedom. She found hers, but it came at a terrible price. If Bastian hadn't saved me, the same fate would have claimed me.

What if she'd only been trying to get home as I had? No one would ever know.

Bastian turned his face upward to the grey rock of the ceiling. "The other six kings wept for their fallen queen, and the seventh king rushed to the mortal realm to find a queen to replace her. But there is a magic that binds this realm together, something more powerful than us all, and it longed for its mortal queen to return. It ached to its very core, almost toppling our entire realm in its sorrow. To punish the king, that force punished us all." His gaze returned to me as I stood completely still, soaking in every word.

Bastian's expression softened like he was looking upon a wounded animal he couldn't save. "With that punishment, your fate was decided thousands of years ago. We'd forever be dependent upon a Mortal Queen. But just like the first, we'd never be able to keep her, always losing her two years after she arrives."

His voice held all the sorrow of the realm, but it still wasn't enough to console me.

His people did this to mine. The fae condemned generations of daughters to die, all because one of their kings chose to stray.

Their crime. Our punishment.

"That isn't fair to the mortals."

"It's unfair to you," Bastian agreed, "but it's torment to us. No matter how hard we fight it, we fall madly in love with you. The lure to you is unavoidable. I can't avoid it myself. But I'm destined to lose you, and there aren't enough stars in the sky to fix that. I'm constantly yearning for you, while forever mourning the queens I've already lost. The pain is unimaginable."

Losing the one you love isn't as terrible as losing your life. "There must be a way to undo the fae king's punishment."

Bastian set his jaw. Any hint of compassion was now covered by the stoic expression he wore so well. His tone hardened. "There isn't. The realm's desires can't be undone. As long as you are a Mortal Queen, you will die." He stood and swept past me. "Do you have a second question? Or have I given you enough disappointment today?"

I clutched my stars. His story was the answer I sought but granted me nothing useful. I had no real purpose here. There was nothing to accomplish to win the right to live.

I was here solely to die.

Clicking heels sounded. A woman as beautiful as the night with hair of stormy clouds and skin of polished glass glided into the room. She bowed her head low. Four earrings adorned her ear. "My King. I need to speak with you. It's about your sister."

"One moment." Bastian regarded me. "Thea, I must take you back now." Urgency rang through his voice and the way he moved. The woman bowed again, but her eyes were on me.

Bastian summoned the chariot and stepped through the doors onto it. I followed in painful silence. I'd just aligned myself with a young king and received nothing in return other than a bleak story and a few pretty stars. My ability to make decisions today was poor.

As the chariot took off, the story played in my head again and again. I mourned for the lost girl and yearned for a way to end the pattern of the queens. It had never been our wrongdoing in the first place. It was the cruelest sort of punishment.

Bastian's story was a far cry from the tales we'd been fed. One where the girls we offered were living in paradise, where this realm was something so magnificent our minds could not comprehend it. The tale was one of sorrow, and it cut me to my core because I saw myself there in that first queen, desperate to escape. Feeling alone. Lost. So confused she was willing to throw herself off the edge of land and into an empty sky just to find a way home.

I held the stars so tight that the glass surrounding them burned my hand. Then we landed in the courtyard outside my palace where I stepped off the chariot.

"Thank you, Bastian," I said. "I needed to know that story." I'd dig through the trails in it, and they were bound to lead somewhere.

Bastian's hands held the chariot rails. His eyes were clouded, so unlike how they'd been when he confessed he couldn't help but love me.

He's only using you, I reminded myself. *The same way you will find a way to use him to get home.* Somehow, this king would be my salvation.

His eyes cleared. "Call me Bash. It'll better suit the alliance. You'll promise not to jump off the island once I leave?"

I nodded, and the chariot rose. Bash's voice floated down to me. "I was right when I first met you. This is going to be very interesting."

11

TALEN CAME DOWN THE STAIRS AS I
entered and immediately spotted the glass in my hand. "What is that?"

I twisted off the top of the glass where Bash had confined the stars
and they orbited my palm with a buttery glow. "Three stars. They
are mine."

Instead of being impressed, his eyes were slits. "Only kings may
summon stars. Which one?" The accusation was clear.

His warning against Bash echoed in my mind. "King Bastian,"
I mumbled.

Talen moaned and put his face in his hands. "Thea, Bastian can't
be trusted."

"Are these stars valuable?" I asked, holding them closer to inspect
their design.

"Just as bragging tools." He huffed. "I don't think you're hearing
me. That fae king is no good. His heart isn't cracked."

I sighed at the odd saying. "I know that. He's using me, but I'll use
him better."

Talen froze, one brow lifted.

I lowered my stars so Talen could see my face. "Bastian wanted
an alliance to secure his position among his islands. I can give him

that. Meanwhile, I'm going to use him to get me home. I won't get attached to him—he's only a tool."

Talen searched my eyes. "You'll guard yourself against him? No falling in love?"

"It won't be a problem. I swear, he's nothing but a means to help myself."

"You're certain? It's unwise for Mortal Queens to form romantic attachments."

"I want to get home," I stated. "Nothing else means anything to me."

A sly grin spread beneath his mask. "Good. In that case, I can't wait to watch you play with a king."

His approving smile filled me with pride. This realm was a series of games, and I'd play them better than any queen before me. That would be how I saved all the future girls who would be bound to this place. To do so meant creating a plan more elaborate than anything this realm had seen from their High Queens, and that started with these stars. To me, they were more than bragging rights. They were proof I could get whatever I asked for, even the stars.

I tossed them to Talen. "Secure these into my throne so they are the first thing anyone sees as they walk in from the courtyard. I want all to know that a king pulled these from the sky for me."

"Consider it done."

"And don't tell anyone about the alliance yet. I want to announce it myself."

His brow creased. "My Queen?"

"If we can put it together in time, I'd like to host a dinner party the day after tomorrow, and invite everyone. There, I will make Bastian bow before me to show his alliance. I will let the realm know I have a fae king working for me."

He held the stars close to inspect them. "You won't convince him to bow. Fae kings are prideful."

"And I'm determined. Bash will bow."

He glanced up. "I'm not certain you have the true spirit of an alliance, but I support this."

I picked up my skirts. The bath called to me from my room, where I could soak in creamy water tinged with lavender and vanilla and plot my next moves until my skin turned wrinkly. "I'd like those stars mounted as soon as you can," I called over my shoulder. "So everyone will see I'm not a queen to be trifled with."

I passed by the blank white walls leading to my chambers. The palace still stood too empty and dull before it opened into my room where color exploded in hues of gold and pink and red. I rubbed my hand over the stone wall in the corridor. Someday, I might like to paint these walls and brighten up the place until it felt more like a home than a cage. A temporary home.

Inside my room, a platter of chocolates rested on the bedside table. A folded note on silver parchment sat beside it.

Stolen just for you.
—Talen

I didn't deserve that fae. The chocolate melted in my mouth with the first bite, and I grabbed the platter to take to the bath. Already the lavish scents filled my nose with their promise of relaxation, which was richly needed after this day.

I paused to remove the little soldier toy from my pocket and place him back on the desk.

"We're still here," I told him. "But I'm going to find a way to get us home to Cal and Malcom. I promise."

A second note on the balcony caught my eye, this one held down by a rock so black it might be ore. Sheer red curtains framed the doors to the balcony, and I pulled them back. Then I pushed the door open, welcoming the cool mist of the night. I'd never get used to this much moisture in the air.

I picked up the note.

Tomorrow there is a feast at King Vern's home. If you'll do me the pleasure of attending, I'll pick you up. In honor of my word, I won't tell anyone we are aligned until you are ready.

— Bash

I read the note twice, then stared into the sky to see if I could find him among the stars with his cloak trailing behind him like a river.

If King Vern was hosting a feast and Bash would be attending, then perhaps other fae kings would attend as well. I almost smiled. My plan took shape, still fuzzy around the edges but brimming with hope.

I'd unite the kings. All six of them. And using their combined power, they would free the Mortal Queens.

Cal's voice prompted me to keep thinking. *They must have tried that before,* he said in my mind, *if they were truly in agony each time the queens died.*

They'd have tried to help, but this realm was obsessed with power, both obtaining it and keeping it. I didn't believe this fate was something that needed to be broken, but rather a wrong that required a penance be paid.

Paid by a sacrifice.

It was a king who wronged the realm. It would be the kings who sacrificed to mend it.

If I could trap them into obligation, then I could push them to do whatever was needed, including draining all their power, to free me. And perhaps the same magical force that first doomed the queens would be satisfied with their sacrifice in return for the loss of the first Mortal Queen.

I'd be willing to let the kings die if that was what it took. I'd be willing to die alongside them. Anything to save the thousands of girls who would come after me from this death.

All I needed was a trap for each of the kings. A cleverly phrased favor, beseeching them to my aid.

I dropped another chocolate into my mouth. A dangerous thought came. Or I stay here and reign, free to visit home whenever I please.

The warm water greeted my tired body and offered peace the day had lacked. I had two years to ask the fae kings to help me, and to manipulate them if needed. That was ample time to save myself.

Only last night I'd been told I would die, but now I had hope, and I sank into the bath contemplating how I'd trick the six fae king into freeing the Mortal Queens.

12

BASH ARRIVED WITH A LARGE
chariot, holding his arm out as soon as he landed. I gathered my
skirt in my hand, the black lace billowing with each footstep and
the tips of my heels peeking out. A gold ring circled my nostril and
jewels hung across my forehead. I'd pulled my hair back so all could
see the seven earrings and know that I was a queen.

I'd eaten my fill just before dressing so nothing at the feast would
distract me from my mission. I'd find the fae kings and ask them
to join me in repealing the hold over the Mortal Queens. Then I'd
spend the rest of the night learning all I could about anyone who
turned me down. I'd use my name and the promise of friendship,
though not alliance.

If they all refused, I'd trap the kings, one by one, and force them
to help me. The power of them together would undo the fate of the
queens. Or forge a new and much better one.

My red-painted nails clung to Bash's arm as he helped me onto
the chariot. He'd traded his cloak for a long-tailed suit and navy
cravat, and he'd painted the right half of his face gold to match his
mask, even coloring his lips.

"You're leaving your little toy behind this time?" He looked
straight ahead as the chariot took off.

"I don't need Antonio tonight," I said. "I can handle this all on my own."

As we passed the palace, Gaia stood on her balcony watching us. When our eyes caught, she drifted back into her chambers and shut the doors. I swore a warning rested in her place.

My dress rippled like a black sea against the twinkling sky we soared through. "Where does King Vern live?"

"The farthest region. It will give us enough time to prepare."

I had to tilt my head back to look at him. "For what?"

"Vern is a cunning king, more so than the rest."

"Even more than you?"

His lip twitched in what might have been a smile. "He knows his limits. But he bested my father many times. I fully expect more games tonight, since he invited the other four kings to watch."

I jittered with relief. Every king would be there.

"You are still new to our realm, and your best move would be to cling to the shadows like a guard against tonight and whatever mischief it brings. I suspect many fae will lose possessions in deals before the stars brighten to morning, and it would look bad for me if you made a wrong deal."

We ducked under an island, and for a moment there was nothing but black. But then we resurfaced, and the stars shimmered in greeting. A cool mist hung in the air and wafted over our cheeks. "Can't have your new alliance be with a foolish girl."

"It wouldn't be ideal. To convince my islands I'm strong, you must also be strong. Tonight, that means following my lead and staying silent."

I tensed. "They will respect me when they see I am strong. If I am quiet, I will appear confused."

"Or you will appear wise," Bash countered. "And you'd be lying if you said you weren't a little confused by our realm."

I gave him no answer to that.

The chariot slowed and his eyes focused on mine. "Being in an alliance means you work in the interest of us both. This is what

I need from you tonight. Trust me, a distant, beautiful queen is something the fae respect."

I wasn't liking this. "Gaia plays that part well. Perhaps you should have asked her to align."

"I did," he grunted. "She said something about my being ill-tempered and walked away."

I bit down a laugh. Above, an island lined by celestial gates loomed, sparkling brighter as we rode close. It quieted me with its beauty.

"Be on your guard," Bash broke the silence to warn again. "I can smell a trick."

I tore my eyes from the shimmering island to see him. "I wasn't invited tonight, so I doubt it's laid for me."

Still, he scanned the home with feral eyes as we approached, shifting closer until he was almost pressed against my side. His hand brushed mine. But when I looked up, his focus was on the fae in the courtyard. They watched us, taking note of our closeness. *This is what he needs,* I remined myself. *He needs to not look cold-hearted.* I left my hand by his as the chariot touched down. He laced my fingers between his as he led me off the chariot. Then, with a dramatic flourish, Bash lifted my hand to his lips to give it a tender kiss.

I invited the warmest smile to my face. It was easier to summon than I cared to admit.

He dropped my hand and turned to sift through the crowd. I stood dutifully at his side with my head held high. Groups had begun whispering upon our arrival, and through it all, a familiar face came into focus. Odette stood in the entryway with a sly smile.

I slipped from Bash's side to pull Odette away. "Spying on me again?"

She ducked under a draped curtain as the marble stone gave way to grass that tickled my ankles. King Vern's home sat outside a forest with many trees peeking up from within the home as if it had been built into the trees themselves.

"I'm not spying. I was properly invited this time—I'm a cousin of King Vern. Distant, as he likes to remind people." She took a sip from a goblet the same color as her ivory gown. Gold accents graced her lips and feet. "Talen mentioned you had a run-in with Bastian. This looks interesting." She glanced at the fae king who stalked through the crowd. "He doesn't come to these very often."

"Is he shy?"

"Some say that. He does look ready to flee at a moment's notice, doesn't he?"

Bash's eyes found mine and his lips tightened. Those eyes darted to the spot next to him then back to me. I sighed. "I think I'm being summoned."

"Have fun," she sang. "I'm here if you need anything. I would happily steal more wine for us."

"Yes, please," I said while moving away, once more grateful I'd chosen an alliance with the House of Delvers.

I didn't pause until I reached Bash's side. "Are you lonely or merely incapable of conversing with people without me here?"

He didn't smile. "I'm watching over you."

"You're very kind," I quipped. Once more, no smile. I gave up and searched through the faces for a gold band of the fae kings.

The entryway opened, as was the custom here, into a grand throne room with King Vern's throne built of twisted wood and ivy climbing to the ceiling. Instead of pillars, trees lined the corridors, and lanterns hung from them. But while both my home and Bash's broke off to stairways, King Vern's spilled into a massive, circular room lined with seating. There was no roof. It was like an arena from back home, one I'd spent hours training in. The very sight of it made me purse my lips.

A man emerged from the crowd to our side. He wore the band of the kings and a beard of silver to match his stormy eyes.

"Bastian, I see you bring a guest." His voice, deep as an ocean, carried a wave of interest.

Bash moved nearer to me. "Thea was eager to join me tonight," he said.

I remembered to put on an adoring face for him. "Thank you for inviting me."

So this was King Vern. His gaze rolled over me for a few seconds before smiling. "I would have made the feast grander, had I known we'd be honored by the presence of a Mortal Queen." In true fae king nature, Vern's beauty stood out. His arms were chiseled with muscle, his light skin flawless, and his smile charming enough to make my knees weak. My own flaws stood out in comparison. Yet, King Vern bowed his head at my presence as if it were I who shone.

Bash looked around. "I doubt that's possible. You must have invited the entire realm." Even to me, hardly knowing Bash, the dislike in his voice was clear.

King Vern drummed his fingers together. "I'm pleased with how many came. I have something quite special."

It was only because of how close Bash stood that I felt him tense. I tucked my hand into his elbow. "We can't wait to see it. Bash promised me you have some of the finest art here."

King Vern spread out his arm. "Be my guest, my Queen."

I pulled Bash away, noting King Vern didn't stop watching us until we'd entered the throne room and were lost behind a sea of fae. The tension in Bash's arm relaxed.

"That was risky," he said. "Art is not common in our world, and Vern owns some of the only pieces. Any other king would have caught your lie." His attention kept jumping from face to face, looking down every corridor and every opening between masses of fae. He wore a frown that deepened with each step.

"If you have somewhere else to be, I can go find my shadows now," I said.

He finally glanced my way. "Not somewhere, someone. I'm looking for my sister, Troi."

Wherever Troi was, Bash searched as if she were drowning and he was the only one who could save her. He cursed under his breath. "Where is she?"

Soft silks of dresses brushed my arms as fae mingled about us, but none of the faces matched someone who could be related to

Bash. They all lacked that resplendent look in the eyes, the strong curve of his lips, the rounded jaw.

"I'd help you search if I knew what she looked like," I said.

At that moment, four drumbeats called the room to attention. King Vern moved through the crowd, but he didn't head for the throne. He stood at the entrance of the arena.

He raised a cup. "We have been blessed tonight. The finest archer in all our realm has graciously offered a show of his talent."

He paused to allow the fae to cheer. Beside me, Bash stiffened. A shot of worry sparked through me.

King Vern held up his hand for quiet. "From that island"—he pointed through the sky to a smaller island positioned like a moon above—"Ian will fire his arrow, and it will hit its mark perfectly."

Once more, the room clapped, this time more enthusiastically. I gawked at the distance.

Bash's eyes closed for a moment as he whispered, "No." When he reopened his eyes, they held fear.

The smile on King Vern's face was more wicked than pleased. "I've recently come by a new possession that is of no value to me. But here, I have found a way to make her valuable." Bash trembled beside me. "Ian will put his arrow through her heart."

The room applauded for a third time, but much less enthusiastically. Whispers rustled through the crowd at whom he could mean.

A moment later, a door at the end of the circle room opened, and a girl with her hands bound stumbled into the light. Her skin was the same warm brown at Bash's, and she had the same sharp nose shape of her mask. Without a doubt, she was his sister.

King Vern intended to kill her.

"Save her," I choked.

"I can't." Bash's breathing was uneven. "My father made a poor deal and lost my sister in return. It was fair, and the deal must be honored. She is now King Vern's possession to do with as he pleases. And this is how he pleases."

My eyes widened. "That can't be right."

He clenched his jaw. "It is the way of our realm. To save her now would put each of my islands at wrong and sentence us all to death."

Troi fought, but her feet didn't move. A post separated her hands so they couldn't touch, but her arms flexed as if she was trying to get them to do so. I didn't know this girl, but I didn't want to see her die.

"There must be a way."

"If she were freed, she could go into hiding. I could make a new deal with King Vern to keep her safe." Bash rubbed his face with his hands, smearing the gold paint. "I need more time to think."

I stared up at the island where Ian stood somewhere, prepared to fire. Any moment now and Troi would be dead. She'd stopped struggling and found Bash in the crowd. A single tear rolled down her cheek.

"Please, all, come find your seats." King Vern gestured to the room. The fae half-heartedly filed in, while the fae king beamed as if he noticed none of the discomfort. Odette's auburn hair passed me by, and she touched my hand.

I grabbed her. "I need a knife," I said.

She frowned but startled me by pulling one from her mass of curls, where it was tied with a ribbon. The fae were now in their seats, and any moment King Vern would give the order to shoot. I only had a second to think of something.

Odette spoke quickly. "If we are planning to stab somebody, King Vern doesn't keep his heart in his body. You'll be in a mess if you try."

Her comment only furthered my frantic confusion. There was so much of this realm I had yet to understand.

Odette stepped toward the arena. "Don't interfere," she whispered. "And if you do, you'd better be certain."

The only thing I was certain about was my heart twisted in a thousand knots while Bash bent as if he'd been punched, his expression that of a lost child searching for something to save him.

"Kill me instead," he called out to King Vern. "Kill me instead of her."

From what I'd gathered, fae lived for thousands of years. He'd said he wasn't much older than me. He was giving up untold centuries to save her.

Troi shouted in return, but her words didn't reach us.

The king's eyes brightened at the idea, but he laughed. "I think not. Another time, perhaps. Tell your father to think twice before accepting deals in the future."

Bash stood back from the room, his expression contorted as the rest of the fae settled into their seats with ghostly faces and averted eyes. I'd planned to strike Vern down, but if Odette was right and that didn't work, I'd need something else. Something certain. Something that couldn't fail.

The idea came to me, and I shivered. But another look at Bash's face set my plan. This would cause me pain, but it would cure his.

"You said the fae love the Mortal Queens no matter how hard they try not to," I said, sliding my hand once more into the nook of Bash's elbow. "I need to know how much."

His gaze broke from Troi long enough to flicker to my face. "We would die for you."

"That's all I need to know."

I slid the dagger into the fold of my skirt. "King Vern." My voice raised. I distanced myself from Bash. "I seek an alliance."

Bash swung his head to me, but I kept from looking his way.

King Vern steadied his hand from giving the signal to fire.

I drifted closer. "I desire a strong alliance, and I can tell you are a strong king. Together we would make quite the pair."

He twirled a finger through his beard. "That we would. What would you offer in exchange?" Even an execution could be paused when talk of alliances was in the air. I only needed his attention a few moments longer.

I took a deep breath and pretended to be almost bored. "First, I need to see that this trick is real. A true king wouldn't hide behind false tricks."

He threw his head back in a laugh. "Watch as close as you like. The archer is true."

Bash was calling my name. I looked at him. "I need an alliance with someone stronger than you."

The hurt in his eyes is for his sister, not me.

I tore my gaze away. King Vern huffed with enjoyment. "Show me your trick," I said as I passed under him. My words crawled as slow as I could make them to give me ample time, while my fingers clenched over the blade. It took restraint not to drive the blade into the king's chest as I walked, but he was not my target. "Show me an archer who can accomplish such a thing."

King Vern's hand raised again.

"Don't, I'll do anything!" Bash had fallen to his knees. I quickened my pace. Troi's glossy eyes bored into mine. I didn't risk a wink. Soft dirt sank beneath each calculated step as I inched along, guessing how close I could get before the fae king suspected I aimed for more than an alliance. Building my courage.

Please don't let me die.

I halted two paces from Troi. This was as close as I dared.

"Show me, my king," I leaned heavily into a flattering tone. "Kill her."

This had to be timed perfectly. At such a distance, we were bound to see the arrow coming before it struck, and that would be my chance.

"Finally." His voice dripped with pleasure and his hand lowered. My wild eyes searched the skies. There it came, the long point of an arrow. At the first sign of movement, I threw myself in front of Troi and slashed with the blade.

Odette's dagger sliced through the rope, freeing one of Troi's hands. At the same moment, an iron arrowhead tore through the back of my shoulder and protruded under my collarbone with a wicked sting. The entire room swayed as King Vern roared.

I was betting on their love for me, praying it was strong enough that he'd free her to spare my life. But I'd intended for the arrow to strike farther from my heart. My arm, perhaps. This was too close.

I choked on something—blood or surprise, I couldn't guess. But my resolve faded in the face of the arrow cleaved through my skin.

Troi was looking at her feet in terror. They weren't bound, yet though she thrashed, they didn't move.

"The only power that works in this room is my own," King Vern growled. He'd chained her there by some magic. He strode through the crowd with the fire of a lion and the scowl of a man I didn't care to cross while Bash raced to Troi to cover her with his body.

"I can't escape," she whispered. She backed away until her body slammed against the dirt wall enclosing us here. She could move for the stairs, but she'd still be King Vern's property, and he could choose not to release her.

Worries for her turned into worries for my own life as the sharp pain began to shred all other thoughts. My knees hit the ground and my vision darkened. "King Vern," I called. But my voice was as weak as my stomach. *Release her or I die*, I meant to say. But all I could see was the arrow in my shoulder, and the word that came out was, "Help."

Bash knelt at my side. "Don't let him heal you."

"You're mad," I gasped with strained breathing. "I'm going to die."

"Don't be so dramatic."

I gaped at him. "Truly," I wheezed. "This is the end."

"Stop it." He almost laughed as he stood. "Vern, renounce your claim over my sister, or the death of a Mortal Queen will be on your shoulders." A rustle of whispers paraded through the fae as Bash stared down King Vern. Whether his mind traced my plan on its own or he came up with it the same way, I was grateful he could stand behind me and push the deal when I couldn't.

Now we only needed King Vern to do his part. Let me die or give in to his love for the Mortal Queens and release Troi.

King Vern's body went rigid two paces from me. He kneeled in the dirt, taking off his robe to fan over my shoulders. "My Queen," he said. Where his eyes ignited with fire moments before, they now flooded with tears. "My beautiful queen."

Bash's words came back to me. *No matter how hard we try, we can't help but love our queens.* Let him be right.

"Let me heal you," King Vern placed a hand over mine, but I yanked it away.

"Only if you release Troi."

He scanned the audience, where all faces were turned to us to catch every moment. His downfall would not be a private one.

"I can't let you die," King Vern said. His muscles flexed and a war seemed to pulse beneath his skin as he clawed his hand into the soil. "I'd never be forgiven."

I'd always thought I could be strong if placed in battle, but this one arrow through my shoulder threatened to knock me out. The darkness in the corners of my eyes crept in. I spoke through gritted teeth. "Release her."

With a growl, King Vern glared up at Bash. "As you wish. Troi is no longer my property."

Appearing strong was no longer my priority. I flung out my hand for King Vern, and he grabbed hold of it. "Bastian?" Bash nodded and without warning ripped the arrow from my shoulder. I yelped in pain.

A soothing sensation flowed through my veins, coiling up my body until it reached the fire in my shoulder and settled in a wave of relief. My next breath came easier, and the one after that was almost normal. Bash held the blood-soaked arrow while Troi ripped the last of her ropes free.

I rolled my shoulder, checking for weakness. Blood soiled my dress, and a crooked scar marred my skin, but it healed without lingering physical pain.

"I had not expected a trick to come from you," King Vern said. Now that he was no longer at risk of bearing the burden of the queen's death, his hardened expression returned. He fixated the entirety of his wrath upon me.

I stood. "If it helps, Bash and I did not plan that together."

"It does not," he grumbled. His stormy eyes held lightning, and I had no doubt he would strike me down in an instant if others were not watching.

Bash reached for my hand to pull me back. "We should go." Troi tossed the dagger back to me, and I caught it.

All the fae stood now, the show at an end, and I dashed up the stairs after Bash and Troi before they could overwhelm us. For the first time since I'd arrived, clouds gathered overhead.

"Whatever he's offered you, you'll regret it!" King Vern's deep voice called after me, sending a chill rippling over my skin. The clouds let loose their first drops. "He is more trouble than he's worth."

Almost every person I'd met had delivered a warning about Bash, and yet I still followed him across the courtyard and onto the chariot where we took off through the night sky.

13

TROI WRAPPED HER ARMS AROUND
her brother, and they held each other during the ride back to his
home. The tall cliffs greeted us with their dull colors, cracked stone,
and narrow streams diving deep into the ground.

"Is Father here?" she asked as we descended.

"I banished him," Bash said, making both Troi and me pause.
Troi recovered first.

"Good. I might have killed him otherwise."

We landed with a soft tap, and Troi practically flew from the
chariot. She breathed in the air of her home and grinned. "So, my
brother is a king now."

Oil lanterns clung to the side of the mountain, lighting up the
palace. The entire first floor was built with windows surrounding
it, so we could see straight into the empty throne room.

"I'm a king," Bash replied. "One who almost lost his sister."

"You two executed that brilliantly." She looked my way for the
first time. "I'm grateful to you. That could have gone very poorly
though, with both the queen and me dead." She was the first
person I'd met who didn't bow before me. Instead she marched for
the palace.

Bash followed her, while I hesitated on the chariot, curling the dagger in my hand. Now that Troi was safe and we'd left the feast, I wasn't certain why I was still here. But at the door's threshold, Bash glanced over his shoulder. "Will you join us?"

Unless I planned to abduct his chariot, I had no choice. I stepped onto the stone. The air ran colder here than at King Vern's home, but a sheet of heat engulfed me with my the first steps into the mountain home, where a river of fire ran in the walls, offering both light and protection from the cold.

Troi walked to the front of the throne and stopped. It was easier to take in her great beauty in this hall, but her eyes held nothing but sadness. "He would have let me die," she whispered.

Bash laid a hand on her shoulder. "He didn't know."

She shot him a look. "Did he think I was bathing in stardust and dining on clams?" She sat at the foot of the throne and leaned back on her hands. "So. Why are you with a Mortal Queen?"

I kept by the door awkwardly, while Bash peered over me. "She's helping me. A bit more than I thought she would, honestly."

Troi shifted forward. "Tell me you planned that tonight. Tell me you knew you'd rescue me."

Bash looked to his feet, and Troi barked a laugh. "Well, that's a small relief, because it was a stupid plan."

"Hey," I said. I didn't need praise, but I'd just taken an arrow to save this girl I didn't know, and some thanks were due. "It worked."

"You almost died," she shot back.

"It was one arrow to her shoulder," Bash said, gaze shifting between us. "You are both too dramatic for your own good."

"I could have died," I agreed. "I'll admit it wasn't perfectly executed. I'd hoped once I cut you free, you could get away on your own, and I thought I'd hold up with an arrow through me better than I did." I twisted the blade under my finger as I went to stand by Bash. The long fireplace coated the grey walls in orange flickers that danced in shadows over his gold-painted face. "But being in an alliance means working for both of us." I quoted him.

"Thank you," he said quietly. "I owe you my life."

I ignored the way my heart sped up when he looked at me as if for the first time. I wanted to believe my intentions tonight were to save a girl from being wrongly killed, but it was only after hearing the anguish in Bash's voice that I'd made my move. Seeing his pain had kept me from thinking clearly. If it was for anyone else, I might not have put myself in such danger.

You are using him. You'd be willing to let him die to save a long line of future queens. This was a game, just like any other, and I could play it just as well as any fae.

I cleared my throat. "I'm just grateful King Vern can be so easily deceived."

Troi touched the skin of her wrists where they'd been rubbed red and raw. "You won't pull off something like that so effortlessly next time."

My brow furrowed. "Why not? I can be clever."

She snorted. "It doesn't matter how clever you are. You made a fool of King Vern in front of the entire realm. All the fae kings now know you are a queen to be reckoned with, and they will be on their guard. Trust me, that was the last time you wing a plan and don't get burned. My guess is the game has already begun to see who can outwit the Mortal Queen who took an arrow to trick a king."

Any pride from my actions turned into fear for what came next.

Troi drew to her feet. "Now, if you'll excuse me, it seems King Vern didn't believe he needed to feed one up for execution."

Her words clung to me as she left. I'd yet to see the repercussions for my actions tonight, but I guessed they'd start with a scolding from Talen for publicly humiliating a fae king without care for the backlash. After that—I'd need to be on my guard.

Bash sank onto the throne.

"Why would you do that?" His expression was more curious than angry. "I've gone over it in my head again and again and I can't figure it out. Why did you put yourself in front of an arrow for my sister?"

"I need you." I gathered my courage in the face of the mighty fae king. Odette's dagger in my hand helped. "Now you're going to give me what I need from you."

Realization dawned in his eyes. "Don't offend me by believing I'm as easy to manipulate as King Vern. You have my gratitude, but I don't technically owe you anything."

"I know. I also know our alliance bans me from deceiving you. But you will honor my request, or you will find being in an alliance with me to be most unenjoyable." I let the dagger pause between my fingers, smiling over it as if I was someone to be feared. Inside, all I could think of was how easily he plucked stars from the sky, and how little effort it would take him to kill me.

His stare was cold, and his lips bent in a heavy frown. He drummed his fingers on his knee so slowly I feared he'd merely stare at me until I relented.

But it was he who relented. "Ask."

I held my head high. "I intend to ask every fae king to stand together and use their power to save the Mortal Queens." It dawned on me that King Vern would now be a difficult fae to convince to help me, but that worry was for another day. Today was for victory. "You will stand with them."

Bash's eyes narrowed, but he nodded. "Fine."

"And second," I said, "you will attend a dinner party I'm hosting tomorrow night, where you will bow before me to offer an alliance."

The room was silent until he roared with laughter. "I'll do no such thing."

I shrugged. "Then I will tell all your islands how horrible of a ruler you will be, and, one by one, persuade them to pledge their allegiance to my name. You will be a king of nothing."

I held my breath for his answer, hoping the stern look in my eyes was fierce enough to sway him.

Bash rubbed his thumb over his lip. From behind his throne, Troi had reappeared with a platter of breads and cheeses, but she didn't come nearer. She wore an amused smile and winked at me.

"I don't bow," Bash said stiffly.

"Then I don't play nice." I moved swiftly away.

"You cannot force me," Bash called out.

"I have other options. If you don't agree, you can consider our alliance broken," I sang behind me. My chest squeezed tight as I neared the end of the hall. "Good luck getting Gaia to join with you. You won't see me again."

When he still didn't relent, I added one last reminder. "You already told me how the fae love their queens. It'll be too easy to beckon the lords to my allegiance. You'll lose your kingdom, all because of your pride."

He hesitated, but I knew I'd won.

"Fine," Bash growled. "I will kneel before you, my Queen." The last bit sounded almost sarcastic, but I chose to ignore that.

The relief in my next breath was more obvious than I intended. "Good." I lowered my blade. "Just watch. I'll be the first Mortal Queen to survive the two years."

Tonight had gone far better than I could have planned, even though I didn't get to speak to four of the six kings. I'd get my chance for that tomorrow night after Bash bowed before me and asked for an alliance he already had. Between tonight and tomorrow, the fae would know my strength.

Troi came forward and set down the platter, then straightened to regard us. Bash's frown deepened at her smirk. "Well done. And you might be the first to survive in our time, but you wouldn't be the first Mortal Queen to live."

Bash shot her a hard look and quickly stood. "Troi." His voice was ice cold, threatening.

"What?" My body went slack. Just as I thought I'd figured things out, another piece of the complicated puzzle came to strike me.

Troi popped a piece of cheese into her mouth. "Legend says another survived before you."

14

I SLOWLY TURNED TO BASH. OUT OF all the thoughts racing inside, the first to spill forth came with a dash of anger. "Liar."

He shook his head. "No, I was protecting you."

I drew myself up and crossed my arms. "My protection is none of your concern. So much for 'an alliance means you look to the interest of both people.' You should have told me another Mortal Queen lived."

"Supposedly lived," Bash said. "It's a tale that many, including myself, don't believe. Troi doesn't even believe it."

"Don't drag me into this." She ate another piece of cheese.

"Drag you? You started this."

I shook my head, hoping if I shook it hard enough, all the confusion would drift away. "One of you explain. I don't care which."

"I will," Bash answered quickly before Troi could speak. "There isn't much to the story. It's been said one girl lived before, but no one knows how. She lived the remainder of her days in hiding somewhere in the fae realm, and apparently her descendants are among us today." He lifted a hand. "That's all anyone knows."

"That's not true," Troi put in. "I know one thing more. The girl was from Ruen."

Bash lifted a brow. "That means nothing to me."

But that last bit of information captivated my mind. "It means something to me," I said slowly. She couldn't have been from Ruen because the fae only accepted girls from the center island. But perhaps she'd wanted to go to Ruen instead of being chosen. She had a Passion for the arts she longed to pursue, enough that she claimed Ruen as her own, even though she never could have belonged to it. *Maybe she was an artist. Like me.*

The knowledge alone wasn't enough to save me, of course. I needed more. "How did she do it?"

"*If* she did it," Bash corrected. "No one knows how. It's just a story, Thea, created by some wishful Mortal Queen or by a longing fae foolish enough to have fallen in love with one." He took off his jacket and hung it on his throne.

"Strip her of all hope, if you please," Troi remarked. "But not all of us are so cold-hearted, brother." She tapped the covered box next to the throne.

I peered more intently. I couldn't identify it the first night, and I got no better look tonight at whatever lay within.

"It's not cold-hearted, it's honest," Bush stated. "I need to take Thea home. I have work to do. Tonight will most definitely have ramifications, and I need to prepare for whatever King Vern is going to do."

"I have more questions," I protested.

"I have no more answers. If you push, I'm counting it as the second question I owe you."

That quieted me. I was saving my final question for a time of need.

In my silence, Bash brushed past me. Troi offered an apologetic smile before retreating to the heart of the mountain with the platter only she had eaten from, leaving no choice but to follow Bash outside. He offered his hand to help me climb into the chariot and withdrew it as soon as I stepped aboard. He rode such a fine line between kind and cold. Luring me in just enough to awaken interest but giving nothing in return.

Stars winked as we passed, growing brighter with signs of morning as we traveled in heavy silence. As soon as we landed, I'd find Talen to ask about the girl who survived. Part of me hoped he'd withheld more information, while a larger part hoped he had no knowledge of it and hadn't kept anything from me.

We settled into the familiar courtyard with the two torches lit in the center, and the black crown embedded in stone. The seven thrones faced us, a reminder of when I'd first arrived. I must have seen Bash that day, but it had all been such a whirl that his face was lost among the other fae kings.

I'd been convinced this new life would be magical then. That was less than a week ago. What new riddles would this next week bring?

I stepped from the chariot and headed to the door.

Bash was at my side in an instant. "Thank you again, Thea. My sister is everything to me. I'm very grateful for what you've done for us tonight."

I paused without turning. The river offered a soft melody by my feet as I spoke. "Bow tomorrow, and you'll never need to thank me again."

A light wind blew past and he left.

The door to the palace stood open to allow both magnificent white thrones to be seen. My breath caught in my throat. Talen had already added my stars.

The three stars twinkled as if still in the sky, like large diamonds demanding attention and making all else dull in comparison. They molded to the palmette at the top, each equal in splendor. It set my throne apart from Gaia's. Now all would know the High Queen of the West wasn't a girl who stood in the shadows, but one who acquired stars from kings.

"I am curious to know . . ." Talen wore his usual top hat and long-tailed suit, combined with ruby-red earrings and a red pin through his nose. He stood at the top of the stairs. "When I said to beware of King Bastian and make an alliance with King Vern, what went through your mind?"

I uttered a short laugh. "I had the best intentions." I gathered my long skirt in a fist and dipped a toe in the river, stirring up the fish.

"I wager you did. Your implementation needed work." He came down to my side to eye the fish as they bubbled at the surface. "However, you've been invited to several events already, including one with King Brock who was impressed by your little performance tonight."

I shook the water off my foot. "Have you gotten replies for my dinner party?"

"Many. And after your spectacle, I suspect I'll receive many more. The entire island will be flooded with fae hoping to catch another look at you, wondering what they missed last time."

"Good." Anxiety clawed at my nerves, settling into my bones where it made a home, whispering how unprepared I was for this realm. I invited a new voice to remind it of how much I'd already done. "When I wake, you can tell me everything you know about the other kings, so I can lay proper traps. I need something from each of them. But for now, my bed awaits."

Exhaustion hung as heavy as one of Lord Winster's wools, and I dragged myself up the stairs.

"I have business to attend to," Talen called from below. "But I'll be here when you wake."

Faithful Talen. I glanced back. The stars in my throne winked once more and I left them behind to claim some much-needed sleep before hosting my first event tonight, an evening bound to be filled with more than food and light conversation. After King Vern's party, I could no longer rely solely on asking the kings for their support. This time I'd go in prepared to trick my way into their favors.

I tossed my shoes to the side as soon as I pushed the door open. The curtains over the balcony swayed with the lightest breeze, and the ever-burning fire heated the wool at its threshold. My shoes had landed near two canvases propped on easels. My paintbrushes sat in a cup on the desk.

Thoughts of the fabled surviving queen and how she'd been connected to Ruen flooded my mind. She might have wanted to Passion for music or culinary, but the hopeful parts inside convinced me she'd been drawn to art as I was. Had she brought paintbrushes with her, too, and longed to adorn these blank white walls with murals? Did her descendants still live among the fae and share her love for painting?

The rough surface of the canvas glided under my fingertips. Would they see my art and think of her?

My hand stilled. My art could remind them of her. My art could be a bridge.

This realm didn't create. They lived in lavish splendor where everything around them was such perfection, they had little use for creating tokens with their hands. Paintings like mine wouldn't enrapture the fae, but they could draw the eyes of the descendants of a mortal eager for a view of where they came from.

It was a long shot. But it might be enough to connect and uncover how she survived the fae realm.

"It's not a plan of Cal's caliber," I acknowledged to myself. Cal would have three plans by now and charts to compare them. "But it just might do."

The idea had formed in a whirlwind of colors and shapes like a painting coming together all at once, leaving me breathless.

The codes.

The hidden messages.

The connection to her descendants.

Sleep could wait. This couldn't. I grabbed my brushes and some jars of paint, then the little soldier toy, Antonio, for good measure, and swiftly headed downstairs.

The throne room again blinded me with its white floors and blank walls, prime for color to overtake them. This palace was large and empty, void of servants or guests or laughter, but that made it the perfect canvas. Soon, the entire fae realm would be here. If one of the surviving queen's descendants came, they'd be sure to see my paintings.

I lifted my brush. I'd cloak my message inside the art. My plea for escape would be hidden right in front of the fae's eyes, but hopefully it would catch the attention of a descendant of the Ruen Mortal Queen who might recognize the bridge from any stories she might have told.

The chances were slighter than I fancied. Still, I dipped my brush in a turquoise pigment and began to paint the famous bridge from the center island. The bridge we called Salvation's Crossing.

15

I PAINTED ALL MORNING UNTIL MY
arms were sore, stopping only to feast on smoked salmon and
sugared vegetables before swirling the bristles in fresh pigment
to begin again. I'd finished the bridge and moved on to another
painting—the center square where the fae always appeared. I drew
the three ambassadors in all their grandeur at the front.

Their vanity would be my tool tonight. This picture ought to
captivate the fae more than the one of a simple bridge, and that
would be how my message could be hidden.

"You've been busy," Odette observed. She circled the room,
lingering before the throne to gaze upon the stars. "That will
garner respect for sure. Bastian?"

"They certainly weren't from Vern."

Odette's laugh rippled. "I still can't believe you jumped in front
of that arrow. What were you thinking?"

*I was thinking of the handsome fae king and how to make
him happy.*

"It was more of an impulse than anything," I said, averting my
eyes. I dabbled at the picture until I was content with the shine of
the fae's hair.

"You should have seen Vern after you left"—Odette smirked—"all worked into a sulk. He hardly spoke to anyone the entire night. It was glorious."

I smiled despite myself. "Any idea what your cousin may plan in retaliation?"

She twisted the lace hem of her gown between her thin fingers. "Vern can be tricky, but this ought to put him in his place for a while. He takes months to plan tricks, giving us enough time to avoid them."

"We will do better than avoid them." Talen's voice reached us before he did. He swept into the hall waving papers in his hand. "We will trick him back. Every king will be coming tonight."

My brush lowered as a wave of nerves hit me. "Tell me about them." I tried to keep my voice from wavering. "I need to know all I can."

Talen eyed me. "I think you should sleep. You haven't done that in almost two days."

My body chose that exact moment to yawn. I did my best to swallow it. "I'm fine. This is more important. This and learning about the kings."

Odette touched the marble beside my painting. "Between this and the stars, you're really making the west side more vibrant than the east."

"That's the plan. The kings, please."

"Alright," she said in an airy tone and settled beside me. "You've met King Vern. Next most powerful is King Brock, who doesn't control many lands nor often participate in games but maintains a fierce loyalty among the fae. You can't even think of a trap against him without someone telling him. He's smarter than the rest and is nearly impossible to fool." She braided the length of her auburn hair as she talked, letting it rest against her cream gown. She was prepared for tonight with gold rings in her nose and crimson lips. I had a lot of work to do, both on the walls and myself, before guests arrived, but Odette could have shown up in a flax sack and outshone me. Any of the fae could.

"Okay, so be careful with Brock."

"Be careful with all of them," Talen said. He kept a distance with an expression that said he was still upset about the arrow incident.

"Then King Leonard," Odette went on. "He is rich, the richest of all, and he hoards that wealth like a dragon, snarling at any who come too close."

"In regard to him, there has been an interesting development," Talen remarked. "Leonard made a poor deal two days ago and owes the lion's share of his wealth to Brock now. That's why I wanted my queen to align with Brock or Vern, but alas."

Odette's brows raised. "Who else knows that?"

Talen's smile was mischievous. "None other than us. Not even his own bride knows."

The word *bride* grabbed my full attention, and I almost dropped my brush. "Are many of the kings married?" I tried to keep my question casual. A wife to a fae king would have to be equally gorgeous and mysterious, even more lovely to behold than those I'd already seen. It was difficult to imagine such a person who saw a different side of the kings.

It would also be a strong alliance for a Mortal Queen to make.

Odette undid her braid to retie it. "Not many kings marry," she put in. "Leonard and Brock are the only ones. When a fae marries, the alliance can never be broken. Spending thousands of years with someone isn't an easy choice."

Even marriage was referred to as an alliance. But to spend thousands of years with a person was almost unimaginable. What were the kings like in the evening when they rolled their sleeves up, poured a glass of spiced wine, and let out all the worries of the day with one long breath? What were they like in the sleepy hours of the morning when their hair was messy and their shirts rumpled?

I attacked my painting more vigorously to clear my thoughts.

Odette tapped her foot against Talen's. "How did you come by this when no one else knows of Leonard's deal?"

He shrugged. "I'm a man of many talents. But, of course, Thea is welcome to everything I know. Perhaps that bit of information could be used to trap him."

Noted. King Brock. Lots of money. "How about the rest of the kings? There are two more?"

"Yes. King Thorn. Young, wise enough, and some call him handsome." He mumbled that last bit and glanced up.

Odette sent him a sharp look that held hidden meaning, but Talen seemed to purposefully ignore it. "Then there's King Arden, with whom the House of Delvers is aligned. He was prepared to align with you through us before you made the foolish deal with Bastian."

Odette, finally satisfied with her hair, looked at us. "What deal?"

"Thea can't make another alliance now that she's with Bastian."

Her mouth dropped open. "You're insane. You need alliances."

"I need Bash," I countered.

"Bash?" Odette rose as her eyes widened.

I bit my tongue. "Bastian. I need his power to grant me freedom, and he's already proven useful. Without him I wouldn't know why you have Mortal Queens, and I wouldn't have tricked Vern the other night. He's agreed to stand with the other kings to free the Mortal Queens, and when those kings see him bow tonight, they will have respect for me as an equal. I need them all to stand by my side to undo this realm's bind on Mortal Queens if I'm to live."

Odette stared at my painting and then at Talen's face, which had gone slack. "I didn't know that was your plan."

Half of it. The paintings would be another.

Talen knelt. "Thea, it's been tried before. It didn't work."

I'd guessed as much. But I was planning on pushing them further. I was willing to sacrifice their lives for mine, and for the lives of the thousands of girls who would come after me. I would sacrifice myself for them as well if it came to that. If I thought on it for too long, or on *him*, I'd break. So I didn't. I only thought of Gaia and of every girl I knew back home who would be kept safe from this deadly fate.

"I will try it again," I said blankly.

"Even if the kings could undo what their ancestors did, you'd need all of them to do it," Talen explained.

"Right." I nodded. "That's what I just said."

He pointed to the kings's thrones outside. "The seventh king is missing. You'd need him too."

His words hit me with a relentless force. I almost cursed. Or cried. Or yelled. Instead, I dropped my brush and stared at the painting of the three ambassadors back home, the last moment my life was normal. If I couldn't find a way there, I'd never see that crowded center or hear the music or see my brothers again.

"I don't suppose anyone has tried looking for the king?" Foolish hope dotted my voice.

"For hundreds of years," Talen replied softly. "That plan can't work."

"It still might. Only six kings rule now, so that has to be enough."

My determination was that of a child, but I clung to it all the same.

"It's worth a try," Odette commented, and I loved her for it. She put her hand over mine. "But be careful tonight. I know a thing or two about trying to manipulate kings, and it comes at a price."

I packed up my brushes. "As long as it's not my life, I'll pay it."

The evening came with the scent of cinnamon in the air, music in the halls, and my tallest shoes on my feet. I sat on my throne before anyone arrived, legs crossed at the ankles and arms draped over the sides with a distant expression on my face. Everyone entering from the courtyard would have an impressive first look of me below the stars received from a king. My dress was a purple so dark it was almost black, and my hair was twisted with black gems throughout.

Gaia was the first to arrive. She took one look at my throne and raised a brow. "That seems a bit much."

Something about her blind acceptance of her fate while I was fighting so hard—to the point of being shot with an arrow and willing to give up my life to save her and all the future queens—grated at me. "Careful," I said. "Those stars would make a brilliant weapon."

She settled onto her own throne, her lips a thin line. Tiny diamonds lined her lower eyelid, shining only a fraction as bright as the stars above me.

"Whatever you're planning, it won't work," she said, keeping her face forward.

Now it was I who didn't reply.

Talen and Odette descended the stairs together, and I was struck by what a beautiful couple the pair would make. They separated at the bottom for Talen to take a spot at my side and Odette to welcome the guests.

"You're fidgeting as much as you did at my coronation," I whispered to him.

He stilled his hands. "The House of Delvers is becoming more powerful than the other two Houses, a thing that hasn't happened for centuries. I have a few deals to make tonight as well to ensure it remains that way."

"You could align with Bastian. I'm certain he would be eager for allies."

"The boy king?" Talen adjusted his top hat. "I'll reconsider that in a thousand years when he's proven himself."

Phrases like that would never stop jolting me.

"Here they come," Talen warned. I resumed my relaxed position just as Odette swung open the doors to let the breeze barrel though.

The fae arrived at the same time, their chariots falling from the sky like rain in a downpour of splendor, masks, and smiles. They swarmed the courtyard and headed straight for the throne room. The first to enter stood tall with his hair long and golden to match the mane of the lion at his side.

I blinked.

The lion yawned while staying close to his master, though no leash held him there.

Talen leaned in. "He acquired the beast recently and likes to show it off. Apparently, it does tricks."

"Fascinating," I said with a strained tone. One bite and I'd be in the creature's belly.

To my delight, almost every fae did a double take when they saw my throne, and each lingering look only fueled my pride.

Many came to my feet to lay down baskets of cakes, jewelry, scarves, or fruit. "For you," they'd say with a short bow. "Our dear High Queen." I nodded graciously to each, asking their name and promising to love the gift. One wrote a book of poems for me and tucked it into a basket. They brought an equal number of gifts for Gaia, their other beloved queen, but their eyes were only for me.

"They enjoy your art," Talen said.

My eyes went to the side wall. As predicted, most fae gathered around the one depicting the ambassadors arriving in our world. Scarce fae had seen my home realm before, and they laughed at how small we seemed compared to them. A few wandered to the other mural, but as far as I could tell, none lingered before it.

"What's the meaning of the bridge?" Talen asked, gathering the latest baskets to place behind the throne.

"Nothing," I lied. "But if anyone makes a comment about it, I want to know."

"I'm sure none will speak badly of such beautiful work."

"Anything," I emphasized. "I want to know anything. Even the most passing comment."

Talen studied me before nodding.

I changed the topic. "Odette looks stunning tonight."

Her cream dress hugged her hips perfectly and split toward the top to become strips of fabric that wove around her neck and arms.

Talen shot me a glance. "Did she say something?"

I gasped. "There's a story there! I want to know."

"It's nothing." He reddened and straightened his already perfect jacket. "She's just a friend."

"I thought friends were worthless," I said, garnering a short look from him in reply. "Your words."

His gaze drifted to Odette. "It's a story best left alone."

That did nothing but feed my hunger for the tale. His eyes held sorrow, leaving me to guess if it was something she'd done to him or a missed opportunity from years ago. From what I knew of Talen, he was sneaky and clever. Clearly handsome, like all the fae. Even for all his friends-are-useless talk, romance must have found him at some point in his long life.

"I do love interesting stories," I said casually.

He hushed me. "Here comes your own interesting story, right on time."

At Talen's raised hand, a lyre came from the wall to play a tune, beckoning the fae deeper into the throne room where they gathered on both sides of the river before their queens. Outside, Bash's chariot landed. He and Troi stepped off.

He'd dressed in a gold suit to match the gold band around his head, the six earrings in his ear, and rings on every finger. Troi stepped away, leaving him to walk alone. His eyes met mine and never wavered, disdain oozing from his expression. It lived in his tight lips and flexed hands. Only once did his eyes flicker away to find the stars.

Troi watched with an amused grin.

I stood and crossed my hands in front of me. All the fae turned to see what I was focused on. They found him, coming down the center toward me.

"Welcome, King Bastian," I said regally.

"My Queen."

His warm, hoarse voice drifted to the corners of the room, mingling with the sounds of the fae whispering among themselves as I held as still as possible until he reached my feet. The copper flecks in his eyes stood out like fire.

Anticipation danced over my skin.

He sighed. Then, as all the realm watched, Bash lowered himself down on one knee.

The whispers silenced and the fae turned to statues. The only movement was the curled tips of the torch fire, the flutter of the three stars in my throne, and the tilt of Bash's head as he lowered it into a bow.

I'd done it. I'd gotten a fae king to bow before me.

"I, King Bastian, would like to offer myself into an alliance with you, High Queen of the West." His deep voice echoed through the hall and to every corner of my heart. Someday, I'd paint this moment. I'd paint it with my finest brushes, then hang it in the hall so I'd always remember what he looked like right now.

I took my time, breathing in the sight of him on bent knee. It was only when he looked up with a glare that I answered.

"It would be my honor."

He stood quickly. "Good." He gave a short nod, then spun away in swift retreat. Without another word, he climbed onto his chariot and fled to the skies.

I silenced the ache at seeing him go. He'd done his job, which was all I needed from him.

The triumph on my face was irrepressible as I addressed the crowd. "Thank you for coming tonight. I hope you find your evening most enjoyable."

I stepped from my throne to join the room. Bash might have done his duty, but I still had a part to play. One king down, five to go.

16

THE FAE WHO CAME ALONGSIDE ME
first had eyes so green they might have been emeralds and a smile
so sweet it must taste better than sugar. His skin was rich brown
and the pull to him almost overwhelming. Right away I knew this
must be one of the fae kings.

"My lord," I said with a bob.

His eyes twinkled. "I think it is I who should bow to you," he
said. But he didn't bow. However, he did offer his arm for me to
walk with him, and the sea of people parted for us. Talen caught my
eye and mouthed a name for me with a wink. Brock.

"Bastian is not one I would have guessed would align so easily
with a queen," Brock said thoughtfully, keeping his gaze forward as
we moved slowly toward the cool air of the courtyard.

"It will be a mutually beneficial arrangement." Half of my focus
was on remembering everything I'd been told about this king. He
was powerful among the others, that much I knew. Was he the one
who owed money? My fuzzy mind gave me little hope of recalling
everything. Talen was right. I should have slept.

"I see. Tell me, do you play chess?" He gestured, and I startled.
A small round table sat in the middle of the courtyard with a board

of midnight-black stone topped with marble pieces. Torches lined our path to backless round seats.

I hadn't set this table for tonight. He had prepared for me.

Uncertainty crept up, weighing down each step. My knowledge of chess was minimal at best.

The glint in the king's eyes told me he'd been playing for eons. "It would be an honor to have a match with you, my Queen." His voice was crisp, and he was built like a wall but moved like a river. I was nothing but a nervous firefly. He sat down.

The lamplight added to the ominous feel of the evening with both light and shadows dancing freely over the courtyard. I kept my back tall so those who watched would see a composed queen. I rubbed my fingertips together, wishing for Antonio to give me strength.

Turn away, my mind said. *Decline to play.*

But Cal had taught me, and he was smart. Turning away would make me look weak, and tonight was to be mine. So I accepted.

The king sat behind black, giving me the honored white. I wiped my sweaty palms on my sides as I sat behind the color Cal had always chosen for himself and made my first move. The cold white pawn was heavier than I'd anticipated.

Brock acted as if he'd expected that and moved his own pawn forward without hesitation. I tried to match his speed but realized I should have waited before taking my first move to plan some variety of stratagem.

With Brock's second move, he advanced his queen diagonally.

I'd never seen an opponent bring the queen out so quickly, but the narrow glint of his eye was too confident to mistake the move for a blunder. Nerves swelled inside.

I moved my pawn forward two.

"You've impressed many fae in such a short time."

"Thank you."

"But I'm not as easy to impress." He moved his bishop. "Winner of this game owes the other a favor?"

No! my mind yelled. But my pride spoke instead. "Deal." If I won, he'd be added to my count of kings who would help me live, and that temptation was too sweet to pass up.

I mentally recited Cal's teachings as I moved another pawn.

Brock whisked his queen into the space before my bishop, across from my king. It was so early in the game that the king had no escape, and the queen was on the wrong side to save me.

The smile on Brock's face was colder than ice. "Checkmate."

I stared at the board long enough for him to stand and begin to walk away. "Wait," I called. I had one more move to play against him. "A second game, one of a different nature. If I can surprise you, you'll owe me a favor."

"And if you don't, you'll owe me a second."

I quivered to think of what he could do with two favors from me. But I nodded. He stood back patiently, eyes dark behind his mask. He was as still as stone, waiting for me to surprise him enough that he'd owe me. I had to trust my information from Talen was good.

My voice was quiet enough that onlookers couldn't catch it. "You owe the lion's share of your wealth to King Leonard, and not even your wife knows."

The stone didn't crack. But after a moment, he laughed. "I hold no secrets from my bride. This might have surprised any other king, but your information is false, my queen. It is not I who owes a speck of silver to Leonard, but he to me."

No. I was too tired. Too eager to play another game.

I'd remembered the information wrong. This loss was worse than the chess match. I'd brought this one upon myself with no help from anyone else.

"That is two favors." He smiled at my misery. "And I call upon the first one now. I don't trust you, High Queen Althea. Your attempt to master this realm makes you less predictable than Queen Gaia, and I don't like things I can't control. You will do me the favor of remaining confined to the Queen's Palace for six months, not even to step foot in the courtyard."

Blood drained from my head. "I'll starve."

"You may have visitors," his pleasant tone sounded as if now *he* was doing *me* a favor. "Make them tend to you."

I was to be his caged animal, bound to a home of white walls and silence, with Gaia as company, watching the realm live through my window. My time was already limited. Now I had even less to bring the kings together to save myself.

He had no idea of the extent of my horror behind my mask, but it crippled me.

He lifted a hand, and a chariot swept from the sky to fetch him. "Farewell, my Queen," he said. "It's good to remember you are but a mortal and not a fae."

I thought they loved their queens, but it was clear they loved this game more. Trickery, deceit, alliances—it fueled them. Their love for me couldn't shake that.

The chariot leapt to the sky, and instantly my feet burned as if they were on fire. His words played in my head. *Not even to step foot in the courtyard.* I had to get back inside the palace. My six months began now. I kept my head low to discourage anyone from waylaying me as I rushed back inside to stop the heat from raging at my feet. With the first step under the arched door, relief came. But with the relief came a wave of humiliation. My failure would be a difficult thing to hide.

The paintings on the wall caught my eye with their brilliant colors. They'd be my only hope now.

The stars in my throne didn't shine as bright, as if they were turning their light from me to match my disappointment. I'd dared to believe I could shine as brightly as they. Instead, I got burned.

I should have slept. I would have remembered that Talen said Leonard owed money, not Brock. The crown of failure was mine to wear alone, and I'd bear it as silently as I could over the next six months, so no one knew what I'd lost.

You are not ready for that realm.

My father was right.

I found Talen's top hat in the crowd as he wove his way to me and held out an arm. His jacket was smooth under my fingers as I took his arm. "Show me the other kings," I whispered. "I need a win tonight."

"They are gone," he told me. "All left at the same time, a few seconds ago."

Was it some message from Brock that pulled them all away? His tongue was not mine to control, and already he might be telling how he bested me out of my own foolishness. Heat flamed my cheeks.

"Then there is nothing left for me to gain from tonight." I marched toward the steps. "Enjoy the music and wine. I will be in my room."

"Is everything alright?" His voice was soothing, but it couldn't quell my emotions.

I paused with my back to him. "No," I said. "I made a terrible mistake, and now I pay the price."

Long after the music and laughter had ceased in the grand halls, I crept barefoot in my satin gown down the vast stairwell, lit by the stars in my throne. The fish swam to the edge of the river like scaly gems on a bright blue canvas, almost begging to be painted. They peered at their midnight guest, but I passed them.

I carried a single oil lamp and held it at arm's length. The room was spotless, not even an empty wine glass or platter of crumbs to show for the night.

My wall paintings lured me. They greeted me with soft colors and the scent of pigments as I set the lamp down with a clink.

Desperate prayers flew through my head. We'd always prayed to the fae on the five islands, but now I prayed to a power higher than theirs to deliver me. I prayed with all my might as I examined the painting for writing along the bridge, a note tucked into the stone, or a faint message hidden nearby. My fingers scratched at the walls, my feet dug into the ground, and my eyes searched madly.

I needed this so badly. I needed there to be a Mortal Queen who had survived, and I needed to know how she'd done it.

My skirts billowed under my knees as I searched lower to inspect the corner where the wall met the stone floor, prying at the marble for a crevice fit for a note. I ran my fingertips over the dry paint, combing for any bump or alteration.

There was nothing. No message. No answers. No hint that anyone had noticed my plea.

Tears streaked my cheeks as I checked it all again. Then again. And again.

I pounded my fist against the wall, then sank so low my head touched the ground. I broke into deep sobs.

Just like that, the last bit of hope I'd held on to drifted away like one of the chariots, lost in an endless sky where I had little chance of finding it again. I was utterly trapped in the fae realm and totally unprepared to die.

17

TALEN HAD LEFT ENORMOUS CHOCOLATE
muffins the size of my head on my bedside table, along with a promise
to bring more paint since he'd noticed I'd run out of blue.

Just as I read the note, he knocked on the door. A silver platter held
fifteen jars of fresh paint, which Talen beamed over.

"Did you grind the pigments yourself?" I asked as I stretched from
my bed. If I focused on how poorly last night had gone, I'd never get up.

He slid the platter onto my desk. "Odette helped."

My feet met soft slippers. I took a muffin and examined each jar.
Talen tilted his head to see my face.

"What, no comment about me and Odette this morning?"

I turned away. "I haven't the strength to pry right now. You can
mention her name once I finish my muffin if you'd like, and we'll see
what happens."

I went to rub my eyes but my hand hit my mask instead. Not even
a week in and already the black mask felt as much a part of me as my
own skin. This realm had changed me that much that quickly.

Talen turned in a slow circle about the room while I pulled on a
knitted sweater. "The air feels like misery. What's wrong?"

I chose that moment to bite into the muffin. He waited patiently while I savored the taste and riffled through my brushes. I needed a few more moments to suffer in my failure privately.

"Do we have more canvases?" I asked through my next bite.

"You're done blemishing the palace walls?"

I swallowed. "You're in a funny mood today, but no. I simply want to send paintings out across the realm instead of confining them here."

"Oh, of course. It would be a crime not to share your art," Talen mocked.

"It really would. I'm going to need at least thirty canvases."

His brows shot up. "That's quite a lot."

"I have quite a lot of time." I took a deep breath and pulled my sweater closer, hoping it would hold me together as I disclosed my downfall. "I made a deal with the wrong man last night, and he's trapped me here as punishment."

Talen didn't move for a moment, then he blew out a breath. "Tell me."

I did, though it pained me to relive it. I never should have played chess against someone who'd been here since long before I was even born, and I never should have made the second deal when my emotions were so high. I added that in so Talen would see I'd learned from my mistake.

He rubbed his forehead. Once more, he looked just like my brother, and somehow it felt as if I'd let Cal down too. In a way, I had. There was precious little time to figure out how to return to him as it was.

"I'm sorry." My voice cracked. "I was only trying to get home."

Talen shook his head slowly, then suddenly straightened. "I'll fix this," he said, tipping his hat at me. "And there are canvases in the closet. I trust you can paint without getting into trouble."

I looked down. "Yes."

"Good. There is also a chessboard in that closet in case you wish to practice." By his tone, I knew he wanted me to practice chess over painting. I bit my tongue and when I lifted my head, he'd gone.

Maybe Talen could fix this and no one had to know about it. But the morning had brought a new surge of will to live, and my plan for my paintings expanded. I'd draw more messages and send them throughout the realm.

"We'll figure this out," I said to Antonio, setting him on the edge of the desk to watch over me as I set up my canvas by the balcony for inspiration. I began a piece depicting the fae realm sitting above my own with a crown centered in my home realm. The word *freed* hid in the sand at the crown's base. I'd take my time with this one, not rushing through, so it was beautiful enough to capture the attention of the Mortal Queen's descendants.

"*Tritshu un kuy*," I recited. *May he favor you.* We never knew who "he" was, but Mother had spoken the words as tenderly as she said "I love you." I needed my mother's blessing today.

My brush had just streaked across the canvas to lay the dark blue base along the top edge, when a dash of black parchment on the balcony caught my eye, held down by ore. *Bastian.* I dropped my brush and went over to the balcony.

The parchment ruffled when I neared, as if excited to have found its recipient. Silver dotted the folded corners.

The beat in my heart was something more than an alliance bond. I took four deep breaths before opening it, enough to remind myself I was using him for my freedom, just as he was using me to secure his reign. Once I was free or dead, he'd live thousands of years and not once think of me again.

I unfolded the note to find his writing.

Since you insisted upon humiliating me at your gala, I plan to host one of my own next week, where I will invite the local lords to witness the strong alliance between us. You will oblige my requests at this dinner. You owe me that.

Unless Talen was clever enough to get me out of this punishment, I could never attend his gala. He'd be furious when he learned how I let myself be fooled, and his alliance with me would be laughable. My mistake was a mark upon his reputation as well.

Without a second thought, I released the paper to the air and let it fall unanswered. I shut the balcony doors and drew the drapes, keeping my misfortune inside with me instead of letting him hear of it. I wasn't ready for his mockery.

The familiar movement of painting overtook me in a sweet release with the brush of bristles over canvas, the thick pigments, the scent of turned soil, and the symphony of shapes, all created at my command.

It was the last bit of power I still held. I might not rule proudly over the fae, but these paints were mine.

Talen returned as I dipped the dirty brushes into clear water, watching the colors ripple away.

He didn't dance into the room or sweep his hat off his head and toss it in the air. Instead, he folded his jacket and set it on a plush chair before inspecting my painting.

"This may be my favorite one yet. Both our realms, joined as one," he remarked.

"Don't do this to me. Did you convince him to release me from the favor?"

Talen bent closer to the painting, and my breath caught before he moved back without finding the message. I rolled my brushes between my hands.

"Halfway. He lessened it to three months."

Still trapped, but at least not for a quarter of my time here.

"You can thank me later," Talen said then bit into a muffin.

"I'm sorry. Thank you."

"Anything for my queen." He gestured to the canvas. "Any particular place you want me to send this? King Bastian's, perhaps?" He grinned wickedly, and I thought of the note I'd tossed over the balcony.

"No." I finished cleaning my brushes to begin a second painting. "I'd rather that particular king remain oblivious to my imprisonment." I switched the finished piece with a blank canvas.

Something about the beige fabric stirred excitement in me with its promise. While I'd painted many pieces before, I'd never envisioned their potential would be as dramatic as my chance of survival.

Talen opened the balcony doors again to let the crisp air in. "Little chance of that, my Queen. The entire realm is abuzz with news of your ill-fated chess match, leaving you no opportunity to hide your misfortune from the fae. They'll know you were bested. Even King Bastian."

I groaned as I leaned over in my seat, resting my forehead against my hand.

"But," Talen continued, "no one will know your confinement has been reduced to three months, and those conditions will remain a secret. When you emerge three months sooner than expected, you will be a phoenix clothed in power and hungry for revenge, and redemption will be yours. I'll make certain of it."

To appear before the realm when no one expected me would be a sight, and that alone lifted my spirits. Talen was a miracle worker I didn't deserve. I would fiercely guard the secret of my early release to make it as dramatic of a return as possible.

Then I'd pray Brock's second favor was a kinder one.

"How?" I asked breathlessly.

Talen passed a finger by his lips. "Some things remain a secret, even from you, my Queen."

I faced the easel once more to start the new piece. "Whatever that must have cost you, thank you."

He sat off to one side as I worked, making content noises in the back of his throat when a new color graced the canvas or when they blended to form something unique. His sounds stopped after a while, and for the next half hour he sat in silence so still I almost forgot he was there until he bent down and took hold of my first painting.

"It might not be dry." I quickly checked for smudged fingerprints along the edges of the starry sky or the bottom where the sand coated the island. Talen wiggled his fingers to prove they were clean.

"What was it like there?" He ran a thumb over the island that stared up at the fae realm. "It looks charming."

I gave a short laugh. "On the other four islands, maybe. I'll never know. But the center island was built for battle, and we were trained accordingly."

"You're a warrior?"

It pleased me that he'd think such a thing. But I shook my head. "No. I was going to leave the center island the day after the Choosing Ceremony. I didn't belong on the center island." I set my brush down to turn on my seat, sliding my feet back into my slippers. "Though, no matter where I'd go, there was one trait that ran true across all islands, and that was our love for this unknown place." I tapped the fae realm, painted over the clouds. "We adore you."

Talen soaked in the sight of the painting. "It's odd. We adore our queens, just as you adore us."

"Obsessed might be the better word," I clarified. "We were wholly taken with the realm we knew nothing of, and every girl wanted to be chosen to live among creatures more beautiful than the night."

Talen's expression changed, and he lowered the painting. "And now?"

"Now?"

"You grew up adoring us. What do you think of our realm now?"

I shifted back to my painting, not answering until I'd found the right words. When they came, they were soft and wistful. "Now I wish I'd taken my brothers and run away to Ruen a long time ago."

18

EITHER TO GIVE ME SPACE OR TO
fulfill his claimed duties, Talen spent the week away while I filled
my room with paintings until the canvases were alive with every
color the realm had to offer—an array of my messages written over
and over, hidden in the current of a river, tucked in the crest of a
flower, or laced in the dark of the sky. Anything a Mortal Queen's
descendant might find.

I'd drawn both the fae and mortals over and over, but the next
live being I saw came with a tap at the window.

Bash stood behind the glass with his face painted gold again.
He tapped his foot.

I'd been in bed holding Antonio while channeling every memory
of Cal and Malcom possible. Bash eyed the soldier toy as I set it
aside. I tightened my thick robe and opened the door.

"Good evening," I said cautiously. The last I'd seen of him, I'd
forced him to bow before me in front of the realm. I searched his
brown eyes for traces of animosity.

His chariot bobbed behind him in little circles, and his long
cloak nearly touched the floor. The buckle on it was silver as was
the ring in his nose. I hadn't seen him wear that particular piece
of jewelry yet.

"I see you're still attached to your little token."

I glanced at Antonio. "I'm quite fond of it, yes."

He made a hum in his throat, then cleared it. "The dinner party is tonight. Get dressed and I shall escort you." He held out an arm and I longed to take it.

Instead, I stepped back. "It seems you're the last in the realm to hear. I've been confined to my palace with no exception."

His arm fell. "How long?"

"Six months."

"Six months?"

The lie burned inside me, and I itched to take it back and replace it with the truth. "Yes."

His jaw clenched. "How?"

I rubbed my eyes. "Chess."

A low growl came from his lips, and with a flick of his cloak, he ascended his carriage. His departing voice was biting. "Then you are of no current use to me."

Bash flew away until he was no more than a speck in the sky, and soon that was gone too. The cold feeling remained, ice upon my heart, not thawing as I rubbed my hands over my arms and retreated inside with my head lowered. I shut the balcony door and let the iron latch fall into place.

He is using you, and you are using him. But the chill in his voice remained.

The paintings crowded me, each holding a taunting sliver of my hope inside them, as if I could paint enough pictures to somehow reach someone who might not exist. I eyed the place Bash had just been, then pressed my hand against my tired forehead. What was I doing? I had no clue how to deal with this fae realm. I'd only been fooling myself.

I'd been in this room for days. Even by Gaia's standards, that was too long.

The door squeaked as I opened it, and a dark corridor stared back at me. I took a torch from my room and passed it from oil lamp to oil lamp until each was lit and the corridor light enough to banish the dark of this realm.

This was how things ought to be. Bright. Alive. Not cloaked in dreary shadows.

My lamp-lighting extended to the stairwell and down to the throne room, until the main section of the west wing was properly aglow. The last lantern connected to a woven cord that plucked a spool of flame from within the iron cage and sprinted up the wall with it. At the top of the rounded ceiling, far enough away that the blaze was but a speck, the cord reached into a glorious chandelier.

From there, the one speck of light rained down, igniting a million candles.

They flickered as if dancing to unheard music, and I almost expected the lyre to peel itself from the wall and play along. The beauty of one chandelier stole my breath with the detail they'd given an ornament that hung so high. If they poured that much devotion into such decor, my paintings must appear crude to them.

My paintings still remained on the wall from the dinner party. I shut my eyes for a moment. I'd been so confident that night.

The wooden handle of the torch fit into the metal sconce. The light danced against my lonely pieces, waiting for someone who never came, as I stood in the eerie silence to look over what was meant to be my salvation. I'd honestly believed a descendant of the surviving Mortal Queen would find it and eagerly help me just because I painted a nice picture. This realm had a way of reminding me how foolish I could be. This picture of Salvation's Crossing couldn't save me. It could do nothing but hang on a wall.

My eyes snagged on the bridge.

I'd drawn myself staring over the railing into the water with a broken crown on my head. But in my rush to finish before the party began, I hadn't had time to draw a reflection, leaving the glassy water clear beneath the arched bridge where a shimmered face ought to be.

But a reflection was there now.

A second girl stared back, one with similar features but a different face. Just like mine, a broken crown adorned her head.

My knees went weak. Someone had replied.

I scoured my gaze over the girl, searching for what she was telling me.

Tears flowed from her downcast eyes to melt into the river. Her bronze skin held tones of a blush, which could mean she was happy or panicked. I guessed the second. But what did that tell me? She looked at the river. Was that significant?

A real river trickled louder behind me as if encouraged by my thoughts. It originated straight from the two thrones of the queens and continued until it ran off the end of the island. Only one idea came to mind. If I hadn't already thrown myself off the island so dramatically, that would be my first instinct, this time following the river.

I put that idea back on the table while searching for another.

Though my figure wore purple, hers wore a slip of red. Ruby red. Blood red. The river and the red could be intertwined. I swiveled to see the real river where the clear, narrow water met the marble, and counted all the red fish. Nineteen, unless I counted that one twice. And there were those outside where the river sliced through the courtyard, but I couldn't go there.

I dared a step out. Instantly, my feet burned.

Nineteen red fish, plus however many were out there. The number nineteen meant nothing to me besides the age I'd barely reach if I didn't survive.

This wasn't the answer. Again, I dropped to my knees by the painting and scanned every detail of the girl's beautiful face. She didn't wear a mask. Had she escaped back to her own realm after all? The very fact that she was drawn into my art signified there was some truth to the tale Troi told me. Someone had found my message and answered.

A queen had survived.

There might be another river in this realm that I needed to find.

Or a place where the color red was significant. Or perhaps her tears were the message after all.

"How did you escape?" I whispered. "How did you survive?"

The thinnest layer of dust collected over her features, and I wiped it away.

The moment my fingers grazed her, my world gave way to a new one.

With a jolt powerful enough to thrust me to my feet, the mighty throne room melted, expanding to open air. The painting faded from my hands, and the river stopped trickling. Sunlight licked my cheeks with a warmth I hadn't felt in two weeks.

My face turned upward. The sun.

I wasn't in the fae realm anymore. I was home.

Very close to home, it seemed. Bodies pressed against mine, stepping on the hem of an outdated floor-length gown with a tight sash that suffocated me. Dust caught in my nose, making its way into my lungs. A hand squeezed mine.

"Don't worry so much. You've got as good a chance as anyone." An older girl with hazel skin and a pointed chin held on to me. "You'll make Momma and Dadda proud."

My skin prickled, while my mind crunched to sort out what was happening.

Banners hung from the square, and the musicians played a familiar tune. Was this—

The figures at the front answered my question. The three fae ambassadors stood there, the same ones I knew, scanning the crowd. The middle fae reached into a glass bowl.

"We thank you for your Mortal Queen," she declared, unfolding the slip of parchment. "Dhalia Mari Severs, will you rule over us?"

The merry crowd roared with cheers and applause that shook the ground beneath my feet. I looked down. That wasn't the applause. My feet were moving.

It should have hit me earlier. But it hit me now. This wasn't just any Choosing Ceremony—this was *her* Choosing Ceremony. Dhalia's. She must be the girl who survived.

The past couldn't be changed, but I tried with all my might. I pressed into the ground to still her feet, I threw my weight backward, I screamed in my head. Not so much as a coil of her thick hair responded. All I could do was experience this as she floated in a daze to the front where the ambassadors stood draped in silver robes and placid smiles.

Last year's chosen stood behind them, the fear evident in her cloudy eyes. Would she tell Dhalia what awaited her as Gaia failed to do for me, so this girl could be prepared for what would come?

The smile on my face pulled at my cheeks. "I'd be honored."

No! I screamed again. *Their realm isn't made for you. Run!*

But the words were lost in her head.

Dhalia turned to the crowd with her chin held high, and her feelings seeped into mine. She'd bring honor to her parents. Slivers of thrill tangled with that thought, until they overtook it completely. She had no idea what awaited her.

"We are ready to leave whenever you are, my Queen," the ambassador spoke in a lyrical tone. They'd moved into the general's house. There was no offer to return to her home to fetch belongings or say goodbye to loved ones, and Dhalia didn't ask for it.

Dhalia's voice wavered only once. "I'm ready now."

She fiddled with a strip of the veil over her blood-red dress until the fae took hold of her hand. The mortal realm dropped away at the icy touch.

The fae realm closed in on me once more with the stone beneath my knees and my painting beneath my hand. I took several deep breaths, long enough to go over the scene once more.

I adjusted my position to catch the chandelier's light on the painting. The girl in red had been me, had been Dhalia, when she was selected. She'd come here to bring honor to her family.

But the vision told me nothing of how she lived.

I touched it again, but my own reality stayed put.

"There has to be more," I murmured, touching it again, dragging my fingers over the entire painting to find another vision. Nothing.

"I need more," I whispered.

My frustration at not receiving the full picture clouded the realization that someone was out there to answer my messages. I wasn't alone. Somehow, I'd found someone willing to show me the tale of the girl who survived the fae, and it could be enough to save me too.

Without the rest of Dhalia's story, there was only one thing left to do. I needed to send another message.

19

THE ONE TIME I LEFT MY ROOM ALL
week, and that was the moment someone chose to visit. Troi stood
in what could only be called battle gear—leather pants, metal braces
on her arms, and two strips of blue paint down one eye over the
red mask. I wasn't surprised she'd chosen a mask that represented
bravery. She was taking a slow circle around my room when I
returned, hardly looking up as I opened the door.

"Troi," I said with a fleck of surprise. "What are you doing here?"

"You, my friend"—she paused to graze her eyes over me—"need
a new hobby."

"I need to be freed, that's what I need," I said, closing the door
behind me.

"Very true, but I can't help there."

I checked the brushes on the towel to see if they were dry yet. I'd
completed seventeen new paintings this week, each with messages
somewhere within, but a renewed energy now simmered, driving
me to paint another.

"How are things?" I dried the largest brush on my skirt. "I have
some stale muffins if you'd like one."

"Bash is fine," Troi replied.

I ducked my head. "That's not what I meant."

She leaned against the pillar nearest to the long fireplace. "He's asked about you."

My fingers stumbled over the paint. Troi went on. "The same way he's asked about many other girls before. He shows interest, only to turn away. His heart has no cracks, Thea. And it won't crack for the girl he knows isn't going to live longer than a blink of his eye."

My lips tightened. "I'm not a fool. I'm using Bash for the alliance, nothing more."

She studied me through black-lined eyes, while her fingers traced the thin copper bands on her arm, creating a low, deep sound much like my thundering heartbeat. After a moment, she moved some of the paintings off my bed.

"As you say. In that case, it's my job to make sure you don't let down Bash as an ally, and that means your chess game needs to improve. Is it true you lost in under a minute?"

"Yes," I admitted, but then added, "Brock set me up."

Her brow arched. "It's chess. That's the point. Do they not teach you to play on the five islands?"

I sighed, moving to the closet to reluctantly produce the marble chess set Talen had left. Troi patted the bed.

"They play there." I set the board on the sheets. "But not as rigorously. It's just a game."

"Well"—she set her queen and king first, choosing white for herself—"here, these games are your life, and you will learn to play them well. I won't have my brother go down at your expense."

"He's lucky to have you." I set my own pieces opposite hers.

She snorted. "If you could tell him that, I'd appreciate it. After . . ." Her voice hardened. "I'm his protector. It's a role I take very seriously. King's Protectors swear off all else—love, friendship, pleasure—for the sake of our kings."

"So when I met you, that was you protecting him?"

Fierce eyes sliced to me, and I froze over a pawn. "I'm so sorry. I didn't mean that."

"You did." She tapped the board. "Go first. I expect your game to be as sharp as your tongue by the time we are finished."

Troi's visits became the fuel that got me through those next weeks.

One month into meeting, I realized she was teaching me more than chess, she was teaching me how to manage in the fae realm. Once I understood that, I began to pay closer attention to her words.

"King Brock is hosting his party in two months, a whole month earlier than most years. It's at his wife's request, of course, who wants to visit the east islands when the stars grow three times bigger to fill the sky with a rainbow of colors. The stars aren't the important part."

I absorbed the information. "The important part is he would do anything for his wife."

She nodded. "Very good. Use that. However, don't ever do that move again."

Her eyes must have seen something on the board that I didn't.

"Your queen?" she pressed. "It's open."

"I'm setting it up for something." My voice sounded pathetic to my own ears.

Troi tightened the wool over her shoulders and took a sip of wine, letting me study the board. When I came up with nothing, she shook her head. "My bishop can take it."

I blinked. "Oh. But then I could take your bishop with a pawn."

She took another sip. "Not worth your queen. I'm going to do it so you learn your lesson." She crossed the board with the bishop and flicked my queen off the table. It rolled to the floor under my mountain of easels and paintings. She grinned. "This is fun."

"I'm glad," I mumbled. The irony of a fallen queen wasn't lost on me.

I picked at the blue paint on my wrist, leftover from another full day of painting. Talen had taken another mass of my artwork across the realm and as soon as my three months finished, I'd find the paintings and examine them. Dhalia's story etched itself into my mind until the details were part of me, every moment ingrained so deeply, it couldn't be forgotten. Her sister's touch, the fae's faces, the scratchy neckline of the blood-red dress. It all sat at my fingertips, waiting for me to piece it together, but I needed more.

I moved a piece, and Troi groaned. "You gave up your queen, then didn't take my bishop with your pawn." She flicked my pawn off the board.

"I'm not focused today," I said.

"I see that," came a voice.

Troi and I both turned to find Bash braced on the balcony wearing a sparrow-tailed overcoat the color of night and a gold, double-banded crown around his forehead. His hand rested on the glass door.

"I've come to see if my ally is spending her six months of isolation wisely, and I find her drinking wine and playing games with my sister." He looked toward the chessboard, where Troi must have been only a few moves away from beating me. Again.

"I am training her," Troi said, as if training me was a grand mission only she'd been entrusted with.

Bash didn't come inside the room, as much as I wanted him to. I longed for interaction with someone other than Troi or Talen. My three months were half up, but they already felt like eternity.

"You're a horrid teacher," Bash said. "Have you given her anything helpful yet?"

"She mainly just mocks me," I replied.

Troi lifted her chin. "It's a style. It's part of my charm."

Bash sighed. "Let me do it."

Troi's eye twitched. But she slipped off the bed and held out her hand. "Be my guest. I have other work to attend to."

She gave him an odd look, somewhere between confused and curious but never settling on either, before stealing his chariot and taking to the sky. Bash took her place without another word and set up the board.

I picked up the pieces Troi had been flicking on the ground. Bash glanced at me. "She's a character."

I set them down, unsure of what he wanted. His demeanor was calm as always, steady and sure in his movement and quiet in speech. "Troi mentioned she was your protector," I said, moving my first piece.

He rested his head in his hand to focus as we spoke. "She forced me to give her the position."

"Forced you? She's tiny. You could resist her."

He eyed me. "She brought three knives to make her demand. I let her have it."

I grinned. Troi might not be someone I'd bond with on my own, but I'd never be ungrateful that we were on the same side. I could use some with her fighting spirit.

There was a pause before Bash asked, "How have the past six weeks been?"

"Lonely," I admitted. He moved his knight forward from behind two pawns, and I matched the move. "How are things with the lords?"

He frowned. "Frustrating. My father was many things, but devoted to Mother was among his most admirable, and the lords related to him in that way. I need you to be free so I can prove I'm capable of maintaining a close bond as well."

I almost laughed. "The two years I'm here wouldn't prove anything against a lifetime. You chose the easy path by asking me to play the role with you instead of a girl who would be here forever."

His hand faltered over a pawn and a splinter of pain crossed his eyes before he blinked it away. "It was a logical move, as is my next one. Since I cannot show you off to the lords, I would like to hire you to paint a portrait of me for my home. If your presence can't be obtained, the painting will show the lords of your affection."

I pressed my lips together. A painting of Bash would do nothing in sending out messages, but I couldn't turn away my ally, especially when I'd already let him down. I nodded.

"Good. Your move."

My focus went to the board. I'd only beaten Troi once, but perhaps the same move could overtake Bash. If only I could remember how I'd set that up.

I hesitantly brought forth my bishop, hoping it had played a part in my earlier victory. I glanced up to find Bash wasn't looking at the board. He was looking at me. Or rather, at my shoulder.

The place where Vern healed me from his own arrow bore a twisted scar much like a coil of hair, pale and warped, reaching for my neck. It bubbled slightly but appeared like any other scar would from years past.

Vern healed it well. Still, I'd wear the mark forever.

Before I could pull my sleeve to cover it, Bash lifted his hand and ran a thumb across the scar with a thoughtful expression.

I held my breath. His touch was all I felt, not the bed beneath me or the corner of the chessboard pressing against my knee.

"I have lived," he said in a hollow voice as gentle as waves kissing the shore, "a short life by fae standards, and yet have met more souls than you would in three of your lifetimes. I've met those strong enough to tear down mountains, to tremble the seas, or to shake the skies—and yet, none of them would have the strength to stand in front of an arrow to save a stranger. Only you, my Queen. Only you."

"My Queen" rolled from his tongue differently than it did off Talen's—which was obedient and polite. From Bash it was endearing, bridging on intimate, and I longed to hear it once more.

His thumb stopped tracing the scar, but he didn't remove it. "Where does such a strength come from? If I peeled back the layers of you, what would I find? What other courage lies there, and what beauty rests behind that mask?" The inflection of his tone was less questioning and more pondering. But I wanted to answer the question. And I wanted to remove my mask and let him see me. I wanted to remove his mask and see him.

His fingers moved again, tracing a slow line down my arm. The silence hung between us as the distance shrank. I wanted more than the look of him. The sensation gripped me with an unrelenting desire. I wanted the taste of him too.

When I thought he might cross the board for me, his face changed. His hand yanked back and he jumped to his feet.

"I must go."

Those three words were all I got. Then he was out the balcony window as if he couldn't flee fast enough and disappeared into the night sky, leaving me with a racing pulse, an unfinished chess match, and the sinking feeling that I'd just lost whatever game we played.

20

A WEEK BEFORE MY THREE-MONTH
punishment was up, when I'd played enough chess and painted
enough pieces that now I dreamed about nothing but artwork of
chess, and finally Talen brought back a painting. "I'd sent this to
Thorn's sector," he said, setting it down on an empty easel. My
childhood home was the focus with the open windows letting in
the yellow sun and fig trees bending under the weight of the heat.
"But it reappeared at the door this morning."

I practically flew to the painting then tried to control my
excitement. The difference this time wasn't hard to spot. Whoever
altered this painting made it nighttime to fit the fae realm.
Hundreds of stars speckled the dark sky, cloaking the center island
in shadows and starlight.

My fingers twitched to touch it, but I wasn't ready to share this
secret with Talen yet, and he'd plopped onto one of the chairs.
Would the painting show him the same vision if he touched it? He
had to have touched it, to bring the canvas up, yet he didn't appear
to have seen something. "Thought I'd come keep you company for
a while," he said. "Odette is on her way too."

"Very kind." I strained a smile.

"I thought so. We've got to make you ready for your reentrance into the realm."

"And what a grand entrance that will be," Odette's chipper voice declared. She stood in the doorway looking like perfection with a silky emerald dress seeping to her ankles and hair set in loose waves. She laid a long covering over a chair and opened it.

Midnight-blue satin layers tumbled free. Odette held up the garment to show off a gown as stunning as her own. "You will steal the realm's hearts in this."

Beads of pearls lined the top like frothing water before they blended into dark waves at the bottom. I'd be an ocean, either raging or calm depending on the set of my expression, returning from isolation when none expected it. Shivers of anticipation ran through me.

"It's everything," I breathed, gently taking the fabric between my fingers.

"I had it made special for you. There is a pocket in here to perfectly fit a dagger."

"Which you won't need," Talen added quickly.

Odette slyly looked at me. "You never know." She recovered the dress and then gazed around the room. "Talen wasn't exaggerating. You've been creating painting after painting."

"There was little else to do."

Her expression turned apologetic. "I'm sorry I wasn't here for company. Now I see you needed me."

"No, I didn't mean for you to feel guilty," I quickly added. "Actually, Troi was here almost every day. I now know enough chess to play it in my sleep."

"Just wait until everyone turns to chess pieces in your dreams," Talen said. When Odette and I both looked at him, he shrugged. "It's happened." He poured a glass of cider for himself and Odette. I swore his gaze lingered on her when he passed it. "Anyway, how did things go on the outer islands?"

Odette sank into a chair before the fire. "Dreadful. I'll never convince them." She held down one end of a wool as I unrolled it. With a jolt, I realized I still hadn't repaid Lord Winster for how he'd tricked me my first night. I made a mental note to revisit that idea when I wasn't so focused on the painting. It wouldn't be right to leave the realm without settling that score.

My stomach twisted at the thought of leaving, and I caught my breath. Once I left, I'd never sit on a wool this fine again. I'd never drink such rich wine from a diamond glass or play chess on a marble board. I'd never fly through the night sky on a golden chariot or sit on a throne below my very own three stars. I'd never see Talen or Odette or Troi again. I'd never see Bash.

"What work do you have along the outer islands?" I asked to keep my mind from traitorous thoughts.

"I'm attempting to broker peace with my cousin Vern. You remember him? The one who shot you? And King Thorn who, true to his name, is as sharp as a thorn." She gave a dramatic sigh. "He has dreamy eyes though."

"Stuck-up snob, if you ask me." Talen's voice was rigid.

"Why would you want to help Vern?"

"It's not him I want to help," Odette replied. "It's his people. Thorn's lands account for over half the farms, and without him we'd all starve. If Vern doesn't make nice, the people could starve, and that includes my family."

Fighting for her family—that was something I could relate to. Antonio watched me from his place, reminding me of my own reasons for not giving up.

"Actually"—she scooted her chair closer to me—"I'm hoping you can be of assistance in that regard."

I didn't want to do anything for Vern, but Odette was different from her cousin. "Want me to paint him a picture? That seems to be all I'm capable of."

She laughed. "No. I want you to sway King Thorn. He's a smart man, but too often led by his heart. And recently his heart has pulled him in a hundred directions, one girl after the other. If you caught his eye, he could be persuaded to follow your bidding."

My ears perked up. "I like the sound of that." I might not have to trick him into owing me a favor. I could smile my way into it.

She beamed. "Good. He'll be at Brock's gala in a week, which is the event we plan for you to make your grand reappearance. Wear this dress, bat your lashes a few times, and he'll be yours. Trust me, he's not a hard catch."

Talen frowned. "Trust you? How close are you and Thorn?"

There was mischief in her eyes. "I've been known to play with him a few times myself. One of those cracks just might be from me."

The fire popped at my feet, almost as if igniting excitement inside me. One more week and I'd reenter the realm and play its games, shock the fae with my early release and dazzle them in that gown. Find the other paintings, collect favors from the remaining five kings, and save both Gaia and myself.

"Thorn's heart cracks easily," Talen was saying. "It wouldn't take much."

The oddity of the saying struck me again. I set my cup down. "I keep hearing about hearts cracking. Why do you say that?"

"This will be fun." Odette held up a finger, stood, and smoothed her skirt as if prepared to put on a grand show. Talen rolled his eyes, but I noticed his lips twitched.

Odette's eyes danced. "Watch. Your mortal heart is made of blood and muscle and . . . other stuff I think. But fae hearts . . ."

Odette situated her hand near her chest with her fingers flexed. As I watched, the skin shimmered, and the emerald silks over her bosom rippled. I gasped. She gave an amused smile. She left her hand there for a second before a transparent structure, similar in shape to my own heart, emerged from her chest.

She held her heart in her hands.

"Our hearts are made of glass. They are breakable. When we experience heartbreak, it literally cracks our hearts, and you can see the places where a fae has experienced pain. See?"

I stood to gape. Her chest showed no mark of what had just been torn from it, even the fabric of her dress was unscathed. The slightly pulsing heart had tiny cracks in two places.

"What are these from?" I hovered my finger over one.

Talen turned away as Odette peeked at him. "It was a long time ago. The cracks no longer hurt to touch." She pushed her heart back into her chest. "Only one fae has ever experienced heartbreak so bad that it shattered his heart and he became mortal. Almost as rare is a grown fae with a heart that has no cracks."

My jaw dropped, and Odette nodded. "That is why Bastian is so dangerous. A fae without a crack in his heart."

The pedestal beside his throne made sense now. It was his heart on display for all to see. He wore his lack of pain as a trophy for the realm to witness, proof of his inability to be broken by love.

"Many girls have tried to crack him," Odette added.

I blinked. "They *try* to break it?"

She gave me a knowing look. "Wouldn't you? To be the girl to make Bastian feel something would bring you clout like nothing else could. The whole realm would be after your heart to see what made it so special that it was worth cracking his."

I had to admit the lure was there to be the girl to accomplish what none other could, but it was in conflict of my mission here, so I shook my head. "I'm sad I won't be here to see that happen."

Odette's eye stayed on me. "We shall see."

Talen buttoned his coat. "I must go," he said abruptly. "I'll escort you to Brock's gala next week." He strode from the room without a second look, leaving an echo of footsteps in his wake to tell the tale he wouldn't.

I looked at Odette. "Talen cracked your heart, didn't he?"

There was a pause before she answered. "He did. He was my first love, and I thought he'd be my last. But we were young then and had no rank in the realm, and Talen wanted more. He got it. Representative for the entire House of Delvers. He ranks above the lords."

She stared into the fire as she spoke, as if the tale was one for the flames and not me. Flecks of smoke rose to take her words with them, and she kept gazing long after she finished. I didn't get the details, but I heard the important bit. Talen wanted more, and he got it. But from the look in his eyes when she came in the room, he'd lost what he most treasured after all.

"For what it's worth, I think he's sorry," I said.

Her smile was sad. "I know he is. He's asked for me to come back many times, but I can't bear it. I wasn't good enough for him the first time. I can't expect him to remember my worth the second time."

It was noble, but my heart ached for them both.

She relaxed in her seat. "Like I said, it was a long time ago." But she wiped a tear from her cheek, proving some heartbreaks can always resurface, no matter how buried they seem. Perhaps Bash was the lucky one after all, not letting his heart be cracked.

There it was again, the low stir inside to be the one he fell for.

You are using him, I reminded myself. *You would let him die to save future mortal girls.* But the mantra was harder to believe now. *You cannot have him, no matter which way this ends.*

"There is one thing you should know." Odette's voice summoned my thoughts back. "Some hearts like mine aren't valuable to others. Some, like Bastian's, are valuable enough to be enchanted so no one else can touch them. And some hearts are bargained with."

I tried to guess who would bargain with their heart before Odette told me, but I couldn't. "That is how Talen reduced your sentence from six months to three." My own heart plunged to my feet.

"What?"

Talen gave up much more than he should have for me, and I hadn't even bothered to thank him properly for it. What he lost was far more valuable than three months.

"Talen gave his heart to Brock for seven years. At any point during those seven years, Brock could crush it with his hand, and he'd be dead."

I might throw up. Odette reached out and laid a hand over mine. "Please, don't let Talen down."

"I won't," I croaked.

I'd been honored before, but I'd never felt gratitude quite like this. Like my chest was no longer big enough to fit my swollen heart.

My gaze fell to the little soldier toy. There were people I'd do anything to get back to. Cal. Malcom. The brothers who were once my entire world. But now, there were fae here I'd fight just as hard to protect. There were parts of my own realm I desperately missed, and parts of this realm that captivated me. Both halves enslaved a piece of my soul, one from years of living there, and one from suddenly sneaking in and making a home before I knew what had happened.

My heart couldn't crack like the fae's did. But someday, the two sides might split me all the same.

21

ODETTE STAYED BY MY SIDE UNTIL dawn when she yawned, stretched her arms, and strolled away. I tried not to envy her freedom, but it pricked me all the same. One more week.

The palace fell into its quiet trance once more, the kind Gaia and I would never be able to fill. The palace was larger than I could familiarize myself with in two years, begging to be lived in. Someday, I would love to fill the chambers with guests, turn the hollow echoes into laughter and make this a home.

"That won't happen," I reminded myself. I fanned out my skirts to kneel on the ground and, now alone, finally held the new painting at arm's length. "Show me how she lived."

Starlight crept over the painting, bringing to life the stars on the canvas like diamonds on a black sheet, until they spread to the air and threw themselves at the ceiling.

The room fragmented before splitting away. What remained was a night sky, stretching as far as I could see. Cool air flanked my arms while silk grazed my wrists as a flowing violet dress hung from my shoulders with billowing sleeves and thin layers of blush crepe skirts.

The sun of my previous vision clearly marked the mortal realm.

Night belonged to both realms, but there was no mistaking the fae world.

I stood at the edge of an island, overlooking another. The second island had a looming tower built of rock at the edge, almost teetering off the side. At the top it shot outward, connecting to a glass orb hanging over nothingness. Tiny lights adorned this orb, and my first thought—or was it Dhalia's?—was how nice it would be to read in that nook, hanging over an empty sky.

"Morten?" My voice called. Her voice was sweeter than mine, like honey and dash of innocence. Dhalia turned, and we looked into the eyes of a man wearing a burnt-orange vest and three nose rings. "Can I align with two Houses?"

His head tilted to the side. He thought for a moment before answering. When he did, hurt rested in his expression. "Are the Delvers not enough?"

Inside, I smiled. We'd chosen the same House to align with. Our first similarity.

"It's not that." She messed with the bracelets around her wrists, and I felt the cold metal just as she did. "I need as much power as I can get."

He stepped near her. "It's unusual to align with a second. But if any could convince the rules to bend, it would be you." Adoration seeped into his every word in a different way than Talen spoke to me. He squeezed her hand, and only because I was a part of her did I feel the affection in the way his touch lingered. The way her hand trembled for his the moment he pulled away.

Fascinating. The Mortal Queen cared for a fae. And he, as Bash had once described such a circumstance, was foolish enough to fall for a Mortal Queen.

A new thought. Was he how she survived?

A string of jealousy wound in my chest. She didn't have to fight alone. His affection for her would lead him to fight alongside her. That was something I didn't have—a true ally. One I could trust in such a way.

From above, a chariot came to land on stone. Dhalia stood in the same courtyard that sat outside my palace, with the same river running through, though the area looked slightly different. There weren't seven thrones at the end for the kings. The trees didn't bear as much fruit. Even the neighboring islands were different.

"Be nice," Morten warned. Dhalia put on a smile.

The new arrival coughed before stepping from the chariot. His ivory skin gained warmth in the flicker of torchlight, and it made his smile appear kind. There was a vibrance to his step as he crossed the courtyard with both hands held out.

They clasped mine as he took Dhalia's. "You are a vision of beauty, my Queen. The fairest High Queen we've ever had."

I felt the aversion inside Dhalia. But she replied, "Nothing compared to your glory, my King."

My attention focused more intently on this man now. He wasn't a current king.

He coughed again and cleared his throat. "I'd love to talk business"—another cough—"but first, could I have some water?"

He looked at Morten when asking this. Morten shifted uneasily. Dhalia nodded to him, and Morten bowed to her.

"Of course, King Ulther. I'll go fetch some."

Dhalia smoothed her dress, trying not to look after Morten.

King Ulther smiled again. "How has your first month been?"

"Fine," she replied curtly. He didn't appear put off by her. Didn't even blink.

"I can imagine it's difficult to understand the intricacies of this realm," he said. He folded his hands behind his back and stared into the sky. "I'll happily help you navigate it."

"I'm fine." Either she was the least hospitable human ever, or Morten had instructed her to be short.

King Ulther inclined his head. "As you wish. You really ought to come visit the western edge of the realm. The lakes are so clear that you can see through to the bottom, and the sands are made from the dust of jades. Peacocks roam through the thicket and eat fruit from your hand."

This realm would never fail to fascinate me.

Dhalia, it seemed, possessed less curiosity than I did. "I think not. I don't care for peacocks." She kept fidgeting with her bracelets and glancing toward the double doors of the palace.

King Ulther let out a defeated sigh. "I see an alliance with me is not in your interests. I might have suspected such from someone aligned with the House of Delvers. If I may, my daughter has long adored the Mortal Queens and picked this out for you. I suspect it would barely fit on your little finger, but I promised to grant it to you all the same."

He produced a silver ring from his pocket, nothing grand. Not even a design was etched into the side, and no gems adorned the band. His shoulders slumped with her rejection, and pity gripped me.

Dhalia stuck out her hand. He dropped the ring into her palm.

An air of mischief wafted about us. King Ulther's smile might be too wide, his show of giving up too obvious, or the ring too simple. I took all of these into account while sniffing for deceit, but it was the smallest detail that snagged my mind.

After coming in with a flurry of coughs, he hadn't coughed once after Morten left.

His ploy came into view, but while Dhalia's thoughts were mine, I couldn't push my own warning through to her. All I could do was watch.

King Ulther's eye twitched as Dhalia inspected the ring, then thoughtlessly slipped it over her pinky finger. I felt what she did, the unmistakable tinge of heat seeping from the ring into her skin.

Her breathing quickened. She tried to remove the ring, but it held fast to her finger.

She didn't hide her nerves. King Ulther stood silently as her gasping intensified and she tore at the jewelry. At that precise moment, Morten came out with a platter and three glasses.

At Dhalia's face, he dropped the platter and ran to her.

"What is it?" Dhalia cried out. "What is wrong with the ring?"

King Ulther's smile was just as broad, but far more wicked than before. He buttoned his jacket slowly, the mark of a job done. "Your acceptance of the ring comes with an acceptance of marriage."

Morten froze.

Dhalia frantically pried at the ring until the spot was raw. "Mortal Queens don't marry. It's pointless for us. Two years isn't enough."

So, in her first month of being here, she already knew the terrible fate that awaited her. I wondered if Morten had told her, and if he did so with more tact than Talen had.

"You will," the king said. "Your refusal of an alliance with me has led us into an alliance far more powerful. I thank you." He had the audacity and the cruelty to bow. "I've long wanted a bride."

Her frantic breathing broke into sobs. Morten wrapped his arms around her in a gesture that couldn't be mistaken for anything other than fondness. King Ulther shifted his gaze between the two of them.

"Careful, lad," he said sharply. "I don't take kindly to those who take what is mine."

He turned away to climb into his chariot. Before he left, he gave one more bow. "This is a happy day, indeed."

King Ulther left as Dhalia sank to her knees. "I'm so sorry," she choked. "I didn't think anything of the ring. I didn't think." Her words burned away in a heave of heart-wrenching tears. Morten laid his hand on her back.

"We will think of something," he stated. "We will find a way to free you from this marriage." His voice hitched. He was as Dhalia was, empty in that moment, and they grasped each other to absorb the shock of what had happened. I felt Dhalia's fear, her horror, her disgust. How her muscles quivered just as mine did, and her lungs squeezed.

And I felt the moment that changed. It hardened into something stronger, and a burst of strength pulsed through her.

"We will have to do more than that." She spoke with resolve. "You and I can't flee to my land anymore. He will find us."

She spoke too quickly for me to process that nugget of information. She wiped her face dry.

"We have work to do. I must be clever enough to escape the fae, but sneaky enough that they'll never even notice."

She walked quickly into the palace. It stood just as it did now, but with rows of mirrors along the white walls leading to the staircase. She, just as I, ruled the west side. There'd been no sighting of the High Queen of the East.

Dhalia paused in front of one of the mirrors long enough for me to get my first taste of her. Dark hair with a mix of caramel hung down her back, the tips curling by her elbows. Her seven earrings were white, as were the bands around her upper arms and the rings in her nose. The crown tattoo on her forehead matched mine exactly.

She turned away as the last detail shook me.

When I'd chosen my mask, the ambassador claimed he'd never served a Mortal Queen who chose a black mask. But he'd lied. I saw him at her Choosing Ceremony, and I was not the first queen to choose a black mask. She wore one too.

As if that detail was the last I was allowed to gleam from this vision, I was sucked away from her body and thrust back into my own, back on the floor by the fire with the wool at my knees and the painting gripped in my fingers.

I took a few steady breaths before setting down the painting and burying my head into my hands. The disheartening snippets didn't show me anything useful. Whoever sent these was playing a cruel game. At the end, I could only pray the answers would come soon.

But wait. I *had* gotten some interesting facts. Dhalia had planned to run away with Morten to the mortal realm. The three ambassadors were the only ones capable of passing through the realms, and he was not one. The details of that plan intrigued me, but if they'd discarded it, I would never know what they were.

And Dhalia thought she'd never be safe in her own realm. That one scared me. If I hoped to survive just as she had, then I'd be following her path.

But that would mean I'd never get home. Because Dhalia never left the fae realm.

22

KING BROCK REARRANGED THE STARS

themselves to form a road leading to his home island, and chariots lined up to glide over the celestial pathway, one by one, settling down on the foothills of his quaint home. It wasn't as lavish as others with curtains of diamonds or pillars of marble with tigers nestled on cushions. Instead, his was more like a glorified townhome overlooking a busy street with brick roads, shops, and swooping banners of all colors.

Talen and I watched from afar, biding our time to make our grand entrance.

The only sign this was a king's home was the grand pavilion on the roof, built as if from light beams and nothing more. Its glow lit up the island.

"He built that for his wife." Talen seemed as taken with the sight as I was. "It's all she's ever asked of him, but he would grant her the realm if she wanted." I longed to meet this wife of his to see if she was as spectacular as I envisioned. Talen spoke as if he heard my thoughts. "Even kings are powerless before great women." He focused on the home as the number of arriving chariots dwindled. But while his face was impossible to read, I had no doubt Odette's image was planted inside.

"We women are not as powerful against the male's pull as we like to claim," I remarked.

That broke his trance. "Tonight you will be. Tonight you will appear to defy one king's command over your isolation, tempt a second king to your side, and I suspect summon blinding jealousy out of a third."

Bash's chariot arrived. It was twice as large as most others, and the navy cloak he was so fond of caught the breeze. I watched his figure the entire time until he landed and waltzed into the townhome as if he owned the place.

Talen's focus never left mine. "Remember your plan."

I stood straight. "I remember." I checked myself once more, adjusting the way the gown fit to my waist and the alignment of the three gold bands around my right arm. I'd left my hair in its natural curls but had allowed Odette to heat an iron rod to wrap a few stray strands around—just the unruly ones that hadn't gotten the message about how important tonight was.

Odette was here somewhere, waiting for our arrival. She'd been tasked with keeping as many fae in the foyer as possible to witness my early release from isolation.

I placed a hand on Talen's arm. "Is that Gaia?"

He followed my gaze and nodded. "She's good friends with Brock's wife and likely came at her bidding. I don't expect her to speak to anyone else though."

I frowned. "Why not?"

Talen's voice dropped. "She was like you in her first few months. Motivated. Cunning. She and the previous queen, Ivory, often worked together to trap the fae in deals. But also like you, she got trapped in a few of her own. One such happened just before you came." With each word, pity crept into his tone. "She lost a deal and was ordered not to speak to her family upon returning for your Choosing Ceremony. She couldn't even look at them. Her humiliation upon losing such a deal must have been great, but I suspect her pain was far worse. After that, she changed."

I remembered how her eyes glazed over her family even as

they reached for her, called to her, begged her to notice them. She appeared so put together, so queenlike. Beautiful, even next to the stunning ambassadors. Much less mortal and more like a fae. I hadn't seen the pain cleaved deep into her heart and how it must have chipped at her with each moment, until she'd come back broken.

Games can be addicting and the high of tricking the fae almost irresistible, until it steals something you weren't willing to give. Gaia knew that well.

I couldn't imagine. Her family's pain would have been massive as well with their daughter ignoring them, and the weight of that knowledge would be a heavier burden to bear. The unwanted image of Malcom came to mind, tears streaming down his cheeks as he said my name and I didn't reply. As he held out his tiny hands for me just to have me turn my nose away. Yet she'd bore that burden.

"Tonight, nothing goes wrong for us. Your appearance is the only move we need to make."

I sucked in breath. "I can appear."

"Good. Then let's begin."

With a gentle stroke of the crossbar, the shimmering wisp that commanded the chariot brought it lower to the island, where lively music and the scent of warm baked pies greeted us. We touched down. I lifted my dress enough to step onto the brick road.

Already, fae paused on the street to gesture toward us. They whispered behind hands and bowed when our eyes met.

Talen placed a hand on my back. "That's the only taste of you they'll get. Let them spread the word that their queen has arrived. The real fun waits inside."

He flashed an invitation to the fae at the door who opened it for us. The home was built from wood and laughter, both stretching from the floor to the low ceiling. Strings of springtime flowers hung in lines from the crossbeams above, dropping never-ending petals like soft rain to the floor. Talen's hand flicked and I stilled. He stood proudly beside me.

King Brock's eyes found us first from across the room, and he nodded knowingly. But true to his deal, the deal that cost Talen greatly, he must not have told another soul of my shortened punishment, for the rest of the fae gasped.

"My Queen," they whispered. The entire room swiveled to soak in the sight of us. Drinks lowered from lips, and conversations hushed bit by bit, first in the entry room then farther back as the attention found us.

"I would never leave you for long," I spoke the line Talen had prepared for me and watched him grin.

Odette smirked as she sipped from a glass, tucked in a corner with her knife at her hip and her watchful eyes hovering over the room. Most of the guests bowed.

And at that, I found Bash. He didn't bow but stood as still as a statue with his lips slightly parted. His cloak hung off one shoulder, and his hand lifted to his chest.

He mouthed something, but his lips barely moved.

My answer was to deepen my smile. The mystery would be what charmed them, Talen had told me. Let me be a mystery.

That was all I needed to accomplish, but we had a second desire for the evening, and that was to charm Thorn into owing me a favor. I moved my eyes from Bash to search for the unmistakable band of the fae kings.

"My Queen." An older fae smiled at me as if what I'd just pulled was a trick we had planned together. "You escaped your bond early. Not many get out of Brock's punishments."

"I'm blessed in my alliance," I said with a nod to Talen. Several others overheard and were acknowledging Talen with admiration.

"Perhaps we underestimated the Delvers," she mused.

"I think you have," Talen said, breaking away to place himself at her side and steer her away. "Are you needing a new alliance? The House of Delvers can do more for you than the Lows or the Berns." His hand moved slightly at his side as if torn between behaving or picking her pocket. *Rich thieves.*

Brock had turned away and resumed speaking with another

king as if he knew I'd be here the whole time, but the king he spoke with glanced at me more than once.

Odette wafted through the crowd to link her arm through mine. "You must see the view from above," she sang.

"Thorn?" I whispered. She nodded.

She pulled me after her, each fae slowly turning away. "That was perfect," she exulted in a low voice. "I'd just spent the hour telling everyone I could about how I missed your companionship, but oh powerful Brock's commands can't be broken, and there's nothing my beautiful queen could do to escape. Then you walked in looking like a goddess."

I gripped her hand to let out some of my excitement. "Thank you, my friend."

"Of course," she said. "Anything I can do for my queen."

She led me up a narrow stairwell to the roof, where a few dozen fae lounged on couches or leaned against the banister to overlook the city. Odette's eyes darted to the left. "Golden hair."

I found his face and gasped.

I'd never fail to be overwhelmed by the splendor of the fae kings. But this one stunned me for a different reason. "I've met him," I said.

"He's been at almost every party you have. I'm not surprised."

I tried to focus my memory. "He approached me at my coronation to ask for an alliance. Said he had the fastest chariot around. I turned him down. But he wasn't wearing the band of a king that night."

At that moment, he looked up. Ours eyes met, and he held mine before a smile crept over his face.

Odette lowered her hand. "Don't turn him down again," she whispered.

I summoned as much confidence as I could in my walk to him.

"So," he said in a voice as silky as my gown. "The queen is free."

"Yes, indeed." I rested an elbow against the banister beside him and swept my hair over my shoulder. His attention traced the movement. "I'm dying for adventure, and if I remember correctly, someone owns the fastest chariot in the realm."

Being near him brought about that same pull all the kings had. The intense desire to stay by his side. His eyes shone like a laugh lived inside them, and he studied me as if he saw no one else, even as others bumped against us while passing.

I told myself it was no different than the lure to Bash and that the attraction was nothing more than the fae realm playing with my heart. But there was something different. With Thorn, I reminded myself to lean close. With Bash, I was constantly reminding myself not to lean in.

Thorn brightened. "You remember me."

I feigned shock. "Of course I do. I couldn't forget you." I trailed my finger in slow circles on the wood near his arm, playing with the rose vines whittled into the railing, letting my finger get closer with each circle. Obvious, perhaps. But he ate it up.

Lamplight bounced off the silver buttons on his undone jacket, the same golden color as his hair. He stroked the hint of facial hair adorning his sharp chin. "I asked you once to ride with me in my chariot. Would you deny me a second time?"

From the corner of my eye, I saw Bash climb the stairs, his eyes skirting in search. I chose the precise moment he found me to place my hand on Thorn's. "Never. Take me out tomorrow?"

Thorn leaned into my touch, letting his jasmine scent wash over me. His chin measured at the top of my head. "I want you to know," he began, "I know you're using me."

My hand faltered, but his clamped over it. His touch wasn't rough, but soft and light enough that if I pushed, I had no doubt he'd let go. For that reason, I didn't push. He grinned. "But that doesn't bother me in the slightest. You'll tire of Bash eventually, and I'll be here when you do."

He kissed my forehead. "I'll pick you up tomorrow."

He withdrew from me, placed a hand on the balcony, and threw himself off. I watched long enough to be sure he stuck the landing before collecting myself in time for Bash to appear at my side.

"This is interesting." His voice seemed strained. "You look lovely tonight, by the way." The compliment was lessened by the grumble in his tone.

I widened my eyes as if seeing him for the first time. "Bash. It's been a while."

He eyed me. "Should I ask about Thorn first, or about how long you've known you were only trapped for three months?"

"I'd avoid either. You won't like the answers."

He frowned. "Remind me. Who are you in an alliance with?"

I set both elbows on the banister, letting the wind blow my hair back from my face. The navy of my dress matched his cloak. Again, the pull to him was hard to control. "I'm aligned with you."

"And what were the terms of the alliance?"

I humored him. "I got two questions and my stars. And you got a girl who had to be around you so the lords think you're pleasant company."

"I'm delightful. And?"

I searched. "And charming? I'm not certain what else you want me to say."

"And you can't make further alliances," he said, nodding toward where Thorn had thrown himself over.

I pulled my hair over my other shoulder and coiled my fingers through it. "What can I say? I like to be wooed."

Bash's frown deepened.

My hands dropped along with my act. "I'm playing him, Bash. That's all it is." I leaned against the balcony to search for Thorn among the busy crowds in the street. They mingled together in groups, never staying in one place for too long, speaking to everyone as if all were friends. This would be a sight worth painting—a night of friendship. But it was easy to play nice with faces hidden behind masks where you didn't have to let your true emotions show.

I'd seen Bash almost as often as I'd seen Talen, and yet his face was nearly impossible to read. But I noted how his entire body relaxed with my words. "You can do as you like." He said it as if he didn't care what I did, but he'd stopped scowling.

"You still owe me that second question," I said.

He situated himself beside me, facing the opposite direction to watch the small group gathered under the pavilion. Gaia sat there with a woman who must have been Brock's treasured bride.

She was the sun. Her hair, her skin, her eyes, they all glowed with undeniable radiance. A white dress wrapped around her generous curves, and her smile dimpled with a laugh that turned heads. She carried herself lightly, perched on the end of the seat while conversing with Gaia, who was her opposite in every way. Dark hair, dark eyes, dark dress. Rigid and closed off as if the air were a personal shield around her. But as the wife laughed, she drew a smile out of Gaia.

Gaia was beautiful, but she'd never be a fae. I glanced to my own dress, wondering how I must look compared to such beauty. Perhaps it didn't do me well to stand so close to Bash, who could make a fae look dull. Next to him, I must look wretched.

"Have you thought of a second question?" Bash asked.

"Not yet. I want it to be a good one."

"I'm curious what you'll come up with."

"I'm half-tempted to ask about your mother," I said. Then I waited to see if he'd take the opportunity to tell me about the one person in his family he hadn't spoken of yet.

He raised a brow. "You'd have to ask officially to draw that out. I'm not giving it away for free."

"Perhaps I'll ask Thorn about it. He probably knows." I shrugged, clinging to my facade of disinterest.

Bash growled. "He ought to. His mother killed mine."

Regret slammed into me. My mouth hung open before I had the ability to speak. "Bash. I-I'm so sorry."

"I'm joking. I wanted to see your expression."

My jaw dropped. "That wasn't funny."

He chuckled all the same, and I swatted at his arm. That only made him laugh more.

"You're dreadful," I mumbled.

"Serves you right for prying. But I'll appease you. My father worshipped my mother until the day she died. But now she's gone, and he's been bitter about that since her last breath. That's the story."

I resisted reaching for him. "Oh, Bash. Was she sick?"

She must have been too young to die naturally. While the fae hadn't divulged at what age they passed, Bash had said he wasn't much older than me, so his mother must have been young as well.

My mind flickered. Thorn's mother hadn't killed Bash's, but murder wasn't off the table.

It could have been an illness, though now that I'd thought of it, I hadn't seen a sick fae yet. Not a sniff nor a cough from any of them. Except for false ones. Perhaps something in the red wine kept them strong, as the transformation Gaia had gone through after only a year here wasn't lost on me. That would be a secret worth learning, and I wouldn't mind obtaining some of the long life with it.

"Not sick," Bash said. "She challenged a fae to a match, and she lost."

"Oh." I had no other words.

"The rules were fair." His voice stayed calm, but the muscles in his cheek ticked. "And it made it easier to steal the throne from my father."

Sickness would have been a kinder death, but in a way, I envied that he knew how his mother died and could mourn her with closure I'd never get. "My mother is gone as well," I said.

I regretted saying anything in that moment where he looked at me a little too closely, like he was seeing beneath my layers into somewhere personal, far beyond where I'd intended to let him in.

"I didn't know that," he said finally.

Others were noticing our closeness and whispered while watching us. This was meant to be my night where I shocked the fae with my reentrance to the realm after being confined and left them breathless with how I'd matured during the three months into a much wiser queen. Yet Bash glued himself to my side, so when they talked about me, they'd talk about him.

He was stealing the moment. I saw that. But I didn't move away, and my warnings couldn't convince my words to stop.

"Some neighboring countries mounted a raid on the center island, and she disappeared when they left. Father went out with a troop of men to search for her, but she was gone—either stolen or killed—and I can't decide which is worse. Either way, I'll never know what became of her." I didn't add the other words, that now my mother wasn't the only person whose fate I'd never see. I'd never get to know what became of any of my family if I didn't get back home. The loss of Mother had haunted me enough, but now it would be joined by wonderings about my entire family.

"She never reappeared?"

I shook my head.

He was quiet for a moment, then he smiled. "Another layer of my queen, and one that's not so different from mine."

The idea of similarities between us pleased me more than it should have. A month ago, I wouldn't have thought I could have anything in common with the majestic creatures of the fae realm who appeared untouchable, much less a similarity with a fae king. Yet here I stood with one at my side, whom I dared to call a friend, and we found common ground.

"And both our fathers fell apart without their wives," I added. "Father was gone for two months searching for her. All he returned with were stories of something called snow and a hardened heart we couldn't thaw."

Bash's eyes widened a bit. "You don't know what snow is?"

"I know what it is," I said, not caring for the bewildered way he looked at me. "At least, now I do. I've just never seen it."

"It's wet. And cold. Highly overrated."

My shoulders sagged. "Oh. I heard it glistened like glass and was as soft as fur."

"I guess that could be said of it," Bash mused. "Not soft enough to keep your father's heart from hardening though."

"Hard like ice."

He studied me for a long while, until his focus was like a weight that pushed down on the shield around me and threatened to see beyond it. Beyond the mask, beyond the games. Beyond my claim of only using him as a means to get home. If he looked too hard, he might see it all.

And if he asked, I would remove my mask for him.

I moved away, and that was when he spoke. "I'm seeing now where you get your strength."

I gave a dry laugh. "I'm from the center island. Strength we have in abundance."

"How lucky for you," he remarked. "You'll find that strength is often a facade here, a cover for sensitive fae who will break if trifled with too hard. We aren't as resilient as we like to claim."

Like how he covered the pain of losing his mother with the claim that it made stealing the throne easier. But the fae told different stories about Bash. "I hear you can't be broken."

He drew back at that. "It's best that way. Keeps me safe." His voice was impassive, like I'd reminded him not to get close.

It wasn't what I wanted him to say, but he hadn't given any answer that I didn't already know. We could find a million similarities to bond us or share a thousand laughs. It would never be enough. He'd share stories of his life but never his heart.

My heart wasn't so easily guarded. I gave it freely with any scrap of affection that came my way. I gave it to my mother, who had well-earned it. I gave it to my brothers, who owned half of it. I gave it to my father, even when his wasn't reachable. And this realm tugged at it, even when it revealed its dangers. I was constantly giving out pieces of myself, searching for a connection.

With one smile, Bash could have it just as easily. But his could never be won.

I forced a yawn. "I should go. I have a ride on the fastest chariot in the realm tomorrow."

A darkness veiled Bash's eyes. "Thorn."

I nodded, searching for clues as to how deep his disappointment lay.

"Very well," he said, frustratingly calm. "Enjoy your time. When you are done, I want to show you something."

"What is it?"

He shook his head, buttoned the gold latch of his cloak, and moved for the stairs. "Tomorrow. Good night, my Queen."

After he left, I found Gaia's eyes on me, even as Brock's wife was whispering something in her ear. The usual warning wasn't there. It had been replaced by sadness and a tinge of defeat.

Gaia had given up saving herself. But I'd never stop until I was dead.

23

BASH PROVED AN EASY SUBJECT TO
paint. His features were molded into my mind with such detail, I
summoned them with little effort. The exact curve of his eyes was
the hardest to capture. I sketched something that didn't do him
justice, then left it to serve as a placeholder until I could see him
again.

I blanketed the background with a night sky, and his looming
mountain home lit up behind him with jutting verandas swathed
in moss on each carved level. The vast windows shone through to
the throne room with his prized glass heart sitting beside it. Bash
stood outside on the edge of the mountain, staring into the night
at his surrounding islands, all situated at a lower level as if bowing
before him.

The hours passed until all I had left were the exact details of
his eyes, which, though a small part of the painting, were of great
importance to me.

Thorn arrived at the door as I cleaned the brushes. His suit was
held together by one ruby button that shone brightly. His bronze
eyes went to my painting.

I expected a polite compliment.

"That's horrifying," he said. "Vaguely threatening."

I frowned until realizing he meant the hollow eyes. "I can't remember the detail of those," I said with a short laugh. "I'm not leaving it like that."

"Ah." He peered closer. "I can help. They are dark and somber, like he's forever attending a funeral."

"He does have a sad look about him," I agreed. "But I think he's just quiet."

Thorn grunted. "It's more than that. I think he hates the world." The way he looked over the painting wasn't with admiration.

"Do I get to know the story between you two?" I asked, setting the last of my dried brushes next to Antonio.

"Everyone has an enemy. I've selected him as mine."

"Truly?" I almost laughed. "Just like that?" I went to my closet.

Thorn rubbed his heel against the soot near the fire, but the blaze in his eyes burned far brighter than any flame. "No," he said. "He broke my sister's heart."

I halted midstep. He let out a puff of breath. "But don't let me drag you into my decade-old feud. It's not yours to carry."

His story clung to me as I slipped behind the curtain over my closet. I'd been mistaken to think that because Bash's heart wasn't cracked, he hadn't experienced relationships before. He might not bear the scars of them, but he held the memories. I shut my eyes for a moment, then shook myself to focus on my task—tricking another fae king.

An ash-colored dress suited the occasion perfectly. Aside from the color, it wasn't much different from the one I wore to the Queen's Day Choosing Ceremony where I went from being a mortal girl to a ruler of fae, but the girl behind the dress was much different. That girl had been in upheaval, her mind whirling at breakneck speed, unable to find her footing. The girl in the dress now, she could hold her own.

I found shoes and laced the strings up my calves.

Thorn beamed when I stepped out. "Beautiful."

Another difference between the girl I used to be and the girl I was now—I had kings looking at me. It still made my head dizzy.

I glanced once more at Bash's painting. Without the eyes, he looked quite ghostlike, but at the right angle it appeared as if he were in the room, watching me curl my hand around Thorn's arm as he led me away.

"Tell me, how fast is this chariot of yours?"

His eyes twinkled. "It can take you across the realm in a matter of minutes. A few minutes more, and you'd be lost in a sea of stars."

"I'm eager to try it."

He grinned. "I've never been honored by a Mortal Queen's company. My chariot shall do its best for you." He opened the doors to the courtyard, where the apples on the trees had deepened into a rich orange color and the leaves were tinged with red—colors that were unseen in the desert terrain of the center island. It still made my breath hitch.

Thorn adjusted his arm to take my hand, and I let him help me onto the chariot as if I couldn't possibly step up without him guiding me. I held my skirt in my other hand and sighed contently when we stood together, facing the skies. Playing my game.

"Ready?" he asked. His golden curls were flattened by a metal band of laurel leaves wrapped around the crown.

"Yes," I replied with my chin up.

He lifted a hand, and the chariot sliced through the crisp air.

It was a speed I didn't know existed. Though this realm offered a strange ability to ride in chariots and not feel like we were being thrown backward, I gripped the rails. Thorn threw his head back and laughed.

The islands came and went too fast to identify them. Was that a river? Were there trees or was it all grass? Even the mountains couldn't be seen at the speed we traveled. Everything was there for only a second before it melted back, giving way to new islands and territories.

If I ever needed to escape, this would be the chariot to steal.

At this point, I wasn't certain we were passing islands at all. Black and flashes of stars were all I could make out.

Thorn raised a hand, the chariot halted, and we hung in the center of nothing.

"Wow." That was the only word I could utter. I'd been right. The islands had pulled away and left us with nothing but endless stars. They dotted the sky in all directions, and any trace of the floating islands of the fae realm were too far away to be seen.

It was just as it had been when I'd jumped off the edge of the island and Bash caught me, but this time I wasn't in hysterics. This time I could enjoy it.

"It's peaceful out here," Thorn said. "No distractions, no games. Just darkness and light." Thorn had kept hold of my hand and now stroked it with his thumb.

I leaned into his side as if this was all I needed in life. Encouraged, he wrapped his arm around me. "It's nice to be away from all the noise," I said.

"Anytime you need an escape, all you have to do is ask."

Can you help me escape now? Take me back to my realm? But I knew better than to ask. He wasn't buttered up enough. Instead, I said nothing at all.

To keep from begging him to take me home, I counted his breaths—seventeen of them—heard when they shifted, caught as if he'd had an idea. He faced the west. "I have something else I want to show you. Something your other alliances would never dare."

The gleam in his gaze was extra mischievous. It stirred excitement within me. "What?"

"You'll see. You're going to love this."

With a snap of his fingers, we took off again.

My hand tightened on the rails as everything distorted around us. Black melted into shades of colors as land came into view, until we were once more inside the realm—though it was impossible to track exactly where at this speed.

The vastness he'd just shown me was one of simplicity and peace. The place he took me next was the exact opposite.

It was lively and brilliant.

The chariot slowed at the threshold of an island and fluttered

down toward it. A million colors burst in every direction, and my
eyes couldn't decide what to look at first. The best way my mind
could label the view was as a carnival, but a more glorious one than
what came through the center island every two years.

"Behold," Thorn answered. "Illusion Point."

The land before us was laden with goldbrick roads, narrow
due to the endless tents parading their wares. The tents seeped
with heavy necklaces, bright charms, rows of bottles and trinkets.
Brick houses were adorned with banners that covered every side,
announcing what lay within. Taverns, enchanters, games, arenas,
shops, or exhibits.

The island was packed so full, some of the buildings teetered off
the sides, as if they were one weight-shift away from plummeting.

"What is this place?" I marveled. The chariot set down on
the only open patch of land near the middle and we stepped onto
uneven stones, where the scent of jasmine bit the air and the bustle
of fae surrounded us. A few tipped their heads at us, but most were
too busy to give us any attention—their fingers in their purses and
eyes darting every which way. Each had a look about them, as if
they were either running from mischief or fixing to get into it.

"This is where the fun is," Thorn said with a roguish smile.

I hesitated. "You're going to get me into trouble, aren't you?"

"I'd never let my queen get into trouble." Despite his jovial tone,
I didn't believe him. Thorn bent his elbow, holding my hand against
his chest to keep me close, and pulled me into the madness.

The fae world was one of grandeur, from the open sky to the
majestic palaces. They had more space than they could ever fill. But
this island looked like they'd tried to squeeze everything into one
area, and it felt familiar. Narrow streets, bright colors, worn-down
tents, and people yelling. Add camels and fig trees and I was home.

That comforted me. I recognized this place. It wasn't much
different from the realm I came from, and that gave me courage
I didn't think I'd ever really felt around the fae. I nodded back to
some as they passed from street to dusty street.

"Games are held here," Thorn explained. He lifted a low-hanging banner for us to walk under. Vendors on the street called out to us, selling fresh fruit and scaled fish. Thorn ignored them all. "The only rule of this island is that nothing is as it seems. You come here to be tricked and hope you can trick someone else better."

Ah, so not like my realm, then. Still very much fae. My confidence faltered.

"Don't worry," he added when he saw the look on my face. "I will keep you in my protection today. But it would be a shame if you never got the chance to visit a place such as this."

"A potion?" A large-bellied man brought a violet bottle to our noses where he swayed it. "It makes you irresistible."

Thorn waved him off.

"I won my chariot from a bet here once," Thorn said as we carried on. "And in another bet, I was able to send a fae off on my chariot at full speed for ten minutes and make him try to return on his own. It took the poor lad three weeks to find the realm again."

My eyes widened, but he grinned. "He was fine, don't worry. The chariot knew its way home, and I'd ordered it to not let the fae die." He said it as if it was a kindness, but I shivered.

We moved past a shop selling the sweetest smelling breads. It was difficult to keep from going inside, but a question spurred me on. "Can fae die?"

Thorn's brows raised. "Why, my Queen, are you planning a murder?"

I shook my head. "No. I'm just curious. Can you die of hunger or old age?"

"Eventually, yes. No one lives forever."

"But you do live for a long time."

"Yes," he said easily. "Much longer than mortals."

Especially longer than Mortal Queens. We kept going with me absorbing every detail of the island. In the distance, an elephant trumpeted.

An elephant.

I scoured around to see it, but a hand found my elbow, one belonging to an older fae with grey hair and a hunched back. Her violet eyes gazed at me from behind a teal scarf. "It's been a while since a Mortal Queen set foot here. Though some might say not long enough."

I stepped back, bumping into Thorn, who tightened his hold on my hand. "She'll be no trouble today."

"Hmm." The woman's croak sounded suspiciously like disappointment.

"Gaia and Ivory used to come," Thorn whispered as the woman backed into the tent, where pools of woven baskets sat, but her eye didn't leave us until a group of loud fae passed, blocking her view. I looked to Thorn.

"I can't imagine Gaia here." I tried, but the image never landed right.

"Not the Gaia you see now, but she was different before. Gaia and Ivory ruled this island, and their tricks put us all to shame. The pair was unstoppable."

I tried to picture Gaia like that, fierce and unrelenting. Cunning. But the only image I had of her was a sullen shadow who clung to the walls and frowned at those who got too close. Nothing deserving of the admiration in Thorn's eyes. She was hardly more than a shell.

I shuddered. Someday that could be me. If this realm broke me and stripped my spirit. "What changed? I know she made a bad deal, but why is she so . . ."

"Lifeless?"

I nodded.

"Ivory died. The better half of the Ivory-Gaia alliance was gone, and all that remained was the ghost of her former self."

I bit the inside of my cheek. *Ghost* was the perfect word to describe her. A vapor of life, clinging to a body.

"It broke our hearts when Ivory died." To his credit, his eyes did glisten. "But for the first time, I think it broke the remaining queen more." We paused in front of a tent, and he coughed his sorrow down to spread out his arms. "This is my favorite place."

It wasn't much from the outside, nothing more than a

blue-and-green striped tent barely reaching the top of his head and about as wide as my outstretched arms. But he held back the flap and stepped inside, bringing me after him, and it all changed.

The tent was suddenly much larger, as large as my home back in the mortal realm, and much taller. Thorn's words came to mind. *Nothing on this island is as it seems.* The smoky air smelled of papaya, and the perimeter was coated with bookshelves of merchandise and racks of clothes. Despite the massive size, it didn't appear like much more than a humble store, yet at least ten other fae stood in this room, with several others in rooms that branched off.

A thin man with pointed ears and a slick beard glided to our side. "It's a blessed day when royalty comes through your door," he said smoothly.

"Percival," Thorn said with a nod. "Have you the shipment?"

"That I do. Right this way."

Thorn released my hand. "I'll only be a moment," he promised. He buttoned his suit jacket and followed the bearded man. I watched them make their way to the back of the tent, where the man sorted through rows of boxes, wondering what sort of shipment Thorn could be here for. But that was not my job today. Charming him was. Acquiring his favor.

Eventually, trapping him into draining his power to free me.

When he looked back, I smiled as sweetly as I could manage and turned away.

The shelves sparkled, though no starlight reached them. The trinkets called to me like I was bait and they were reeling me in. Shiny bottles with crisp labels were aligned in perfect rows on the shelf. I wondered what they held inside. Whatever it was, it was strong enough that my hand involuntarily moved to the caps. I had to know.

"You're a pretty thing."

A voice snapped me back to my senses and my arm dropped.

A woman approached to boldly lift a lock of my hair and twist it between her bony fingers. "We are so fortunate to have our Mortal Queens. And you are fortunate to have the attention of two fae kings." Her sharp nose was like an arrow. "Tell me, girl to girl, which do you fancy more?"

I stepped back, knocking my hip against the shelf. Bottles clattered. The woman's silver eyes pierced mine. "I don't fancy either," I said.

She smiled as if she saw through the lie.

She lifted her arms, her long sleeves draping down to her waist. "Kings are tricky. I can grant you your heart's desire, whichever one that may be." Another sneaky smile.

Now I saw her game. "I'm fine," I said. Her breath hit me with how close she stood.

"Are you certain? You won't be here long, and you don't want to take your time making them fall in love with you. I can give it to you like that." She snapped her fingers. "All it costs is one look inside your memories."

If I could have slithered back farther, I would have. Already the bookshelf dug into me as I tried to keep back. I didn't want anyone looking into my memories.

"I'm certain. Thank you."

"Elda." A man appeared from behind the woman. "Leave our queen be." His voice was demanding, though his face was as calm as the seas of the five islands.

She sized him up for a moment. Then her face twitched, she clicked her tongue, and she waddled away. "As you wish."

The man wore a velvet coat with two layers of brass buttons reaching from his collar to the end at his knees. The vivid red fabric rivaled a fire. "Not many girls turn down their heart's desire," he commented. He didn't crowd into me as the woman had, but instead gave me room to move away from the shelf. His tone was soothing, if perhaps calculating. "Makes me wonder what your true desire is."

It wasn't one of the two kings. A month ago, the question would have been simple—to get home. But now? A tiny piece of me whispered it was to guarantee my family was well, while finding a way to remain here. That last bit had seeped into my heart, teasing me with uncertainty.

I offered a simple answer. "I don't make deals with people I don't know."

"Then I assume you'll be uninterested in mine, but I'll present it all the same. He pointed to a necklace of emerald green. "This is the cheapest item I have, but perhaps the most powerful."

The necklace twisted lightly, showing off all its angles. I glanced up to be certain Thorn was still deep in conversation with the bearded man, paying us no heed.

"It's rare," the fae said, keeping my attention. "This lets you control anyone you've seen without their mask."

I looked at the necklace with new interest. Faces here were a powerful thing, or so I'd been told. Now I saw the first proof of those words. I bent closer to the lackluster shine of the emerald, catching my foggy reflection from within. "One could control them?"

"Fully."

If I possessed this and saw an ambassador's face, I could force them to take me home. However, I hadn't seen anyone without their mask. New webs of plans stretched before my mind, weaving trails I could follow. Tricks I could run. Moves I could make. A chance at going home.

But you don't know if you want to go home.

I shook my head, forcing the idea away for now. "It's worthless to me. I haven't seen anyone beyond the mask."

"Not yet, I think. But perhaps one day." He turned to riffle through other objects while I mulled that over. Next, he presented a thin gold watch with its flat face decorated with a teal band. Simple, by fae standards, but he held it like a treasure. "This lets you freeze time."

I gingerly took the watch to feel the weight of it. "For how long?"

"Twelve minutes," he replied. "Press right here"—he pointed to the side—"and you will be the only one who can move for twelve minutes. No one else will even know that time has passed. But it can only be used once. After that, this will be nothing but an ordinary watch."

My mind jumped. "Could I remove someone's mask in that time?"

He grinned as if very pleased I had thought of such a thing. But he shook his head. "Sadly, no, or else I'd use this myself."

I held it, struggling to pass it back. Even without removing masks, I could do a lot in twelve minutes, if used at the right moment. I could search somewhere or someone. I could think through a situation. I could move with a twelve-minute head start. "How much?"

"One memory."

My gaze snapped up to him. "A memory?"

He nodded, a carved smile on his face. "I'll choose one of your memories and take it. You'll see it one last time before it's mine."

I ran a finger along the band. One memory wasn't asking much. Behind him, Thorn was shaking hands with the other fae, and I panicked. If I had this, I wouldn't want anyone else to know. I had to choose now.

Stopping time was worth a memory.

"Alright," I said, almost biting my words. But once they were out, he snatched hold of my hand, not giving me time to take it back. The deal was struck.

24

THE METAL OF THE WATCH PRESSED
into my skin with the strength of the fae's grip. A memory hit me,
one I hadn't thought of for a long time.

Mother sat on the floor with her skirt fanned out on the marble
beneath her. She had flowers pinned to her hair, yellow flowers I'd
picked for her that day. Malcom perched on her lap with his soldier
toy in his mouth.

I came through the door with a teapot to pour water into cups
and pretend we were at a fancy party, like the ones father went to
with his general friends. Some of the water spilled on the floor, but
mother said nothing.

There was a snap, and Mother gasped. She pried the soldier toy
from baby Malcom's mouth. The arm had broken off. She swept a
finger through his mouth to remove the broken piece and passed
both to me to throw out. But Malcom cried, so she gave the toy
back, slipping the broken arm into her pocket.

That was how Antonio broke his arm. The distinguishing detail
that made him Malcom's favorite. *He was hardened by battle,* he
said when he was older.

"That's fine," Mother said with a smile as she took the teacup I
offered her. "Some of the best things are broken."

"Is there tea in the fae realm?" I had asked.

I shut my eyes. Always so obsessed with the realm I couldn't touch. Mother's eye twinkled as she lowered the cup. "There is. Finer tea than we have here, and sweeter." She cast her eyes upward, her expression was pure longing. "Everything there is better."

Cal called for her, and she shifted Malcom and got to her feet. *"Uhnepa te,"* she said in her language, stepping past me. I repeated it before snapping back to reality. My hand freed.

Thorn finished shaking the other fae's hand as if no time had passed.

"Why that one?" I asked, clutching the watch. "It's meaningless."

The fae's jaw was slack, and his eyes glazed over. He now forced a smile to his face. "It doesn't matter. It's mine now."

And with those words, the memory was ripped from my mind.

Something was gone. I knew he'd just taken something. I scrunched my eyes, trying to bring it back. Trying to remember what I'd lost. But it was out of reach.

I felt out of sorts. "What was it? Can you tell me what you took?"

"Do not worry," the fae said. "You won't miss the memory."

The gap was like a burning hole in my mind. I had to know. "But what did you take?"

"A simple one to you, but of great value to me." A strange look passed his face, and he glanced toward Thorn. He leaned closer to me and spoke quickly. *"Uhnepa te."*

I staggered back. "Where did you hear that?"

"Your memory."

A drowning chasm inside opened. "You stole one of my mother?" I had limited memories of her, and each one held a precious place in my heart. After she left, I spent nights going over each one to get another moment of her. Now this fae had taken one of them, and he could see it anytime he liked.

His lips twitched, and he ran a thoughtful hand down his cheek. "Where is your mother?"

I shoved the watch into my pocket. "That's for me to know." Never mind that I had no idea.

He looked at Thorn again, who was now coming toward us. His voice was almost breathless, "I'll give you anything if you tell me where she is. Anything."

The power that came with the offer tugged on my desires, luring me in with what I could get from it. But the confusion as to why he cared gave me pause.

He grabbed my wrist and dug his fingers into it. "Anything."

I yanked away. "Why?"

"I need—" Thorn reached us before he had time to finish speaking. The man quickly bobbed his head and took a step back.

"I'm here anytime you want to visit," he said. The sneaky smile had returned. "My offer still stands." He was looking at me like one of his prized trinkets, and I felt very much like I was bottled up inside a jar.

"She doesn't want to make deals today," Thorn said firmly. But the man had already turned and slipped away.

I tried to wear a casual face as I struggled to retake my memory, to understand why the fae cared about my mother, and to figure out how to use his offer to my advantage. My face must have been an odd twist of emotion since Thorn frowned.

"Are you alright? What did he try to offer you?"

I cleared my throat. "The power to control anyone I've seen without their mask. But I've never seen someone without one."

"You won't," he stated. "No fae gives that up easily. But you don't need a trinket to control someone once you've seen their face—you'd already own them."

So there was the trickery of that fae. But still, "When fae marry, do they reveal their faces?"

Thorn placed a hand to his own golden mask. "If they do, they are very foolish. Never give that power to anyone."

We walked back out to the street, and I tucked the warning away inside along with every other warning I'd been given so far. It seemed this realm came with a heavy dose of caution.

Thorn's jacket swelled at the pockets, and I eyed the spot to guess what he'd picked up from the shop. From the few items I'd seen, it could be anything. My own souvenir weighed in my pocket, and I kept a hand over it while Thorn's head turned from side to side, eyes sweeping each narrow alley we passed, over each face that turned to us, and each window within sight. Looking for someone, or something.

A whiff of pastry and blueberry wafted by, and I breathed it in to fill up on the taste of it.

"Do you want to try some?" Thorn asked. "Madame Rola makes these tartlets I swear are worth killing over." He jutted his chin to the wooden shop at our right where a wide sign read "Rola's Rolls."

"As long as I don't actually have to kill anyone."

"Ah, but where's the fun in that?" Thorn said airily as he led me through the narrow glass door and into a parlor with rounded chairs, dainty tables, and a long bar at the back loaded with sweets.

"What's the trick here?" I asked. Silver platters held stacks of sugar-dusted rolls, tarts and crepes, puff pastries, and jelly biscuits, each enormous and each tempting with luscious butter and creamy frosting. "There's got to be magic in those desserts."

When I'd been in the other shop, the bookshelves drew me toward them against my will. These didn't do that. They didn't need to. My will said to devour them all, and perhaps that was more dangerous. They were tempting without magic.

Thorn sniffed over the counter. "I'll show you." He pointed to a fan by an open window, directing the sweet aroma outside. Two passersby stopped and were led by their noses inside.

"That's the trick. Rola makes delicious food you can't resist. And her recipe is guarded tight. Trust me, I've tried to get it."

"And he'll never have it." A woman appeared from behind a black curtain, drying her hands on a towel hung over her petite shoulder. "But I'll always have a raspberry pudding with molten chocolate drizzle for my best customer."

Icing coated strands of her pale hair, which she tucked behind her ear as she pulled two small bowls from under the bar and set them on top, each jiggling with pink pudding. Beside them were two perfectly square cubes of fudge. She didn't ask for payment but looked at Thorn expectantly. Thorn stuck out his hand, and she brought her own finger to his. I crept nearer. When she pulled her finger back, it was stained with blood.

Thorn pressed his fingers together, but a tiny drop appeared as soon as he let go. His blood, I realized. She'd taken blood from him. Madame Rola held up her finger with Thorn's spot of blood and disappeared behind the curtain. When she reappeared, it was gone. "The girl?"

Thorn moved in front of me. "You can have two more from me instead."

I shifted from behind him. Her eyes, as brown as the fudge before us, held his for several moments before she finally nodded. She reached back out and took two more drops of blood, while the other customers browsed the assortments without batting an eye.

When she'd finished, Thorn wiped his finger on a napkin, scooped up the pudding, and strolled outside. I took one more peek at the woman before she disappeared behind the curtain again, then followed Thorn.

Thorn led us to the back of the shop, where a small courtyard sat inside a circle of lush trees, a marble bench between each. He passed me a bowl.

"What was all that about?" I asked.

"No one really knows. She's never caused problems though, so I assume her intentions with the blood are harmless. Frankly, I think she feeds on it."

I shivered. "Nasty."

"Even I, who would eat anything, agree with you. But this"—he dug the spoon deep into the pudding—"this is scrumptious."

I eyed the pudding, eerily similar in color to blood. "Is there anything bad she can do with it?"

He shrugged. "If there is, I don't know it, and she hasn't done it yet."

He wasn't bothered, and when I stole a glance back at the shop, Thorn nudged me. "She doesn't have your blood. You're safe."

I turned back to the pudding. "Let's see if this is as good as you claim."

"It's better," he promised.

We tried a bite at the same time, and all my tastebuds melted at the rich flavor. Before I swallowed, I went for a second spoonful, and then a third. He was right, this was good. As I ate, I let myself sit close to him, sending flickers of touch between us. My foot swayed, rubbing against his, and I allowed my elbow to graze his arm. I sent him little smiles between bites.

If he was falling for the charm, he didn't show it. Perhaps I wasn't as good at flirting as I'd hoped.

His attention was frustratingly everywhere but on me. Thorn surveyed the courtyard as if someone might be lurking there, taking his time with his own dessert while I swiftly devoured mine.

Then he paused, staring through trees. Intricate candles rested on the branches with flames reaching to lick the leaves and curl over the bark, never burning anything. If someone stood within their shadows, my eyes weren't skilled enough to see through this blasted eternal night.

Thorn at last began to eat again, giving one more glance to our surroundings. An odd smile came to his lips.

"Four months in this realm, three alliances made, one king fooled, one king who bested you, and one king who took you on the chariot ride of a lifetime." He took another bite. "Quite the adventure."

I set my empty dish aside. "It's certainly been something." *Five kings left to get favors from, one mystery person leaving messages, and my life on the line.*

"Your alliance with Bastian interests me most."

I knew little of trying to charm gentlemen, but I knew speaking of other men wasn't the way to do it. Even in the fae realm. "It was made impulsively," I said quickly. "But I don't want to talk about him. Tell me more about you."

"I am a man looking for an alliance myself. My kingdom has been stagnant for a while. It could use change."

I leaned an elbow against the back of the bench, tilting my head while hoping my hair fell over my shoulder in an alluring way. "An alliance?"

He set his half-eaten pudding aside. His eyes rose to meet mine, and I could feel him reeling in. One more smile, perhaps a kiss, and I'd convince a second king to owe me a favor. Odette had been right. King Thorn gave his heart away too easily. It almost pained me to play with it this way. Almost. His wounded pride would be worth my life. But then he spoke.

"Knowing Bastian, he made you promise not to make any further alliances, didn't he?"

My plan unraveled. I opened my mouth but nothing came out.

"That's fine, I don't need that from you. But you need something from me, don't you? What do you need?"

I let my elbow drop and contemplated him for a while before replying. "One favor. That's all I ask."

"For what?"

Again, I met him with silence. He sat back and watched me as if he had forever to wait. He had ages. I did not.

"I want to unite the fae kings to undo the command of their ancestors to bring Mortal Queens here, and free us from the death that awaits." Almost the full truth.

His eyebrows shot up. "All of the kings working together? That's never happened since I've been alive."

"It can happen if you all owe me a favor."

He took a gulp of air, scanning the courtyard again. His eyes caught on the tree line, but when I looked, there was only darkness and hints of colorful tents beyond.

"It won't work."

If I had a year for every time someone had said that to me, I'd soon live as long as the fae. "Then it won't hurt to agree."

He grinned. "Deal. I can grant you a favor. But I'll need something in return."

"I can't make an alliance."

"I know." He played with a coil of my hair. We were quite the contrasting pair—him like the golden sun and me with the first hints of night. "What I ask is in repayment for my sister." I wrinkled my forehead. His face came closer, until his breath brushed over my nose. "Grant me this, and you will have your favor. I suspect you were willing to kiss me to get your favor anyway. One kiss, and it's yours."

He hesitated only for a moment, letting his nose rest near mine and his eyelashes flutter shut. His gentle hand went through my hair and he paused, taking in the scent of me. Waiting for me to accept.

One favor, one kiss. It would be the easiest deal I made.

I hesitantly put my lips against his.

He tasted of the pudding and of satisfaction. My hand gripped his arm, pulling myself close.

Kissing someone I didn't have feelings for ought to feel flat, but the feeling that rushed through me was anything but dull. It was intoxicating. Deep. Longing. The lure of a fae king at work. Mortals couldn't resist their charm.

I kissed him for far longer than I intended. I suspected he'd let me kiss him forever if I didn't stop.

I forced myself to pull back. His eyelids opened and he held my gaze for a moment. Then he smiled broadly. Something twinkled in his eyes with the promise of secrets I would never get to know.

"That was all I needed." Once he'd broken away, the overwhelming desire to be close to him faded, and guilt rushed in.

I shouldn't have done that. It was funny how one bad decision could bring the clarity you lacked before you made it, but it was always too late.

He stood unfazed and offered a hand. "The favor is yours. If you ever need anything else"—a wicked gleam danced in his eyes—"I'm always here. But first I should escort you home. I suspect another fae king wishes for a word with you."

He laced his long fingers through mine and guided me from the courtyard. Leaves rustled behind us. But there was no breeze.

I glanced back, where shadows lingered between the trees. Beneath them, I swore I saw someone.

But they pulled back and left me with questions I'd never get to ask.

Thorn said he wanted payment for what happened to his sister. Bash broke his sister's heart. He'd been scanning the trees, waiting, biding his time. Unease clenched me. The figure in the courtyard.

"Is Bash here?" My words were breathy.

Thorn grinned. "Would you have kissed me if he was?"

I didn't have the answer to that. I spun around, staring deep into the trees. The noise of the island suddenly boomed too loud, and the pressure in my head exploded. I shot Thorn a devilish glare.

"Answer me. Is Bash here? Is that why you had me kiss you?"

Thorn continued to walk without me. "The deal is made," he said lightly. "But my advice I give freely." He stopped and turned. "Strategize with your head, never your heart. Your head can save you. Your heart will only lead to him, and ruin lies there."

25

BASH WAS WAITING IN MY ROOM
when I returned, pacing the floor like a scowling lion. His frown deepened when he spotted me in the doorway. I held my head high. I had nothing to apologize for and nothing to explain.

He, however, did. "What were you doing on Illusion Point?"

"You summoned me," he replied in a tight tone. "I thought you did. But Thorn—" he bit down on his words.

So that was what Thorn had been doing while I was selling a memory. He was summoning Bash.

"I have nothing to explain to you," I said. "I've done nothing wrong." I bent to untie my shoes and make certain the watch I'd acquired from Illusion Point was concealed.

"You'll need those," Bash said abruptly. He stopped pacing to gesture toward my feet.

"My shoes? If you're taking me somewhere to yell at me, my room works perfectly fine."

"I'm not going to yell at you," he said flatly. "You make your own decisions."

I retied my shoes and stood up. "You're just going to glare at me then? We can talk about it if you'd like."

"There is no need," he said. The air in the room stilled like the entire realm held its breath to watch the fallout of me kissing another fae king.

Bash's eyes darted over the floor in the way that Cal's always did when he was sorting through something.

This pleased me. The glass-hearted fae king cared. I knew it.

"Bash, whatever you need to say, I can take it."

"There's nothing to speak about. If Thorn wishes to kiss you, he can. If he falls in love with you, it will be his heart that shatters when you leave. It will be him who falls apart when you aren't here anymore. It will be him who mourns you for eons to come."

My breath caught as Bash went on. My hand went to a chair to steady me as the words tumbled from his lips, and my ears caught the hints of desire and hurt mixed together. His gaze wasn't on me. It was on the walls, the fireplace, the paintings, anywhere but on my own, as if his words exposed too much of him already and he wanted to keep some part hidden.

But the words were giving him away.

"If he is foolish enough to love a mortal girl, then let him. But you aren't his to cherish. You never can be. You will die someday, while he lives on, empty without you. Kings were not meant to love fragile mortals who are fated to die and leave us alone. The pain of that is too great. And he can't . . ." his voice cracked and his head dropped. His next words were whispers.

"I can't, Thea. I can't do it."

I didn't need to take off his mask. I saw him now. I saw his pain. His heart wasn't cracked because he never gave it, but it was chipped in its own way from the pain of trying to protect it. Keeping himself from loving others was a burden he bore so he would never know the sting of loss.

I went to his side. "Bash—"

He stepped away. "I told you. We can't help but love you. But this?" His hand briefly touched mine, and his voice was barely audible. "This will break me. I can't do it, Althea. I can't love you."

A tear carved its way down my cheek. "I'm not asking you to."

His thumb brushed away my tear. "You don't need to. I never stood a chance."

We stood silent for a long time. Close, but never touching. Letting the world move on while we stayed in that moment of unexplored feelings and warnings of what would happen if we crossed the line. I painfully reminded myself that I couldn't have a future here. Everything I did had to be for the sake of the queens who would come after me.

Your heart will only lead to him, and ruin lies there.

I couldn't offer him a future, but I could offer my painting. In that moment, it was all I trusted myself to do. I went over to it. "It's not finished," I said, turning the painting toward him. "I need to do your eyes still, but here it is."

He came and took the painting in his hands. I bit the inside of my cheek while waiting for his response. I'd never painted a portrait for another person before, and the anticipation of how he would like it was almost unbearable. Especially because it was *him.*

But I hadn't expected the moisture in his eyes.

"It's remarkable," he said slowly. "I can take stars from the sky, but that's the extent of my power. I can only steal beauty. But you? You create it." His eyes lifted to me. "You are it."

How could he expect me not to care for him when he said things like that?

He set the painting down. "It's perfect. Thank you."

He stared at it for a while longer before speaking again. "Come. I have something to show you."

He didn't take my hand as Thorn had but strode to the balcony where a cloak hung on the glass doors. He took it down and tossed it to me. The fabric settled in my hands, almost toppling me over. Hints of a cinnamon scent clung to the thick fibers.

"What's this?"

"For our adventure."

Firelight caught on the bristles of the cloak, bringing out the deep velvet color, almost more purple than red. White-and-grey speckled fur lined the hood and seams, grazing my ankles when I flung it over my shoulders. I exhaled. "This is glorious."

"There are mittens in the pocket."

I reached inside. On the five islands, where the sun beat against us as if attempting to scorch us from the land, mittens were not needed. I doubted they were even made there. But I identified the two wool mittens in my pocket. "Where are we going?"

He stepped onto his chariot and beckoned me. "I'll show you."

He still didn't take my hand. Not as I stepped up next to him, not as the chariot took off, and not as we flew through the sky. He kept a respectable distance, which in the small chariot meant he was pressed against the opposite side.

I can't love you.

"Here."

I looked down. We were in his kingdom, on the very island where his palace lay carved into the mountainside. But instead of settling in his courtyard, the chariot took us to the top of the mountain. I drew in a breath as the chariot settled.

It didn't settle on rock. It sat on snow.

"You didn't."

"You said you've never seen snow," he said. "I brought you to some."

He waited for me to step down first. I held my skirt in hand while staring at the snow beneath us, so pure and soft. A blanket to cover the mountaintops and stare over the realm. "It's magnificent."

The snow gave a small crunch as my foot broke through the surface, then surrounded my toes with bitter cold. I laughed. Another step, then I dropped to my knees and buried my hands.

Bash laughed behind me, then stepped off the chariot to join in the fun. I ripped off the mittens to let my fingers slice through the snow and feel it for myself.

"It's so odd," I said, squeezing some between my hands. "It's both soft and hard at the same time. Wet and dry."

Bash knelt beside me. "I suppose it is. I wish I could see it through new eyes and experience it for the first time. I'm afraid it's lost its wonder for me."

I rolled it over my palm, then let the snow fall to the ground. It left little patterns where it hit. Water soaked through the cloak and into my knees, but I didn't care. Starlight cast a glow over the snow, giving it a pale, blue color. Everywhere else, it was always night—dark and endless. But atop this mountain, the snow reflected the stars, and it brightened the entire realm. It didn't need lamps or firelight to shine. It did that all on its own.

"My kingdom is one of rock," Bash said. "But this patch of snow proves there is some beauty here." He turned his head west, where the other islands in his domain lay, holding his chin high.

I dusted off my hands. "Do the lords consent to your rulership yet?"

He shook his head. "No. But we are getting there. My alliance with you has helped."

Despite the cold, a warmth knitted inside.

"It's a beautiful realm," I said. "You are fortunate to rule over it."

"As are you."

"That's not the same. It's not mine. Not really." I recalled Gaia's words from when I first met her. "It's a beautiful world I can never belong to."

"Not to me," he said softly. He stood, revealing wet patches on his own knees.

I stood next to him and tightened my cloak as I gazed at the realm from this view. The mountain cleaved into the island beneath us with iron lamps at periodic intervals to illuminate Bash's grand palace. The other islands shone from afar, each town built around mountains of its own and homes with glass walls cut into the rock, like caverns of caves.

Above were the infinite stars in an endless sky, bright enough to see the realm by. I shook my head. "What could be more beautiful than this?"

He surveyed it all. "My world is one of obvious beauty. It's big and easy to see. But yours?" He sighed. "I want the quiet beauty of waves touching a shore. I want the broken beauty of sunbeams seeping through a forest. I want the still beauty of an orange sunrise. We don't have that here."

I could have stayed in that moment forever, listening to him speak of gentle beauty, thinking it was the perfect phrase to describe him.

"Then come back with me to my realm," I said. "The land is like that there. You can walk down as many sandy beaches as you want."

He gave me a sideways glance. "Are you using me to get you back to your realm?"

"No," I said, and somehow the words didn't taste like a lie.

He looked away. "I can't. Only ambassadors can cross the realms, and if I had an ambassador return you to your realm, you'd never leave it. I can't bring myself to do that."

Bash moved for his chariot while I stayed planted. "You would rather leave me in your realm to die than see me go free?"

He hunched like I'd stabbed him. "I don't want you to die. You've no idea the deep love we have for our Mortal Queens." How many times had I heard that? "Our delicate, beautiful Mortal Queens. Return you to your realm and lose you to ours? Never."

The sharpness in his voice made me grit my teeth. "That is not love," I called after him. "It's obsession. It's possessive greed."

"Oh, no. It's captivation," he countered. "And it's endless. No matter how many games we play with our queens, we still love them more than we love ourselves. We will not lose you to the mortals." He said that word as if it was a sickness. As if *we* were the twisted ones.

Bash mounted the chariot. "I will not hurt you. I could never do that. But I also cannot save you, no matter how many times you ask it."

"There must be a way," I persisted. Surely those who held the power of the realm at their fingers could free me. Bash had made it clear he loved the queens, and more than that, I suspected him of caring for me. Yet the man I saw here was different from the one who'd confidently plucked stars from the sky. He was bent in on himself as if it were he who would die and not me.

"There isn't. I've been through everything and spoken to anyone who might help. When I got the summons for help from you today, I was already at Illusion Point searching for something to save you."

Pain rippled through me. He'd been there for me, and his reward was to watch me kiss King Thorn.

"Bash, I'm sorry."

"Don't. I needed to see it to remind me never to care." The cold of the snow was nothing compared to the indifference in his tone. "You can collect favors from the kings if you want. But if we were strong enough to save a queen, we would have done it by now." He ducked his head. "Enjoy the beauty of the realm now and be grateful you don't have to see the darkness that settles over our hearts when you leave it."

I slowly went and joined him on the chariot, leaving a wide gap between us.

He needed to see the kiss, and I needed to see him fall apart because of it. I needed the reminder that this thing between us was too frail to survive, and to hear him say he couldn't free me, even if he held the power. His attraction to me was nothing but the lure to Mortal Queens, and my attraction to him was nothing but the pull of a fae king.

That would not save me or the girls who would come after me.

In the end, I had to be willing to let the fae kings die to repay the punishment this realm placed upon them. I had to be willing to watch Bash die.

I set my gaze forward. "Take me home."

26

THE NEXT MORNING. I TOOK MY

time to wake, slowly pouring a cup of tea to sit on the balcony with as I stared into the darkness and thought of my brothers. Trying to summon a deep-rooted peace. I breathed slow. I cleared my mind. The peace didn't come.

It wouldn't have lasted long anyway. A minute after I returned inside, a flash of color came from outside. Troi swept close on a chariot, then lept from it to land on the balcony. Before I could say hello, she'd drawn a sword and pressed the dull end against my chest. "What have you done to my brother?"

"Nothing." I staggered back, bumping against a large mirror. She—and her sword—moved with me. I lifted my hand to push it away, but she held fast.

Her eyes narrowed to slits. "Lies."

"I saved your life. You won't kill me."

"Try me," she hissed. Her hair was in braids twisted at the nape of her neck and her brown eyes were closer to black. "What did you do to Bastian?"

I risked easing away. Her blade didn't waver but she let me move.

"I didn't do a single thing to him. What's wrong?"

"He's a mess. He's frantic, flying all over the realm, offering favors for assistance that leads him nowhere. He's going to get himself in a lot of trouble."

"That could have nothing to do with me. I haven't asked him for anything."

"And yet he wasn't like this until you." But Troi sheathed the sword at her hip, where it clung to her leather pants. "You did something to him."

I moved to the mantle to gather my brushes. "Do you always dress like you've come from battle?"

"Do you always send men into frantic messes?"

"Your brother makes his own decisions. I'm not influencing them."

She barked a laugh. "Please. I see how you look at him. But when you leave, I'll be left to pick up the pieces, so you'd better leave him whole. A broken king cannot lead us. Bastian is too young to recover if he fails so soon."

My mouth went dry. Little did she know how her brother refused to fall for me. How he kept himself at a distance so he wouldn't feel anything when I left. If she knew how strong his desire not to care for me was, she wouldn't be here. Bash didn't need any help not loving me.

"You have nothing to worry about," I said firmly.

"I am his protector," she reminded me. "And I will protect him from you, my Queen." Then she was out the door.

The entire realm had a fascination with their Mortal Queens, but that wonder didn't grip Troi. I had no problem believing she'd slit my throat if she needed to, and without much prompting.

"Goodbye, Troi," I muttered. "Always a pleasure."

I twirled a brush but found no motivation to paint. When I turned, Bash's painting grounded me. "I don't need your judgment," I said as I draped a cloth over it. My hand went to my chest where Troi's blade had pressed. "And, please, tell your sister not to kill me."

The door opened and I whirled, hands up in defense. Odette stood with her eyebrows raised.

"You look like I intend to murder you."

I lowered my hands. "I thought you were Troi."

She laughed, the sound as bubbly as champagne and brighter than any star. Nothing like Troi. Dark grey fabric hung from Odette's shoulders in a woven pattern to create a dress that accented the hints of red in her auburn hair.

"Sorry to disappoint you. I thought we could have a night together." She flung herself on the sofa before the fire and kicked up her feet. "By the way, one of your paintings is in the courtyard looking rather sad and lonely."

"Really?" After again hearing Bash tell me nothing could save me, I could use some wisdom from Dhalia.

"It's just sitting there."

I tried not to look too interested and tied my slippers slowly. "I'll go fetch it. I'll be right back."

I donned a shawl and went out, my pace quickening with each step. The lanterns in the corridor and stairwell were still lit as the day wasn't quite over, and their light led the way to the courtyard where the fish bubbled to the surface in the river to say hello.

A painting sat on an easel in the same place where King Brock had bested me in chess.

I tried not to think of my great loss as I turned the painting around.

I gasped. This wasn't one of my pieces. It was entirely new. Dhalia stood in a white gown overtaken by lace and layers, a rosette train caught in the wind behind her as she stood on the balcony in her black mask and stared into the night. Morten loomed behind her, pressed against her back as he bent over her shoulder.

Dark lines traced her eyes, but a tear marred them. All the colors of the painting were dull in comparison to those eyes and the glint of tears pooling in them. Her sadness was the entire focus of the painting. In a moment, it would be mine to endure.

I readied myself to feel her emotions, then touched the painting.

Mist clung to my cheeks and gathered at the curve of my neck where Dhalia's hair was curled in small ringlets. I'd been wrong, Morten wasn't pressed against her. He braced a pace behind, only hovering over my shoulder.

"It will be fine," he said.

Dhalia shifted, and he flew back.

"If this doesn't work?"

Morten's exhale was like a breeze stoking embers of anxiety within Dhalia, and they stirred inside me. I tried to send my own feelings to soothe her, even knowing it couldn't help.

"It will work. Just keep your gloves on until he touches you."

Tight, cream gloves adorned her hands, stretching up to her elbow. How had I not seen them earlier? Now I searched for other details I might have missed, anything that could be useful. A half empty glass of wine sat next to an entirely empty bottle. Every surface was covered in candles, the edge of the bed, the table, the desk, the shelves over the mantle. A pot of roses marked the entryway so it was the first thing someone would smell when coming in.

The stars had dimmed, indicating nighttime. A few chariots still roamed the skies, and Dhalia glanced at them obsessively. She fidgeted with a strip of her gown then let it drop. I didn't need to share her body and thoughts to know that nerves clung to her like the mist.

"Be brave, my Queen. He will touch you."

Morten retreated into the closet, letting the double doors close nearly all the way, leaving a slender crack I had no doubt he'd be staring through the entire night.

Dhalia placed a hand to her chest to steady herself. Then she traced a path to the center of the room, her heels clicking on the marble, and stood tall. She faced the door with a raised chin.

The door whooshed opened, and King Ulther took up the entire space of the doorway, his dark skin warm against the firelight and his grey suit as crisp as stone. The signature golden band of a king crossed his forehead above his gold mask, and his brown eyes absorbed every inch of Dhalia.

"My King," she said. Could he hear the vibration in her voice? She swallowed.

He took a tentative step near. "You are a magnificent bride."

My failure to put that together sooner showed a significant flaw in my understanding. This was Dhalia's wedding night. Her dress alone should have told me that. Now the nerves made sense.

"Everyone knows you tricked me into this," she said. It wasn't a threat, but her tone was as sharp as a knife. "None will think this a love match."

He chuckled. "Love is not as powerful as this alliance. Never before have a Mortal Queen and fae king been joined in such a bond."

"I want more than that," she said. Dhalia took her time to sit herself behind her vanity and gaze into the reflection, shaking her head as if what she saw displeased her. She dragged her hands through her tight curls. "If I'm to marry you tonight, I want more than an alliance. My time is limited and I—" she allowed her voice to crack, yet what I felt inside her was anything but sadness. It was calculating. Determined. "I want something more."

King Ulther's eyes widened. He took in the candles as if seeing them for the first time. He moistened his lips. "I can't promise that."

Dhalia's nerves hardened into stone, and her mind quieted until only one thought remained like a mantra repeating in her head.

Defeat him.

This was her battle cry, her wedding dress her armor, her words her weapon.

She twisted a strand of hair between her gloved fingers. The candles she'd set on a short table flickered when King Ulther drew near her.

"I don't need promises. I need happiness. That's all I hope for anymore."

He said nothing, but I sensed his unease. His steps were gruelingly slow, and his throat bobbed as he swallowed.

"Can you do that, my King?" she pressed. "Can you make me happy? If I marry you tonight, will you make me forget that I die next year?"

His hand pulsed toward her but hesitated. He was close enough that he could kiss her, and I felt Dhalia resisting the urge to look at the closet.

"My King"—her voice was husky as she drew a finger down his chest—"make me forget I'm to die."

His self-control snapped. His hand seized her waist to draw her close for a kiss.

But none of that happened.

When his skin touched her dress, King Ulther's body stilled. The only motion from him was a twitch in his eyes as he struggled. Frozen, I realized. She'd frozen him.

"Don't worry, my King." Dhalia's voice was rich with triumph. "I can release you. But not until you release me."

"What . . . did you . . . do?" So he was able to speak, but every word was strained, and Dhalia grinned through it all.

"A charm was placed over my dress." She pulled on the fingers of the gloves, removing them and tossing the fabric aside. "The first person to touch it would be frozen, but only if they touched it willingly." She smiled. "It was too easy."

She walked in a circle around him, pausing only to wink toward the crack in the closet. "My two demands are simple. If you fail to oblige me, I'll leave you trapped forever, and once I die, there is no one who can save you. So I'd think very carefully about the next words you use."

King Ulther's eyes narrowed, but he grunted.

"First, you will release me from being your bride. I find I don't care to be tied to you."

She stopped right in front of him, waiting for an answer.

His lips trembled. "Fine."

"And second, you will help save me. I will not die here."

A low rumble came from deep in his throat. "No."

She arched a brow. "No? Then you are of no use to me." Dhalia crossed to the desk and blew out candles as she opened a drawer. The slick hilt of a trailing blade with a white-horned hilt slid into her hand. She held it up while turning around. "But I'm generous. I'll ask again."

"I can't," he protested. "It's . . . not possible."

"The two of us are clever enough to think of a way." She made a big show of cleaning the blade before pressing it to his neck. "Let's explore you changing your answer, shall we?" Dhalia had fire in her belly. She pressed the blade deeper. She was dangerously close to killing him.

I saw the moment King Ulther gave up. "Fine."

She withdrew, and the hold over him gave out. He stumbled, then gathered himself. "It won't work. I can't save you."

The frustration inside her was the same as my own at hearing those words again. "Try."

He finally relented. "Let's sit. We will think."

Dhalia blew out the candles on the bed and rested against it. "I already have an idea."

27

TRUE TO THE PAINTINGS' RELIABLE
nature of showing me just enough to leave me with a million more
questions and an infuriating need to see the rest of the story, the
vision ended.

I wanted to go over every detail again to analyze if I'd learned
anything, but when I turned around, I spotted Gaia coming down
the stairs in a flowy dress of cream and blush, her hair pulled up
simply, and shoes on her feet. From her hurry, she had somewhere
to be, but she moved in a frantic way as if someone followed her.
Like she was trapped.

She came into the courtyard but seemed not to notice me.

"Are you alright?" I questioned.

Her gaze sprang to me, and she flittered the other way. "Eight
months," she was whispering. "Only eight months."

"Gaia? What's wrong?" I followed her as she flung a hand
upward to call upon a chariot.

When she looked back at me, her cheeks held a pale color
instead of their usual bronze complexion. Something wild was
in her eyes. It gripped her and it frightened me. She spoke more
clearly now. "Eight months until I die."

"Oh, Gaia." I crossed to take her hands. "Look at me. Look at my face, Gaia." Teary eyes found mine. I had to tell her. "We can fight this together. There was a queen before us who survived. We just have to outwit them."

She squeezed her eyes tight and shook her head. "No. I don't want to die."

I gripped her hands harder. "Then don't. Fight."

"I-I'll end up j-just like Ivory." A tear rolled down her cheek as she raised her eyes to mine, her voice soft as a dying wind. "I tried to save her, but I lost her."

Tears threatened my own eyes as it sank in how much Gaia lost when Ivory died. She seemed to melt before me, filled with nothing but dread and heartbreak, sobbing as she eased out of my grip to bury her face in her hands. Her shoulders heaved as she wept.

Behold, the stoic Gaia. Broken.

Her cries filled the courtyard. No one understood the feeling inside Gaia better than I did.

At least I had friends to lean on when despair consumed me. Gaia had none.

"Join me," I said impulsively. "I have a friend over, and we'd love to spend the evening with you."

Gaia raised her head and quieted. She wiped her tears with the back of her hand and steadied herself. The chariot she had called for was here, waiting. "I have plans."

"Really?" At her dangerous look I scooted back. "I'm sorry, I didn't think you were attending events."

As quickly as she'd pulled herself together, her sanity slipped away again, until she was as I'd found her moments ago. Lost to herself.

"I can't die. I can't die." She raked a hand through her hair. "I can't die." Her words were mindless rambles between cries and tainted with hopelessness.

"Gaia?" I put a hand on her arm, but she yanked it away.

"I don't want to die," she said loudly while running to the chariot. She turned to give me a last look, and something in her face terrified me to the core. It was a look I imagined must have been pasted to my own face right before I threw myself off the edge of an island. Ignorant desperation.

Odette would have to forgive me. I chased after Gaia but her chariot rose and carried her away.

I'd never called upon a chariot before, but when I swung my arm in the air as Gaia had, one emerged from the night. "Follow Gaia," I instructed. The golden wisp leading the chariot understood, and it rippled forward like an enchanted ribbon.

I followed Gaia north through lands I didn't recognize. I kept her barely visible in front of me, close enough that I could be certain the chariot followed, but far enough that she wouldn't catch me doing so. It was only when we slowed down that my gaze dropped and I gasped.

Gaia had fled to Illusion Point. The land where nothing was as it seemed, and tricks could await in any corner for prey—especially a girl in her unraveled state.

A shiver ran up my spine as her chariot landed in the center of the crowded town. She stepped off without looking around and darted through the tents. She knew exactly what she was after.

Thorn's story came to mind of how Gaia and Ivory had ruled this island together. She was familiar with these crowded streets, but she was different now. *She'd be an easy target.*

"Take me down," I instructed. "Before she gets herself into trouble." The chariot obeyed and we landed as Gaia's chariot took off without her.

The narrow street was lined with boxed lanterns that hung low over the red cobblestones. The path was empty, except for one gentleman and his cart. I gathered my skirts to follow where Gaia had gone. The fae shifted his cart toward me, almost knocking me down as it blocked my way with its oversized wheel.

"No, thank you," I said without glancing at him as I skirted the wheel.

He threw a powder in the air as I went, a thick red dust that lodged in my throat and burned my eyes. It clung to me for a moment before simmering away.

I whirled around.

The man was built like a cart, wide and short. He glided as if on wheels himself. At my expression, he shrugged and slunk into the shadows. I rubbed my eyes and moved after Gaia.

All the shops on the left side of the street held round doors, blooming flowers under the windows, and weathered signs on a post. I blinked and the shops shifted, and suddenly they were all different. Some were taller, some low, some bright, and some carried all the black of night inside them.

Another blink and they were back to what they were before.

I shook my head and stared at the street, but that too had moved. Where it veered to the west earlier, it now split in two directions, north and east.

A few steps and it all shifted again.

I turned in a slow circle. With each moment, the landscape shifted further, until I couldn't tell which way I'd come from. The man with the cart stood in the center of the road with a wicked gleam in his blue eyes.

"You did something."

He shrugged. "Perhaps. But you won't likely find your way out on your own. Or"—he produced a furled parchment from his silky robes—"this will guide you."

I glared at him, and he tucked the parchment away. "I'm a kind soul, so I'll inform you that choosing the wrong path leads to you owing me a favor."

I scowled. "How is that fair?"

He leaned down and picked up the cart holds. "You come to this island. You expect to be tricked." He bowed. "It's an honor to play with you, my Queen. Choose wisely."

They had a delusional sense of honor here.

The man and his cart disappeared just as the streets shifted once more. Now four roads presented themselves, each bedecked in sparrow-tailed banners, shops with fae mingling about, and scents of frosted cakes.

It split again. Now five roads.

Again. Six.

With each moment I waited, the options grew, and my odds of choosing the right one slimmed. A clever thought came. If I didn't know where I wanted to go, I couldn't choose the wrong way. Any path could take me somewhere, and I would rather be anywhere than here. Every direction could give me that.

I'd worry about finding Gaia later. For now, I willed the desire to be *somewhere,* avoiding all thoughts of a real destination, and stepped forward.

A strong hand tugged at my arm.

Thorn pulled me away from the road. His eyes flashed. "Artru?" He scanned the area until the man with the cart, his head bent reluctantly, stepped from the shadows. Thorn's tone was curt. "No."

The man's shoulders sagged. He plunged a hand into his deep pockets to pull out a handful of silver dust and tossed it into the sky like a million twinkling stars that settled over my face.

With my next blink, the island righted itself.

"Any path you chose, he would claim was the wrong one," Thorn said, looking after the man who had now gone. "You couldn't win that."

I rubbed the dust from my forehead. "That doesn't seem fair."

"Lucky for you, I'm here." He smiled.

Suspicion edged my mind, and I pulled back to examine him. Why was he here? How did he know I was in trouble? Was this only a deception to appear as my hero?

His smile faltered. "What is it?"

"Nothing." I glanced back to the roads. "Actually, I'm searching for Gaia."

He stood stone still before letting out a low whistle. "The queen has returned." His eyes roamed over the island. "It isn't ready for what she can do."

"I don't think *she's* ready," I replied. "She's in hysterics. I followed her here but then"—I waved my hand—"the dust and the splitting roads."

"Understandable. My business here is done, and I'll gladly help you search. It should be an interesting night."

I noted the twinkle in his eyes, begging me to ask him why. I humored him. "Why?"

He looked around then leaned close. "All the kings are here at the same time, save one."

My brows raised.

"Yours." My cheeks heated at that, but he went on. "He doesn't care for this island. I haven't seen him here in fifteen years, until he showed up two days ago."

For me.

"What of the missing king?" I asked.

Thorn sighed. "Alright. All the kings are here except the stuck-up one and the missing one. But now both our queens are here too." He lifted his hands gleefully. "This island is practically trembling with possibilities."

I tried not to think of what that could mean. I had to find Gaia before she did something rash. "She went that direction," I pointed.

"After you," Thorn said, still giddy.

We searched through narrow, winding streets and into shops both rundown and pristine. We checked alleys and taverns and more. We even stopped by Rola's Rolls, where we purchased some tartlets. Thorn offered to pay for me again.

"It's alright." I stuck out my finger and she hungrily stole a drop of blood. It was worth it for the impressed look on Thorn's face, and I buried my unease deep inside. I squeezed my thumb against my finger.

"Let's go. She's clearly not here." I took my wrapped tartlet.

Madame Rola's teeth bared in a knowing smile. "Lost a queen, eh?"

I stiffened. "What do you know of it?"

She clicked her tongue. "You don't have enough blood in your body to know."

Thorn knit his thick brows together. "Do I?"

Again, she clicked her tongue. "No. But it wouldn't matter. The queen came to get a slice of marzipan cake. She and Queen Ivory used to do that together, but only after their task was completed. Whatever game she came to play, she's played it."

My face drained of color. "What game? Did she say anything about it?"

Madame Rola slyly turned away to rub the already clean counter with a rag and whistle to herself. The melody was low and enchanting and entirely irked me. Thorn placed a hand on my shoulder.

"Outside," he whispered.

I sent Madame Rola a daggered look as we went out the door. Her song clung to the air, following us.

"I know where we must go," Thorn said.

My attention snapped to him. "How?"

"That song she's whistling? It's played here. It comes from the heart of the island, where ravens gather on twisted vines to watch the games being played. It's where seven thrones are set up for the seven fae kings, and two large pedestals sit behind a table set with the largest chess board in all the realm. The rest of this island is made of little tricks and jokes, but the center? It's where the kings go to make their deals. I almost lost my kingdom there once, and that song played as I scraped by."

I paled with each word. "Gaia went there?"

"She must have. I didn't think she'd ever return."

"Because of a bad deal she made?"

His expression flickered. He squared his shoulders. "Because Queen Ivory died on that chess table. She was found in the middle of the night before you came, her body torn among the chess pieces."

If I was pale before, I was a ghost now. My stomach knotted. "Who killed her?"

Thorn's voice was strong in its sincerity. "None of us would kill a queen."

Bash had said that. Talen had said it. Had Odette told me the same thing? I felt as if I'd heard it a million times, but this time it landed like a rock that sank to my feet.

The realm had taught me many things. Watch your words. Guard your face. Shield your true intentions. But if it had taught me one thing more than anything else, it was this—the fae were dirty liars.

None of us would hurt a queen.

We love our queens too much. We can't help it.

My beautiful queen.

I'd been told it all before. But the tale of the realm placing a cruel fate upon the fae—to love their queens, only to lose them—was beginning to sound too convenient. In a land where lies were told as easily as breathing and people found their delight in tricking others, it would be an easy lie to maintain, and I'd never know the truth of it until my final moments.

It was easier to wonder how Ivory died than to picture her dead upon that table. My mind gave her features similar to mine, Gaia's, and Dhalia's. Bronze skin, oval eyes, thick thighs, and thin lips. A fire in her belly from Dhalia, a gentleness in her touch like Gaia's, a determination like mine. Dead, just like we all might become.

I was in danger of losing my teeth if I ground them any harder.

"Take me to the kings," I demanded. "I'm in the mood for a chess game."

Thorn eyed me but obliged. We maneuvered through the bustling island, ignoring those who called to us as we passed, no matter how tempting their promise of everlasting happiness or true love might sound. Thorn kept close to my side and stared everyone down as if he were my bodyguard instead of a king.

I didn't mind. I preferred him close. It made it easier to keep an eye on him. My ability to trust was especially low tonight.

Pure white gates reached through the dark skies. We moved from the busy streets to stand at the threshold of the center. A sliver of a river cleaved the land, and eight identical bridges formed a circle, each leading to that center.

That center.

Over the bridge and beyond the gate, we came upon the arena. Seven thrones made of black iron lined one side, where the ground dove deep with seats carved from dirt and paved in travertine. Thorn fell back so I could walk ahead but kept himself close behind me. With his golden beauty and strong presence, it wouldn't matter that he placed himself in the back. He'd be the only one people saw.

I was wrong. All eyes fell to me.

"Don't look away from the thrones," Thorn warned. "You wanted to come here. You play by the rules. Keep your eyes on the thrones until you sit down, then you can search for Gaia. She's not here though."

"How do you know?"

"She'd be on her throne."

I only saw seven for the fae kings, but as we descended the stairs, two more came into view. Where the kings' thrones were black, ours were white as the moon and faced the other way, as if the kings were our opponents.

Vivid green grass wet our feet where the thrones faced the chess table. It was three times as large as any board I'd seen before, and two men sat around it now. King Brock was one of them. The other kings–Vern, Leonard, and Arden–watched on.

One seat open for Bastian. One for Thorn. And one for the missing king.

"I may regret this," Thorn muttered. He squared his shoulders and ignored each of the kings' penetrating stares as he followed me to the white thrones. When I sat down, he stood at my left as if a servant.

I fanned out my skirts. "What is your plan here?" I asked, already scouring the seats for Gaia, though I knew she wouldn't be there. Hints of her could remain–in a whisper or in a glance, or in the ripple of whatever she'd done here.

"You can't form an alliance, but I'm aiming for a tight friendship." Thorn said. "And it never hurts to be in the company of a fine woman."

"See if you can find Gaia. That will earn my friendship."

His eyes roved in search, but they went to the chess game more often than not. To Brock's opponent's credit, he lasted much longer against King Brock than I did. Humiliation still made me wince at how easily he'd taken me down. But this fae stood his own, tightening the corners of his mouth each time Brock made a move, then retaliating with a sense of victory in his smile. Then Brock would move again, and he'd frown. The process repeated over and over, with neither of them saying a word, until Brock moved a rook from behind a pawn to set up the trap.

Pride fluttered in me. I'd seen that coming. Not only could I have avoided it, but I saw a way the man could have won. It was a move Troi made on me.

"What did he lose?" I asked Thorn.

"Nothing," he replied. "But he came asking for an increased budget for his crops, and now he won't get it."

My eyes widened. "That's how such matters are decided?"

"When we're in a good mood."

"And when you're not?"

Thorn gave an airy wave of his hand. "We string him up to a board, stand on the other end of the island, and fire an arrow. If it misses, he gets his request."

I gaped at him. "That's barbaric."

"It's entertaining."

The man stood from the table and bowed. From the seats, the fae cheered and threw favors, their white handkerchiefs falling like diamonds from the sky. The man departed with his head held low, and I pitied him and those he represented who needed more crops.

That reminded me of something. I turned to Thorn. "I have a matter to discuss with you."

He cocked his head, waiting.

"It's for a friend. I need you to agree to the alliance with King Vern." Across the yard, Vern leaned on an elbow, talking to King Leonard beside him.

Thorn scowled. "I don't care for the man."

"Neither do I," I admitted. "But some of his people are reliant upon the crops your kingdom brings in, and without you, they'll go hungry."

"Would you say they are restless without it?" he asked, thoughtful.

"I'd guess not having food would make one irritable."

He studied the ground, then looked up and nodded. "I'll make an arrangement."

Odette would be thrilled. And I'd help my friends after Talen had given his heart for me. It wasn't a favor of the same magnitude, but it was something. Over at the table, Brock stood and offered the challenge of five hundred pounds of silver to anyone who could best him. All I pictured was Talen's heart in his hands, at his mercy, likely to be crushed if the House of Delvers lost favor in Brock's eyes.

The other kings laughed when no one would take on Brock, who went to sit on his throne. About a hundred fae sat in the rows of seats, wrapped in circles above us. They mingled with each other, but always kept an eye on the chessboard.

"Gaia is gone, and no one would freely tell us what she did," Thorn said in a low voice. "You'll have to ask her yourself when she returns to the palace."

I frowned. "If she's there. She looked wild when she left. She's desperate to survive past our two years."

Thorn's face tightened. "We are all desperate for that."

None more than myself or Gaia. I had my two favors, one from Bash and one from Thorn. But the remaining kings sat before me, and I still needed to collect favors from the four of them.

Starlight bounced off the chess table. It tempted me. I'd learned so much from Troi. . .

I took a deep breath. Precious little time was left if I planned to save both myself and Gaia. I needed those favors. I could get at least one more tonight. "I want to play."

28

THORN MADE A NOISE IN HIS THROAT.

"Are you certain that's wise? Didn't Brock beat you in five moves last time?"

I grimaced. "First, I didn't know you knew that. Second, I've practiced since then. It's almost all I did during my isolation."

"I thought you painted during isolation."

I huffed. "Your knowledge of me is unsettling. I can beat him, I know it."

"He won't eagerly play you a second time. Your optimism is suspicious."

I ran a finger over his sleeve. "Then you will. Let me beat you easily with simple moves. Then appearing on a high, I will challenge Brock."

Thorn laughed. "Willingly make myself appear a fool? I'll pass."

I thought quickly. "I need those favors. Please, I'll grant you the friendship you asked for."

His foot tapped against the grass. "And I want a painting like the one you made Bastian."

My attention turned from the kings to him. "Why?"

He shrugged. "It will brighten up my throne room. Do you want to trick Brock or not?"

"Deal." I stood and turned to Thorn with a loud voice. "I challenge you to a game." My voice drew the attention of all the fae, but I kept my eyes on Thorn.

He sized me up, then said in an equally loud tone, "I accept."

He pulled out the white chair for me then sat at black. I made certain the kings were all watching as I took my initial move, the same pawn I used first against Brock, as if I'd learned nothing.

Thorn moved his pawn to face mine. I moved another.

We played back and forth, not speaking, until I saw a way to win. I moved my knight into place, with only my bishop left to position.

Thorn swept his rook into a square that blocked my bishop's path.

"What are you doing?" I mumbled.

"I don't want to look too bad," he said. "Find another way."

To spite him, I took his rook, and he moved his king away. It took nine more turns to set up something again, and this time he let me have it.

Thorn threw up his hands as I declared checkmate, then stood and bowed so deeply that his nose almost touched the table. "My Queen," he said.

I made my smile huge. "I win!" I laughed and the crowd cheered. Then I spun to the kings, eager glee still on my face. "King Brock, I challenge you to a rematch."

There was a rustle of excitement among the fae and, one by one, the kings turned to Brock. He sat motionless, considering me. Then he spoke. "What do you want?"

"A favor," I said, as I stood from my seat. I could hear Thorn resetting the board behind me. He then came around to my side.

Brock's eyes narrowed. "And if I win?"

"Whatever you want."

Thorn's eyes flickered to mine in warning, but Brock grinned. He rose, removing his cloak and straightening the rings on his fingers. His green eyes gleamed.

"Did you know," he remarked, taking a step toward me, "that every other Mortal Queen at this time had already acquired five additional alliances to go with their original House alliance?" Another step. Nerves tensed through me. "But you . . . you have only made two. Lord Winster and Bastian." His lips curled at Bash's name. He stopped a pace away. "That makes those two alliances very strong. Bastian has some lands I desire, so that their inhabitants pledge themselves to me, but I suspect his alliance with you is keeping them on a leash."

His eyes landed on mine. "I win, you annul the alliance with Bastian and distance yourself from him."

I froze. I wasn't prepared to do that. Cutting ties with Bash would be like cutting off a piece of me, and a surge of regret tore through my veins.

You can't lose Bash. It's not worth it.

But I thought again of Gaia's face streaked with tears and our desperation to survive. "Deal."

The word was out. There was no backing down now.

Thorn took his place beside the other kings to watch our every move. My hand lingered over the pawn I had previously moved first before suddenly choosing another.

Brock's lips tightened. I wore an innocent expression, but he'd see the cunning underneath soon. He moved a pawn, and I moved my knight out.

He eyed me. "You're playing different."

"I'm playing to win."

He moved his knight. I moved my pawn to give my rook a wider range. His bishop advanced, and his focus drifted to his knight again.

The minutes stretched by, each one spent with us huddled over the board in silence, eyes prowling the pieces. A smile that frightened me crossed Brock's lips, until he whispered, "You've gotten better. You are a worthy opponent now."

I had nothing on his hundreds of years, but those three grueling months with Troi of relentless gameplay had taught me well.

He fell silent again and the game continued. I kept my play slow, deliberately. Minutes were soon hours, and each time he moved his piece opened trails that my mind followed into potential moves, while I knew he was doing the same.

Nearby, Thorn would fall from his throne if he leaned forward any farther. Sweat glistened on his creased brow. If Brock won and my alliance with Bash broke, the path would be clear for an alliance with Thorn. I wondered who he cheered for in this match.

If it was for me, he had nothing to worry over. The play Brock was setting was familiar. Only because Troi bested me this way four times. Did she finally show me a clever trick to get out of it if I acted soon enough?

I acted, sliding my king forward.

Not even the slightest flicker crossed Brock's face, and uncertainty pricked me. But he thought for a very long time about his next move, and when he finally made it, I spotted a tremor in his hand.

Troi did better than teach me to avoid this trap. She taught me how to use it against him. His bishop was too far away now and would have to pass through two pawns to get back, while his other pieces couldn't be maneuvered in the way needed to help.

I moved my knight. "I'm generously informing you that I shall soon win this match."

His eyes narrowed, flicking once to the kings beside us before falling back to the board. "I could take that with my rook."

"Then it's out of the way for my own rook. You could come at that with the queen or else my knight takes the queen. The rook could also take the queen then, if you'd rather. Or perhaps you'd like to avoid all that, and my knight will simply take the queen now. However your queen dies, which she will, I can move a piece next to your king."

His lips tightened. "I see that." He moved his king the other direction.

I chuckled. "That made it easier." I moved one piece. His frown deepened.

"Choose how you die," I said.

He sighed. "You needed a win. So be it." He took my knight

with his queen. Two more moves and I said the word I hadn't been certain I'd get to say against him. It tasted like sweet retribution.

"Checkmate."

He sat back in his seat and spread out his hands. "The Mortal Queen has won."

The fae exploded into cheers again, reminding me of their presence. I stood and took a bow as something beyond pride struck me. Though I was surrounded by powerful creatures and magnificent kings, they bowed to me as an equal, and for the first time I felt it. I no longer felt faded against their glory or out of place here. The high of winning lifted my spirits and whispered promises of many more times like this if I stayed. *You were made for this realm,* it whispered. *Your father was wrong. You are ready. You are a queen.*

Brock, to his character, didn't pout upon losing, but wore a grin as if it were all in good fun. As if we were simply two friends playing together. Behind him, Thorn stood and applauded vigorously.

"My Queen, you've earned yourself a favor. Would you like to use it now?"

Three kings down, three to go.

Yet something else tugged at my heart, and I swallowed.

Two deep breaths was how long it took to make up my mind. Talen had come through for me, and now I'd come through for him. I prayed fervently Dhalia would reveal her secret soon.

"My King, I ask that you give me Talen's heart in the condition in which he gave it to you."

His brow furrowed and he came around the table to examine me with a peculiar look, as if still analyzing a chess game, and I held my head steady until he'd finished. His voice was low, meant just for me. "You are the first queen to ask for something that wasn't for herself." He tilted his head. "And here we thought black meant mischief. Perhaps it means kindness after all. You'll find the heart when you return home."

There was no regret over the decision I'd made but purely joy that I'd get to hand Talen his heart back and the anticipation of seeing his surprise.

Thorn left his throne for my side. "You got your favor," he said.

"No." I shook my head. "I got something much better. I'll get the favor another way."

29

I SCOURED THE EAST SIDE OF THE
palace like a hungry tiger, desperate for traces of Gaia, but the
halls were empty, and the walls wouldn't give up the secrets of their
queen. Soon, the sound of laughter drew me back to the west side,
and I pocketed my worries for Gaia for the moment.

Talen's voice caught me, and my pace quickened. He sat inside
my bedchambers with both his top hat and grin lopsided and his
feet on a velvet footstool, while Odette stood across the room
behind an easel. One of my paintbrushes was in her hand.

She held it up to me like a toast when I came through the door.
"Alas, our great teacher is here. Tell us, wise one, how to make
trees appear less like gumdrops."

I peered at the painting as I undid my sandals. She'd tried, quite
dreadfully, to paint a forest. What she got was a half canvas of dull
green and lines of brown.

"What is that meant to be?" I came closer and squinted at the
bottom. "A tree stump?"

She swatted me away. "It's a bunny."

"No," I said. "It's definitely not. Where are the whiskers?"

Odette blinked. "Bunnies have whiskers?" That sent Talen into
a fit of laughter as Odette begrudgingly handed over the brush. "I

give up. I don't know how you paint for hours upon end. It's quite frustrating."

I swirled the brush through a pan of water, taking care not to drip anything on the sleeves of my dress. "If you ever have the urge to try again, I'll gladly teach you."

She put her hands over her chest as if I'd just offered to make her the godmother of my child. "You'd do that for me?"

I glanced to Talen. He just grinned. "How was your evening? Odette says you left her."

"Abandoned," Odette corrected. She pointed a sharp finger my direction. "Rudely abandoned."

I set the brushes away and checked through the glass balcony doors to where I suspected Brock would leave the heart. Sure enough, a golden box sat on the banister, dangerously close to the edge. One violent wind and it would topple over the other side.

"I'm sorry to have left you, and sorry you ruined a canvas. But I think this will make up for it." I opened the doors and collected the box. A twisty design deep in the gold marked the smooth edges before meeting in the center at a lock. I opened it. There, a glass heart sat inside a bundle of scarlet velvet.

I couldn't help myself. I noted the three cracks.

The box shut with a snap. I wouldn't pry.

I turned with a smile growing on my face. Odette was collecting her mountain of curls on top of her head, complaining she had nothing to pin them with, while Talen stood by the heat of the fire, looking over her painting with an expression that told me he found it far less horrendous than I did.

I cleared my throat. "I have something for Talen."

His white brows raised. "You didn't have to get me anything. I'm here to serve you."

He might technically be charged with caring for me, but Talen was no servant. He was more friend than ally, and this would show him that I cared more about him than what I could get from him. I proudly passed him the box.

With a dance of excitement, he opened it.

His mouth unhinged. "Whose heart did you steal?"

"Yours. And I didn't steal it. I won it."

Odette gasped and Talen almost dropped the box. I put a hand to his arm to steady him as disbelief rolled over his face.

"What did this cost you?" His voice was thick. He slowly took off his hat and set it on the bed. "It must have cost a lot."

"Nothing," I lied. Only the loss of a favor. "But I would have paid a heavy price for it."

He wrapped his hands around the heart and let the empty box fall to the floor. His eyes fixated on the fragile glass. "Why would you do this for me?"

This moment, drenched in gratitude, touched me far deeper than receiving a favor from Brock would have. Among us, the shields had begun to fall, stripping bit by bit as a friendship deeper than an alliance formed until I was no longer on guard for hidden motives or sneaky tricks. I could breathe.

This realm was becoming dangerously more like a home and less like a prison.

"Oh, I suppose I forgot that friendship means nothing," I said. Talen's eyes met mine with a twinkle.

Odette wrapped her arms around me with tears in her eyes. "Thank you," she whispered.

"Of course," I whispered back. "For the girl who gladly handed me a blade even when she thought I planned to murder a king, and the man who gave up his heart to save me from my own mistake, I would do anything."

Talen lifted the heart with a contented sigh and eased it back into his chest where it belonged. His face brightened like he was complete now, and his eyes grew moist.

"Thank you, my Queen."

I wiped my own cheeks. "Look at me, making everyone cry. Let's get back to the real issue, which is where we are planning to hang this masterpiece." I lifted Odette's painting. "I say in the throne room."

Her eyes widened. "You wouldn't dare."

"I might," I said with a wiggle of my brows. Talen grinned, but his hand was still over his chest, and his eyes still sent a million thanks my way.

Once more, he reminded me of my brother. My thoughts of Cal were fewer and far between compared to when I'd first arrived, and my feelings for Talen were no longer reflections from missing my twin. He'd earned them in his own right.

"Find a place to hang that while I change, or else I swear I'm putting it in the throne room," I warned.

"Quick," Odette squeaked. "Throw it off the balcony."

I laughed, making for the closet. I looked back at them before changing, as happiness settled in my heart with a peace I thought I'd never feel here.

I was more than happy. I felt at home.

Guilt threatened to replace the happiness—guilt that I didn't miss my real home as much as I ought to. Guilt that I was thinking about staying here. Guilt that when I thought of my future, it was a fuzzy picture of nighttime and lanterns hanging off the edges of islands, and chariots that burst through the sky as the company of fae surrounded me.

If surviving the two years meant I had to go home, that was what I would do. But if it offered the chance to stay here . . .

I looked at Odette and Talen once again. Sure enough, they'd chucked the painting off the balcony.

If offered the chance to stay here, I wasn't certain I'd say no.

I woke to an unforgiving wind curling through my hair, and the curtains over the open balcony door whipping against the wall. Between the two open doors, which I swore I'd shut, was a painting of a girl I'd come to recognize standing on the very balcony the canvas now sat upon. Her hair was pulled back from her face with the force of the wind and her eyes were pink with tears.

My head fogged as I sprang from the bed, and I placed a hand against it. It throbbed from lack of sleep. I grasped a goblet to let its cool water spill down my throat, apologizing to my body that it was all I could offer at the moment. Whatever Dhalia was ready to show me, I was ready to see.

My eyes went to the skies first as if to catch a fleeting glimpse of whoever had left the painting, but the endless twinkling stars gave no sign of a visitor. So I knelt with the painting, holding it atop my skirts.

"Tonight, you will tell me your secret," I whispered.

In the painting, Dhalia stood staring into the vast night. I spoke the command begging the image to oblige. "Tell me how to live."

I touched the painting.

The mist came first, clinging to her lashes and swarming at her cheeks with a dense heat. Next was the beat of heavy rain that pounded in her ears like relentless drums, vibrating to her bones. Inside her body, I felt it all. The beat of incoming rain, the chill against her skin, and the wild anticipation building in her chest as if she planned to take on the world.

Dhalia fidgeted with the coil around her upper arm, twisting it as the sheer red dress was weighed down with the rain, but she paid it no mind. Her eyes were on the skies.

She wiped her cheeks. Their dampness was not from the rain.

Morten burst through the doors. "You're going to catch a chill," he said. "Now is a dreadful time to get sick."

She sighed but turned and slowly kicked the door shut behind her with her foot. "I'll be fine. The rain washes away my nerves."

Morten wore a suit the same dark green shade as Odette's trees, and the corners of his lips were pinched. "It's almost time. Are you ready?"

Her entire body shivered, but I suspected it wasn't from the cold. "I am." She pulled her hair into a simple braid that would look sloppy on anyone else, but as she tipped toward the mirror, her reflection was devastatingly beautiful. Like a wild, carefree woman born with natural beauty.

But her smile was sad. "Do you think Portia suffered?"

He paused as if hoping an answer would come if he waited long enough. Dhalia went back to messing with the band on her arm. I'd noticed she was usually steady in how she held herself, but tonight she was shaky. A part of her was always in motion, a tapping foot, restless fingers, her teeth worrying over her lip. More than that, I felt the wave of unrest rolling in her stomach.

At last, Morten answered. "No. I like to believe none of the queens suffer."

But his downcast expression told a different story.

He put a hand on her elbow. "Come," he said. "The ambassadors will gather shortly."

"And then we get a new queen," Dhalia said flatly.

Morten fetched a purple cloak to drape over her shoulders. His amber eyes searched hers. "Can you do this? Today is important. Today is your freedom."

She squared her shoulders as I homed in on the details of the vision to understand what freedom they spoke of. "I am focused. I am ready to do what must be done." *Lies. She wasn't focused at all.*

"Everything will be fine," Morten assured. "King Ulther came through on his word, and the way will be open for you today. After this, you will be the first queen to live."

She cast another look outside, where rain blanketed the balcony. "Portia deserved to live too."

Morten's arms wrapped around her to pull her into his warmth. She wound her hands around him, but the emotion inside her was more frightened than comforted. Not frightened by him, I could tell. Frightened by something else.

He spoke into her ear. "So do you, my love, and we will save you."

Her breathing was shallow and her knees wobbled as she stood. I suspected I knew what today was, and that explained her jittery composure. It wasn't much different from Gaia's yesterday. Nor from my own if Gaia died.

"I'm going to miss everyone," she whispered.

"You'll be missed too." Morten held tight until her shaking stopped.

"I'm ready."

"Good," he said, pulling back to adjust her hair and take her in. He stroked a thumb over her cheek. "Happy Queen's Day, my beautiful queen."

The vision ended.

It was the shortest vision I'd had of Dhalia, but perhaps the most useful. She still guarded the details of her plan, not letting me see into those thoughts, but today she gave me something almost as helpful.

I now knew that her hope for survival hinged on Queen's Day, the day of the Choosing Ceremony, and that she had to wait for the ambassadors to enact her plan. And King Ulther would make the way open. She had a way home.

With the victory of that realization came the bitter sting of the situation. I thought Dhalia survived by continuing to live here in the fae realm. But that must be wrong. She survived by escaping at the Choosing Ceremony. It was why she had to wait for this specific day. It was why she said she'd miss them. Dhalia didn't outlive the two years in the fae realm. Somehow, she escaped back into her realm and lived there.

My heart sank. The tales the fae believed were untrue. Dhalia didn't survive here. She had to leave this realm.

If I wanted to live, I would have to leave too.

Bash mentioned they'd tried that before, and the queen still died. Dhalia must have found a way around that. My knuckles tightened over the canvas until the wooden frame groaned in protest. "This isn't what I wanted," I spoke to the night. I begged it for a different solution. "I don't want to run back home. Let me stay but still live."

Outside, the first drops of rainfall came, mirroring the night Dhalia made her escape. I took that as my answer. I'd asked for a way, and I had it. If I hoped to live, I couldn't have a place in this realm.

I bit back tears. Dhalia might have found one way, but I could find another. I could still trap the kings into freeing me. I could find the missing king if that was what it took. I would live.

But if not . . .

My eyes strayed to the watch on my nightstand, sitting next to Antonio. If I didn't find a way in the next eight months to save both myself and Gaia, then I'd have a backup plan. I stood to take the device in hand, watching the second hand tick by.

At the next Choosing Ceremony, if I didn't find a way to live by then, I'd use this watch to stop time and escape.

My fingers tightened over the band. *Don't make me use this. Let there be another way.*

The rain fell harder, slamming against the balcony. It marked the first rain I'd experienced since arriving here and accomplished drowning out all thoughts in the roar of cascading water. I craned my neck to find the grey clouds gathered over my island. It seemed none of the other islands carried a storm tonight—only mine.

I set the watch down gently, switching to hold Antonio in hand. *I'll be back, little one.*

I'd lost sight of what mattered. This realm had distracted me. Malcom deserved a sister who came back for him, not one who lost herself in the lavish fae realm. Once more, guilt gnawed at me. By now, that guilt had made its home in my heart, and it didn't plan to leave.

I'd been right. The two sides were tearing me apart.

Malcom needed me. Cal needed me. We were family.

But I wanted to stay.

I set Antonio on the desk and breathed out. This didn't need to be decided now. I had eight months to find another way to survive. I'd deal with where I planned to live later. Eight months to be at peace with leaving one realm behind.

Eight months until I betrayed half of my heart.

30

LORD WINSTER SENT A PLATTER OF fruits and loaves of honey bread the next morning with a note saying, "From your ally," as if I'd forgotten he existed. In truth, he'd dwelled in a far corner of my mind, but as I sliced a grapefruit with a knife, I debated how I could repay him for his warm welcome into the fae realm.

Now that I'd been here for a while, his little trick didn't feel so horrible. But I'd made a promise to get him back for it, and that wouldn't be forgotten. I had no doubt Talen and Odette would help me scheme something grand, and we'd be laughing about it for months to come.

My pondering paused as a wisp—the first I'd seen unattached to a chariot—sped through the open balcony doors. The translucent ribbon shimmered with gold dust that tangled through my hair and cupped under my chin, pulling my attention outside. There, its chariot waited in the sky a step away from the banisters. The wisp coiled around my arms to nudge me toward it.

It took me a moment to realize I was being summoned.

"Give me a moment," I said, taking a last large bite of sugary bread. The wisp nudged again. "I'm not even dressed," I protested. "I'll be right there."

Seeming content with that, the wisp waited.

I set the food aside. "Any hints on where you're taking me so I know how to dress?" I asked. It didn't answer. "If I show up in the wrong attire, it'll be your neck."

The wisp understood and darted into my closet, winding through the clothes until settling over a blue silky gown with capped sleeves.

"Simple, yet comfortable," I said, taking it from the rack. "Good choice." I tied it on and slid two rings through my nostril, adding a few copper rings for my toes that peeked out from golden sandals. I pulled my hair back with a band.

"Appropriate?" I asked the wisp. It fluttered at my back and pushed me toward the balcony. "I got it, thank you."

I stepped off the balcony and onto the chariot. As soon as my feet landed, the wisp took its place at the helm of the chariot to pull us away.

It wasn't the fastest chariot I'd ever been on, so I guessed it wasn't from Thorn. It wasn't the large one Bash usually rode in, either. Perhaps Odette had summoned me.

We climbed through the sky, stars winking like diamonds around us. We passed a few other morning travelers who bowed their heads to us. A cool breeze chilled my sleeveless arms, and I wrapped my arms together with a reminder never to allow a wisp to choose my attire again, no matter how confident it acted. The wisp slowed and I peered over the edge.

"You are from Bash," I said.

Bash's mountain home was lit up against the constant night. As we approached, he descended from the sky on his own chariot to land in the courtyard. I stole a glance to the top of the mountain, where the snow he'd shown me sparkled like a white sheet, almost as brilliant as the stars.

Bash waited for me. That sneaky wisp dressed me in the same color as him, though the saturated blue did far more for him than it did for me. My heartbeat quickened as we drew near.

"You summoned?"

He offered a hand as I climbed from the chariot. "I've something to show you," he said. I was startled by the slight tremor in his fingers.

Bash let go of my hand and strode to his place, removing a parcel from his jacket as he went. I struggled to keep up.

"What is it?" I asked.

He didn't turn his head. "You'll see," he called back.

Iron grated against stone as Bash opened the doors. As soon as I was through, he let the double doors shut. With a snap of his fingers, the fireplace along the walls burst to life, the hungry flames banishing the cold draft.

He stopped and ran his eyes over me. "You look lovely. Now . . ." He undid the twine around the parcel without giving me time to absorb the compliment. He tilted it toward me. A dull lump sat inside.

I blinked. "It's a rock."

He stood close enough that his cloak fluttered against the skirt of my dress but made sure his body didn't touch mine. He chuckled. "It's not a rock. It's a mirror."

I squinted. "Bash, that's a rock. A very large rock."

"My Queen, if you'll give me a moment, I'll prove you wrong." He held it closer to me. "It's a mirror to the mortal realm and it was very difficult to acquire."

I caught my breath. With a slight smile, Bash placed his lips near the rock. He glanced at me. "Their names?"

My voice was distant. "Cal and Malcom."

"I desire to see Cal and Malcom Brenheda, siblings of the High Queen of the West."

My heart sped up until it was a pounding drum in my tight chest, and my palms grew sweaty. Forget Bash's desire to keep distance between us. I pressed myself against him to see the stone as its face shimmered white. I squinted against the blinding light. When the light dulled, an image was visible.

Tears filled my eyes as the scene came to life.

My brothers. Cal tucked in his loose cream shirt with frayed strings that was two sizes too big. He'd always insisted he'd grow into it. Malcom had grown into his. How was that possible? It had only been four months, yet my little brother was looking more grown up than before. He wasn't playing with his toys. Instead, he was in the kitchens with his sleeves rolled up and flour dashed across his chin.

"Did you get the eggs from the market?" Cal asked, stoking the fire. His dark curls were damp from the heat, and he wiped them back with his palm.

My first tear fell at the sweet sound of his voice.

"I did." Eliza answered, coming into the image to produce a basket from a cupboard. Lilies were braided through her blonde hair and fastened to the collar of her yellow dress.

I didn't look like I belonged in the fae realm, but Eliza did. Her slender body drifted through the room as she arranged flowers and kissed both my brothers' heads.

She passed the eggs to Malcom, who cracked and folded them into the dough.

They were in our home kitchen, but it was unlike I'd ever seen it before. The few open cupboards were swollen with food—butters and jams and breads and vegetables. Vegetables that didn't look like they were stolen from Daven's crop. And flowers, bright marigolds, adorned the windowsill as if they had money to spare on mere beauty.

That was why Malcom looked different. He was plumper. He'd been eating well.

Eliza dipped her fingers in a burlap sack and flicked flour across Malcom's cheek. He laughed, deep and full.

My second tear fell.

"I have news," Cal announced. "Abbas accepted me. I begin lessons at full moon."

My mouth dropped at the name. Abbas was a legendary scholar all the islands cherished, often moving between them to teach in schools. He must have come to the center island after I was chosen, and somehow Cal caught his eye. I had no trouble picturing Cal waiting outside his class every day until he exhausted the man into teaching him.

Malcom clapped, while Eliza wrapped her arms around my brother. He returned her embrace with a wide smile.

"Who needs an apprenticeship?" Eliza declared. "You'll get better training from Abbas, and any island would want you."

"It won't come with a stipend for years." Cal brushed a strand of golden hair from Eliza's face. "We might have to wait to buy that old manor."

Her eyes danced. "We don't need a stipend. We are doing just fine on the pension."

They were doing more than fine. My anxious worry faded. Happiness radiated from each of their smiles in a way I'd never seen before, clinging to their cheeks and the light in their eyes, and it changed them. They didn't need me to steal from the market or let out the hems of old clothes anymore. If the money I'd saved under the floorboards was still there, they wouldn't need to use it for a long time.

Malcom went over to finish kneading the dough and laid it over a pan. Cal took the moment to squeeze Eliza tightly and whisper in her ear, *"Uhnepa te."*

Bash's muscles tightened as my heart did the same. The vision faded away. As Cal's wild curls and Malcom's floured chin disappeared, I whispered, *"Uhnepa te."*

The mirror was only a rock once more.

We stood silent in the throne room, listening to the crackle of the fire as I absorbed the scene, wishing I could be there with them. Torn between wishing they were missing me and being thankful they were fine.

They were happy. Cal had training without leaving for his Passion and could stay with Malcom forever. And from the way Malcom gazed at Eliza, he had the motherly presence he needed. They feasted on sourdough bread and imported cherries instead of scrounging for old figs.

"They don't need me," I said slowly.

"No." Bash placed the rock back into the parcel and walked to the throne to set it on the dais. My eyes trailed to the place where his perfect heart sat, still covered, beside it. "They don't need you at all."

Hearing it hurt. My face pinched.

"Thea, that's a good thing." Bash looked at me as I struggled with my tears.

"I know," I sniffed. "I don't know why I'm crying." My voice came out sounding very unflattering. "Happiness, I guess? And a little sad. But they are doing better than I imagined."

"There shouldn't have been any doubt," he said firmly. "They have the Mortal Queen's pension and your blood in their veins. They are strong."

I choked back a sob. "They don't need me," I repeated. One less thing to worry about in a realm where worries were as numerous as the stars. And perhaps one answer, as well. I didn't need to fight to return to my siblings and give up the part of me here. There was no use in breaking myself when they didn't need me. I could stay without guilt.

I could stay.

I wiped my cheeks dry as Bash cocked his head like he was trying to read my thoughts.

"Thank you," I smiled tearfully. "That was the best gift anyone has ever given me."

He raised a brow. "A glimpse at your family? You haven't received many good gifts."

"No, the permission to choose my own desire."

He paused a few paces away, rocking on his heels twice before stepping closer. A small gap resided between us, then he crossed that too.

Everything in me stilled, waiting for what he would do next. Then, in an action that was unlike him, he reached for me. His hands took mine and he folded them together.

"They don't need you at all," he said quietly. "But I do."

My body numbed. "Bash."

"I need you." There was no hesitation. His dark brown eyes shifted between mine.

"One more time," I breathed.

His hands stroked up my arms to brush my hair back from my shoulders. "Althea." I quite liked the way my name rolled from his tongue. "I need you. Don't leave this realm. We will find a way to keep you here. Alive."

My next breath was a sigh of relief and disbelief mixed together. Had the thrill of seeing my brothers again corroded my mind, or was Bash, the beautiful fae king, asking me to stay here with him?

"What happened to keeping your distance from me?"

"Forget that. It was an impossible wish."

I searched his eyes. "I've had enough tricks," I told him. "If you are playing me, it's not okay."

"I would never," he promised. "I'm ready to fight for you if you'll let me. We will defeat this fate of yours together."

All breathing functions had stopped. All thoughts vanished. All ability to see anything other than him faded away. His voice settled along my hairline.

"Please, Thea. Please, let me fight for you."

"Yes," I breathed.

I could have waited for him to kiss me, but it was a thousand times more gratifying to press my lips to his and see the way his eyes widened in 'surprise before closing as he leaned into me.

Kissing him was exactly as I imagined it would be. His hands wrapped around my waist to draw me closer, and heat radiated between us. My fingers laced through the coils of his thick hair and down the curve of his neck, obsessed with every detail of him. I was drunk on the taste of his lips, which was sweeter than any wine Odette could steal. He was glorious. And for this one moment, he was mine.

When he pulled back, he stayed close, his nose rubbing against mine. "I'm a fool to have fallen for a Mortal Queen," he said.

"I'm glad you did, or you would have left me falling on my own."

He grinned. "I'll always catch you when you fall."

He kept my hands tucked in his as he let out a deep sigh. "We have work to do. If you're going to survive the two years, we need a plan."

"Oh, I have plans," I told him. "I've been scheming for a while."

He raised a brow. "Perfect. I have a plan, too, but you're not going to like it."

"Does it involve me staying here?"

He nodded. "It involves you becoming a fae."

31

I STEPPED BACK AND GAPED AT HIM. "Is that possible?"

Bash grinned at my surprise. "It's tricky, and I don't possess the ability to transform you, but it is possible. You see, other queens have been determined to get back to their realm to survive." He kicked his cloak away. "I think the trick might be to stay here."

I thought of Dhalia escaping at the Choosing Ceremony. This couldn't be how she survived. She ran. I wanted to stay.

"Alright. I'll do it."

Bash spoke carefully. "My Queen, you need to think about this for a while. Becoming a fae comes with many complications. Your heart will turn to glass. You will cease to age at a normal rate. If you don't like it, you'll have thousands of years to regret your decision. And fae . . . We can't walk in the mortal realm as you do. You'll be trapped here just as you are now."

Little did he know how fond I'd grown of this cage.

But . . .

"Would I never see my brothers again?"

His eyes were sad. "You'll see them at next year's Choosing Ceremony and no more. Same as if you'd died."

I weighed the options in my mind—live among the fae or live

among my family. Live for centuries or live for less than one. Bash or my brothers. Whichever way I chose was sacrificing one in favor of the other.

"You don't need to decide now," Bash said. "In truth, I'm uncertain it would work."

I twisted the ends of my hair between my fingers. "How would we try?"

"Well," he wrapped his fingers around mine. Now that he'd touched me once, it was like he couldn't stop. "The power belongs to the three ambassadors. They are this realm's connection to yours. It's a way of keeping some balance to the power here. The queens rank higher than the kings, then the three Houses rank below them. Next are the representatives, one for each House. After them are the lords. Then the ambassadors."

I hadn't realized that Talen, as a representative, ranked so high. But hadn't Odette told me as much? How he'd traded her for that power?

"Okay," I said. "So we need an ambassador to help us. I can ask one to assist."

He shook his head. "She won't. Making a mortal a fae means transferring power to you. You'd get her power and they'd lose it. One must be tricked into it."

I blinked. "We both rank far higher than them. Can we not force the exchange?"

"The ambassadors rank low, but they hold their power with pride. None would give it up willingly. Trickery is the only way."

Of course trickery was the answer. "How?"

The corner of his mouth curved upward. "Rumor has it, Lord Winster has seen one of the ambassador's true face. With that, we needn't force her. We must only ask, and she will be required to say yes."

That sounded like forcing to me, but if it worked, I didn't care about the technicalities. The mixture of relief and disappointment was an odd sensation. "I need Lord Winster."

"Correct. But only a little. Call upon your alliance to gain power over the ambassador, and her power will be yours."

It sounded enticing when he said it, like he was personally inviting me to a magical event where I'd find eternal happiness, and there was no way I could refuse. It almost made it worth having to interact with Lord Winster again.

He lifted a hand. "There is a small trick though."

"There's always a trick here, isn't there?"

"It wouldn't be fun any other way." His lips lifted into a smile, but the look in his deep-set eyes was as if he were a moment away from losing me, and he could hardly hold on. "Mortals cannot hold the power of a fae. So for that moment, between taking her power and becoming a fae, you'll need something to harness the energy. I can get a bracelet that will do so, but I'd have to steal it. I'll be doing this at great risk."

I took a deep breath. "I speak to Lord Winster, and you steal a bracelet. We turn me into a fae."

"Then put the bracelet back before we get caught," Bash added. The hard set of his shoulders pulled tight, like this were the most important bit.

"That doesn't sound too complicated," I mused.

"Here's the trick—" Bash began.

I stopped him. "Just for my own knowledge, how many tricks will there be?"

He was quiet for a moment, something delicate dancing behind his eyes, then said, "This is the last one, promise."

"I can handle that. What is it?"

"It's no small matter to steal this bracelet."

That was no surprise. "We will give it back," I pointed out.

"We must. But it's a crime to take it in the first place, even as a king. And I'm already on thin ice with my lords after I took the crown from my father. If they find out I stole this power token from them to help take the power from an ambassador, it will be considered an injustice. I could lose everything."

My chest constricted at the gravity of what failure could mean for him. "Maybe we shouldn't. You may not know this, but Lord Winster is not a favorite of mine. This plan may not work."

"I'm aware it's fragile, but there is no other way to become a fae. You need the strength of this forbidden bracelet to take her power."

I felt all knotted inside with no clear vision on how to untangle myself. "I don't want you to lose your kingdom."

"I appreciate that." He took my hands and my heart fluttered. "I don't want you to die."

I bit my lip. "Tell me the plan once more."

He smiled down at me. "Speak to Lord Winster, steal the bracelet, steal the ambassador's power, return the bracelet. That's it. We could do this in a month if all goes well."

"No," I said too quickly. His eyes widened, and I evened my tone. "I will do it at the next Choosing Ceremony. That way I get to see my brothers once more before the change takes place." At least that would give me a chance to explain my decision to them so they wouldn't feel abandoned, and to tell Eliza how grateful I am to her for caring for them so well.

Bash brought a thumb to my cheek. "Of course."

I looked straight into his eyes. "And there are no more tricks involved?"

He shook his head. "That's it."

Outside the wall of windows in Bash's mountain castle and across the cobblestone terrace, sat the two chariots with their wisps circling each other as if in conversation, stopping briefly to watch other chariots dart by. I watched with them, taking it all in with a new eye. This realm would soon be mine as well. I'd have a rightful and permanent place here to call my own, and someday its magnificence might even lose its wonder as it becomes a familiar home.

Bash rested his chin atop my head with his arms around me, and I was happier than I'd ever been. I basked in his warmth. I shifted and caught a glimpse of his heart on the pedestal beside his throne and realized I couldn't feel it beating in his chest. Because his heart wasn't there. Someday, my heart would stop beating, too, as it hardened to glass.

"Has there ever been a fae queen?" I asked.

He pulled his chin back to glance at me with a rakish gleam in his eyes. "You think I'm making you my queen so soon?"

I lifted my chin. "I don't need you. I'm a queen in my own right."

He held me closer before answering, his voice now soured. "There was one once. The first Mortal Queen became a fae before her king betrayed her." He snarled his words at the mention of the king betraying his queen, where previously he'd told the tale casually.

"Ah, that's right. The king who ruined it for the rest of us."

"I can't despise him too much, though," Bash said. His lips brushed the top of my hair. "Without him, I wouldn't have you."

As someone who'd never shared a romantic connection before, I could listen to such words all day and never tire of how cliché they sounded.

Bash kept me tucked in his arms as snow began to fall outside, and while I'd thought sitting snow was beautiful, falling snow was glorious. Amid the flurries, Bash gave me his promise.

"This realm will be yours, as will I."

While I smiled up at him, he met my lips with his. When we parted, I gave him my promise. "I will stay in this realm with you."

The delight and satisfaction in his eyes would be what I took with me to Lord Winster's home. I climbed aboard the chariot.

"Take me to the lion's den. I've got one battle left."

32

NOW THAT I'D GAZED UPON THE
homes of kings, Lord Winster's manor didn't appear as magnificent
as it did quaint in the way it was nestled into a bed of cliffs at the
edge of a sea. Instead of being lit as bright as the sky, only one trail
of torches lined the pathway to his front door, and a few bright
windows crossed the pane of his brick home. They flickered in
greeting as I crossed them.

"Stay near," I ordered the chariot.

Last time, I'd tried to radiate the confidence I lacked inside,
but this time it was easy to muster as I knocked on the door. Lord
Winster hadn't met the person these few months had turned me into.

But I hadn't met the child who answered the door.

I startled. "Oh! Hello. Is Lord Winster home?"

The child popped her thumb from her lips to twist her head
around. "Papa?"

I needed the time it took him to answer to recover from the
shock. Meanwhile, the girl with golden curls and a pink dress
jabbed her thumb back into her mouth to stare at me through eyes
that were eerily like her father's.

He appeared, coat unbuttoned and hair ruffled, to sweep

the child up in his arms. She rested her head against him while staring at me.

"My Queen," he said. "What an honor. Come in." He opened the door farther and welcomed me into the warmth of his home. He set the child down and bent to be at her level. "Camille, go tell Nanny we'd like some tea, please, and you can have a cookie."

She ran down the hall in a patter of eager footsteps.

I studied him until finding what was different. "You shaved the mustache."

He touched his upper lip. "She said it itched."

"I didn't know you had a child."

He chuckled. "I have three. Someday I hope for three more. Come in. We can rest in the sitting room. The hearth has warmed the rugs." He steered me to the same room where I'd once painted for him and his guests, the same place I'd decided to join in an alliance with him. It seemed fitting to be in that room as I called upon our alliance now. I sat on a beige lounge chair with a curved back near a doll house, its associated toys sprawled across the room.

Lord Winster sat across from me. "Did you receive the breads I sent?"

"Yes," I said absently before truly remembering, then repeated the word more firmly. "They were delicious, thank you. That one with lemon zest was my favorite."

He beamed. "Mine as well. I'll send some more."

"You don't have to," I told him. "There is something else I need." I checked to ensure no one else was nearby. "Is it true you've seen the true face of a certain ambassador?"

Lord Winster's smile dropped. "What of it?"

"How much control do you have over this ambassador?"

His lip twitched. "A fair amount. Why?"

The words caught in my throat. For Lord Winster to have seen her true face, he might have tricked her into it and would care little about how he lorded his power over her. But another possibility was that she had removed her mask willingly for him, which would make this a more difficult ask than I'd anticipated. From the way his fingers curled tightly over his armrest, I guessed which it was.

"As your ally, I need your help."

If she had removed her mask willingly, and there was a bond between them, he wouldn't agree to steal her power. I ought to have thought this through before my arrival, but for now, I did the best I could. I came up with a lie. "I have questions about my selection, and I need her to answer them."

His fingers relaxed. "Then ask her."

That confirmed which ambassador it was. "I did." My lie continued. "She won't tell me. I need to force her."

He drew his thick brows inward. "You wish for me to order her to tell you about your selection? What are you so desperate to know?"

It took unbelievable effort not to squirm. "Simply details of the day I've forgotten. I need you to order her to say yes to anything I ask."

The answer hung in the air as Camille returned, her ringlets bouncing as she trotted in, spilling tea from the rims of glass cups. Lord Winster stood to take them from her, and she settled on the floor with her dolls while he passed a cup to me. He didn't seem to mind her presence at our meeting. He lowered into his chair once more to stew over the request, blowing on the tea. His brows were knitted so tightly, they formed one straight line, and the steam from the tea made a home in them.

"I've never asked you for anything," I said in a sweet manner for Camille's sake, but with a hard look in my eye for Lord Winster's.

He frowned. "I know. And as peculiar as it is that you haven't formed a multitude of alliances, I'm grateful. But to betray Hellen like that . . ." his voice trailed off.

I sipped on my tea. "Was she"—I glanced to Camille—"special?"

Camille paid us no attention as she brushed a doll's hair with a silver comb encrusted with diamonds. Lord Winster was very focused on his tea. "Once. Not now. Still . . ."

This one request was all I needed to grant me freedom, and I felt his answer swaying unfavorably. I set down my tea harder than intended. I could offer him something in return for this favor, but we had an alliance, and that meant we worked together. I was no longer concerned about guarding my words because of Camille.

"I need one day where she says yes to anything I ask. That's all I request, and then I will remain your grateful ally. If not, our alliance is over."

He set down his own cup. "My Queen, I would not deny you as an ally. You may have what you wish. One day."

"Queen's Day," I specified. "That is the day I need."

"Queen's Day it is. Is that all?"

I stood. "You've proven yourself an ally of the highest value. Thank you."

He bowed his head but did not rise as I stepped around Camille's toys. The girl was parading her doll from one dollhouse to another but stopped to wave at me as I started to leave. I could sense Lord Winster's sullen gaze boring into my back, but I felt only excitement at the ease of the meeting. I'd come prepared to fight. Instead, I'd been given tea and left victorious without a struggle.

Camille was speaking, "Come along, Gaia. We have a party to go to."

Without thinking, I whirled around, looking for my sister queen.

"Okay, let's go," Camille replied in a higher voice. She danced two dolls around a three-story house with blue windowsills and yellow flowers painted on the side.

My heart skipped a beat. The dolls had familiar tattoos on their foreheads and seven earrings in their ears.

"Is that me?" My voice sounded breathy. I couldn't guess which one was Gaia and which was me, but Camille held up the doll with the ruby red-dress and the longer hair, just as I'd looked at my coronation. The other doll wore a silver gown that sparkled from every angle with its hair in three braids wound together.

"I love my Mortal Queens," Camille declared.

I couldn't tear my eyes away from myself as a doll. It was more frightening than flattering.

"Do you just have two?" The question came before I could stop it.
Camilla paraded the dolls into the house "Of course. The others
are dead. I only keep the dolls for the living queens."

A shiver spread down my spine. I took slow steps away.

That wouldn't be me. Thanks to her father, I would be the one
doll Camille could keep forever. As the door closed behind me, I
heard Camille's pretend conversation. "Here, Gaia. We'll have one
last party before you die."

33

TWO CRATES OF DRESSES. ONE FOR
each Mortal Queen, arrived with the morning stars. It took both
me and Odette to haul mine up the stairs, where we unhinged the
top to an avalanche of ribbons, laces, and pearls.

Odette gasped. "I want to be a Mortal Queen and have"—she
fished a note from the pile and read it—"*Lord Madrid* send me more
gowns than I could ever need." She plucked a deep-red gown from
the center and held it to her chest. "It clashes with my hair, but look
how pretty it is!"

"You would drown in that. We'd need a month to find you
among all those layers."

That only pleased her further.

I selected one as deep a blue as Bash's cloak, lined with silver.
"Should we be touching these?" I wondered aloud. "What if
it's a trap?"

Odette brought another dress to her face and sniffed it, then
laughed at my appalled expression. "Talen routinely checks for
traps, so if this is here, he must have allowed it through. Still, I like
to be certain."

I stroked the blue one. "As long as it passes your, um, test. You
can keep that one."

A delighted gleam lit her eyes. "You might change your mind about that because"—her voice dropped into a whisper— "there's a hat."

I was already halfway through buttoning the blue dress around me, which squeezed my ribs hard enough to tighten my breathing. Odette donned the hat and spun around. "When you're gone, I want all of these."

The tightness in my chest wasn't from the dress anymore.

Odette looked up, a frozen look on her face, as she lowered the hat. "I didn't mean that."

"It's fine." I turned for her to do up my last buttons, gathering my hair over my shoulder.

"When you die, it's going to be like a part of me dies with you," Odette said as she finished buttoning and came around to face me. She gathered my hands in hers. "I mean that. Your death will kill me." She'd changed quickly from the girl doting over gowns into a friend more serious than I'd ever seen her.

She continued. "You've no idea how hard it is to give our hearts to the queens just to lose them again and again. It's torture of the worst kind. It's the cruelest part of this realm."

I squeezed her hands back before she could start crying on me. "I'm going to be okay."

Her head tilted, and her hair fell to one side like an auburn river. "You're so brave."

"I mean it." I pulled my hands from hers. "I'm going to be just fine." My mouth opened to tell her of my idea to become a fae. She could be of great help deciding what I, as queen, should look like when I was no longer mortal, and how I could reveal my new power to the realm. She could celebrate then. Instead of having only a year and eight months left, we'd spend centuries as sisters.

Her gaze drifted over my shoulder, and she blinked. "There's a letter for you."

It sat on the balcony beneath a chunk of ore, bearing the black parchment of Bash's messages. "Remind me I have something to tell you." A soft breeze caressed me as I opened the balcony doors. "I think it'll make you happy."

I lifted the lip of the envelope and pulled out the note to find Bash's words.

Don't speak of our conversation to anyone. You never know where alliances lie.

I highly doubted Odette or Talen held a secret alliance with the silver-haired ambassador, but I glanced at Odette all the same. She'd gone back to sorting through the dresses. Her eyes went to the note but darted away when she caught me looking.

Don't speak of the plan to anyone. Odette wouldn't betray me. She was in my House alliance, so she couldn't. *No,* I reminded myself. *She can't* trick *me. But she could betray me.* I was certain there was a difference.

She'd find out soon enough, and then we'd celebrate in style. My lips would remain sealed for eight months until I became a fae.

"What is it?"

I crumpled the note into my pocket. "Just a kind note from Bash."

She flashed a sly grin. "Intriguing. But what was it you wanted to tell me?"

I closed the balcony doors behind me. "I was thinking we should invite Gaia to join us. I believe she's lonely."

Odette waved a hand. "She gets invitations to three dinners every night and more gifts sent to her door than any queen before her, so her loneliness is of her own choosing. But do what you like." She chortled. "I'd be the luckiest girl in the realm to have two Mortal Queens as my companions for the night."

"I'll go fetch her." I hurried down the stairs to the grand throne room, where my three stars shone as bright as the chandelier.

Woven baskets of plump, vibrant oranges sat on the two thrones with a note atop each, and I immediately went to them.

"The fae are especially generous this week," I mumbled, plucking an orange from the top. *Would they be as giving when I was not a Mortal Queen but a fae one?*

I dug a nail into the thick skin and the citrus scent sprayed out. I crossed the bridge as I carefully peeled back the outer layer. Gaia couldn't say no to the oranges and the dresses, and perhaps after a few drops of Odette's wine, she'd divulge what she'd been up to on Illusion Point.

I wound up the stairs on the east side and knocked on her door. Then I opened it.

The orange fell from my hand. Gaia's room was a mess. Three bags sat in the center, while everything else had been torn from its place and bundled against the wall or a chair until nothing was left as it should be, not even the bed. Blankets hung from the canopy, and Gaia sat between them.

Head between her legs, shoulders shaking.

The breath left my body.

Odette and I had been laughing and trying on dresses while Gaia had been like this.

Guilt further gnawed at me as I realized my fae plan for salvation didn't include her. I caught a breath. It could though. She could steal some other ambassador's power, and we'd rule as fae queens together.

"Gaia."

At my voice, her head sprang up to reveal bloodshot eyes. "What are you doing here?" Her braided hair stuck out in every direction, and the circles under her eyes were as dark as her pupils. Her olive-green dress was damp and one fist was clenched.

"I live here," I said calmly. "And I'm going to do much better about coming to visit you in the future." I stepped through the mess on the floor to get to her. "What happened?"

She shivered. "I have no use for this room anymore."

Again, speaking nonsense. I sat beside her and touched her leg. "I found a way for us to live."

She began to shake her head, then she looked at me. Something in my expression must have convinced her and her eyes widened. "How?"

I glanced to the door and whispered. "We become fae."

Now she did shake her head vigorously. "No. I don't want to stay here. I don't want to live here. We both have to leave."

"Why?" I asked her. "Life is good here. What is waiting for us back home but stubborn fathers, families who have moved on, and no purpose? We are queens here, and the fae love us. There is nothing in that realm that rivals what this realm has."

Her eyes changed, and for the first time, she didn't look as if she'd lost her mind. She looked as if she thought I had. "This realm is a lie. It's a trap. We have to leave it and never come back." She opened her clenched fist. "I have my own plan."

A watch sat in her hand that would have been identical to the one I'd acquired from Illusion Point, except hers was silver where mine was gold, the band made of rosy leather.

I looked up at her. "I have one of those too. It stops time."

Her hands clutched it, her knuckles bone white. "This one is different." There was a dangerous tone to her voice. "Mine doesn't stop time. It speeds it up."

Another striking difference in the watch stood out, so obvious I wondered how I didn't see it before. Hers didn't have normal numbers but counted from one to seven before beginning again.

"How will this help you?" I asked.

She took a deep breath and looked at her packed bags. "This will get me past my death date. Once I've shown I can survive, an ambassador will take me home."

Fear gripped me, and in turn, I gripped Gaia's arm. "What are you doing?"

She pulled her arm away and clutched the watch to her chest. "Surviving."

The watch was what she'd gotten from Illusion Point. This watch would propel her past her fated death day, but where would it leave me? "Have you thought this through?"

Tears pooled in her eyes. "I'm tired of thinking. All I've done since I got here is think and read into people's words and faces, and guess at who is on my side and how I can survive. I'm exhausted. I don't want to think anymore."

And then she jabbed the button on the side.

In shock, I watched the little hand as it began to turn, slowly at first, then whipping itself around faster. Once, twice, three times. Then too fast to keep track.

A wind howled through the room, clawing at our hair and ripping at our clothes. The hand spun around and around.

I dug my fists into the duvet beneath me as the wind whistled in my ears. Gaia's lips trembled. She dropped the watch on the bed.

The hand spun on.

I tried to reach for it, but the wind thrust me backward, and objects in the room flung between us.

"When does it stop?" I yelled.

"I don't know." She buried her head in her hands and screamed.

Again, I fumbled for the watch. It spun and spun and spun.

Each time the hand passed the top was another week. If this worked the way Gaia thought it did, we'd lost months already.

"How do you control it?" I was frantic now, shaking Gaia to get her to focus on me.

Her head lifted and she cried out, "Don't stop it! I need to let it go long enough that I outlive two years."

The wind was a hurricane now, throwing chairs against walls and nearly deafening us. The watch sat unfazed on the bed as the world went into a panic around it.

The hand spun on.

I couldn't breathe. This was taking too much time from me. I'd lose the chance to see my brothers and become a fae. She'd take me straight to my death.

"We have to stop it!" I screamed. Gaia put her hands over her ears.

I threw my gaze to the windows. Outside, flashes of light zipped across the sky in an indiscernible nature. Were those chariots? Or were they stars peeling from the atmosphere? Was time crashing by for everyone else or just us?

My hair flapped over my face and as I pulled it back I realized it was several inches longer than it should be. Panic swelled inside.

The watch spun on.

And on.

And on.

"It's been too long!" I shouted at Gaia.

She was now looking at the watch as if keeping track of how much time had gone by. I reached for her, but suddenly she took a shuddering breath. With the next wind that came, her neck snapped, and she fell back on the bed.

With that, everything was silent.

The watch ceased moving.

The wind fell, the room stilled, and the stars outside froze from twinkling.

My hand shook as I picked up the watch. It let out a rhythmic ticking sound.

I eased up to my knees at Gaia's side.

"Gaia?" I whispered. Her eyes were lifeless pits staring at the ceiling. I gently shook her. "Gaia, it's over. It's over."

She gave no reply.

I'd never been good at checking for a pulse. But right now, I checked a hundred times. My fingers roamed over her wrist and her neck, pushing into her skin to search. I cried her name. I shook her a little harder. I squeezed her hand.

On the hundredth try, or perhaps the thousandth, I gave up and sank to the floor, trembling.

Gaia got us past her fated death day. But she didn't survive it.

Like all the queens before her, Gaia was dead.

I dropped my head into my hands and wailed.

34

I WAS A CORPSE TRAILING THROUGH

the halls with no direction. My feet led me away from the horrors of Gaia's violently torn room and down the hallway. I paused at the threshold of the grand stairwell to take in the sight of the throne room.

I noticed my three stars first. They were dulled. What light remained was peeking through a curtain of thick cobwebs that clung to both of the thrones in a grey shawl, crawling along the legs of the chair and over the seat and blanketing themselves down the sides. Large black spiders climbed through the webs. It was terrifying.

The cobwebs had made a home throughout the entire room—hanging from the chandelier above, wrapping around the banisters, and coating the bridge over the river that now ran black instead of crystal blue. The fish must have died.

Worst of all, a darkness clouded everything in a heavy fog. It was thick enough that I felt it on my skin and feared if I breathed it would swallow me whole. The haze had taken everything—all the beauty of this realm—and turned it to horror.

How much time did I lose? This room makes it appear as if hundreds of years went by. But if I'm still alive . . . It must have been some point between the end of Gaia's rule and the end of mine. I kept Gaia's watch in my pocket, wishing I'd broken it minutes ago. Months ago?

Tears blurred my vision.

I stumbled down the steps to face the two thrones, running a finger along the thick layer of dust. My feet kicked something and I looked down, then jumped back. The basket of oranges still sat there, now decayed with black bugs crawling paths through the rotten mess.

I had to squint to see my paintings on the opposite wall. The colors were faded with another bitter reminder of the time that had passed.

Though it was tricky to see, I saw the realm with clarity for the first time, and it was nothing but death.

I'd been ready to stay here. I was going to trap myself in this realm forever.

Gaia might have lost her mind, but she was right about one thing. Mere mortals weren't made to withstand the intoxication of the fae realm. I had to get out.

Trumpets called from outside, drawing my attention to the courtyard where an army of fae gathered beyond the doors. I froze, unsure of whether to go to them or run. I didn't want to see anyone right now.

But over the crowd I spotted the silver hair of one of the ambassadors, and I knew what today was.

It's Queen's Day. They are going to the mortal realm.

The silver fae bowed her head to the crowd and stepped on a chariot where the other two ambassadors waited. Their cheeks were sunken in, and they wore black clothing.

I must have looked like a mess. I had no shoes on, my hair was horrendous from being blown about, and tears painted my cheeks. But I picked up my skirt and ran toward the courtyard. An uneasy plan formed in my mind.

"Today," the ambassador was saying, "we restore the realm. We will bring back not one, but two girls to fill our hearts again." *They planned to trap two more girls. Their cycle was repeating.*

The fae clapped, but it was a weak noise.

Using both hands, I threw the doors open.

"You will bring only one back!" I called out. I stood firm on my bare feet near the black river and stared down the ambassadors. "And you will take me with you, for it is my right as High Queen of the West to see my realm once more."

An odd thing happened then. My words drifted over the courtyard and like a ripple, the fae clasped their hands to their chests, then knelt before me. The three ambassadors straightened, not as if struck, but as if coming to life again. Their chests expanded and color seeped into their skin. Smiling—even the silver fae— they joined the rest of the fae in kneeling. In a column around my body, the darkness separated, forming a sphere of light the fae marveled at.

The island was a murmur of praises. "My Queen. My beautiful queen. You have returned to us." They spoke in hushed voices as they gazed at me with tears streaming down their cheeks. "The queen has returned."

I stood watching, numb. They thought Gaia and I had left them. I wished that had been the case.

From where the seven thrones of the kings were placed, King Brock rose to his feet. I had difficulty looking at him because Bash was beside him, his hand also on his chest looking like he could scarcely breathe. At his side, Thorn winked like this was an elaborate reveal he and I had planned together.

I longed to board his chariot and ride away from all this. But I had a bigger plan that than. I stole a glance at Bash. What had he gone through in this lost time? Was he still prepared to make me a fae? Did I still want to become one?

Brock was speaking, "On behalf of the fae, we welcome you back to our realm. We were incomplete without you." Everything about him grew more vibrant with each word and, at my feet, the river turned from black to a dark blue. The stars above brightened.

Was the land healing? Had it broken without its Mortal Queens?

Eyes never leaving me, Bash stood as if to come to me, but I took a step back.

"Allow me a moment to prepare myself to leave," I stated. "And I will go with the ambassadors to the mortal realm."

Bash's face fell, and I turned quickly away. I pushed back through the doors to steady myself and find my room. The glass doors closed behind me to quiet the fae's whispering. I passed my paintings on the wall and the image of Dhalia beneath Salvation's Crossing. She was meant to be the key to my survival. I turned away from that too. I had to follow her footsteps. I had to leave him behind.

I'd just reached the stairwell when the doors opened, and both Talen and Odette rushed in from the courtyard.

"Where have you been?" Odette asked. Her auburn hair was loose around her shoulders and her cheeks were rosy. "Why did you leave us?"

"I didn't." She flung herself into my arms.

"You did," she said, voice breaking. "You were gone so long. We couldn't find you anywhere."

I shivered to think of the fae prowling the land for me and Gaia. "Gaia was trying to save herself, and things didn't go as planned." The pain of her loss pierced me.

Odette pulled back. "She's gone?"

I nodded slowly, swallowing the lump in my throat.

Talen stepped closer. "We've endured eight dark months without our Mortal Queens, and we are grateful to have even one of you return." His eyes glistened. "Queen Gaia will be mourned greatly."

I resisted glancing back to her rooms where her body surely still lay. The room would need to be cleaned before the next queen arrived.

In the short amount of time since I'd first come down the stairs, the cobwebs had started to fall from the throne and disintegrate at its feet. The black spiders scurried off to hide in the shadows as the chandelier grew brighter with each passing moment.

"What happened? Was the realm dying?" I asked them.

Talen bowed his head. "We cannot live without our queens."

I swallowed again. The river was even more blue than black now, and I understood what I'd previously missed.

"It's more than needing us," I realized. "You feed off us."

"Thea—"

"No." I walked away from them. "That's it, isn't it? You cannot live without mortal girls in your realm. And we cannot survive it. You only live because you sacrifice us."

There was pain in Talen's eyes. "We would never hurt you."

"Then leave us in our realm." My voice shook. "Die yourself."

It was at that moment Bash walked in—and he stilled. I didn't take time to absorb the look on his face as I gathered my skirt and climbed the stairs. Talen and Odette stood frozen, but I could hear Bash behind me.

I hurried and made it to my doorway before he was in front of me. He reached for me, but I held myself away from him, opening my door and brushing past him. It might have been only a day for me since I'd seen him, but it had been eight months for him, and I saw that in his eyes. How he'd fallen for a queen and then lost her. How he never imagined I'd be back.

I didn't want to be back. But now that I was, one thought plagued me. *I must get out. And loving him stops that.*

"I thought you'd left me," he said, coming into my room. Everything looked just as it had before I'd gone, minus the flurry of dresses Odette and I had been going through. Those were now folded into a crate by my closet door. The fire was lit, and a book lay on the armchair beside it as if I'd only stepped out. My canvases sat on their easels with my paints in closed jars beside them, my brushes cleaned and ready. The beginning of Thorn's portrait stared at me. I turned away from it.

"I should have," I said. "Mortals don't belong in this realm."

He stepped toward me as I slipped into the closet and shut its door between us. His words came through.

"But fae do. Tell me you will stay with me. I can't lose you twice."

My heartbeat faltered. He was begging. I stepped into a shimmering gold dress.

"Thea," he pled. "Let me help you. Whatever you need."

"Can you save the queens from dying?"

"I can save you. After that, we will figure out how to save the rest. You have my promise."

I opened the door, and he kept his distance respectfully. I didn't close the gap, but I didn't move away either.

But his eyes . . . so much pain. "What happened to you?" His voice was barely audible.

"I found out what it means to be a Mortal Queen," I replied. "It means death."

He reached for my hand, and I fought against the sliver of peace it brought. Stupid fae kings and their irresistible touch. Against my will, I stepped into him and he folded his arms around me. He held me close, saying nothing for the longest time.

Then he lifted my chin with his finger. "You will not die," he said. "I won't let that happen."

I wanted to believe him, but all I could hear was Gaia's neck snapping. He reached into his pocket. "This will guarantee you live."

He offered a golden bracelet with pink gems to clasp onto my wrist. "I took the bracelet anyway, just in case you came back for me. We can still make you a fae."

I blinked. "I want to be free."

"With this, you will be."

"Or I'll be trapped forever."

He met my eyes. "I cannot force you into this decision, but I can guarantee my love. Althea Brenheda, I will love you every day for every year of our long lives if you choose to stay with me. This"—he tapped the bracelet on my wrist—"assures you will live a long life. The fate of the Mortal Queens will not be yours."

True to the nature of this realm, I didn't have time to make a decision. But either way, stay or leave, I knew I'd give Bash the same reply. I'd decide later if it was a lie or the truth.

"You're right," I told him. "Make me a fae. Let's do it tonight when I return from my realm."

Bash smiled and tenderly cupped a hand to my cheek. He hadn't changed in the past eight months at all. He was still the same man I'd seen last. Thick lashes, crooked grin, and eyes that soaked in the sight of me like he couldn't get enough.

"I'm going to make you my queen," he said in the gentlest voice.

"And I'm going to live." *One way or another.*

He held my palm to his lips and pressed a kiss into it. "Keep your long sleeves down to cover that bracelet," he said. "If the lords knew their king stole from them, I'd lose my kingdom. Don't let anyone see it, not even Odette."

"I won't," I promised. "It's our secret."

"I will see you tonight," he said with a wink.

I nodded as he left.

I quickly turned for my desk. Faithful Antonio was poised on the corner guarding over the room. I opened my bag to find my watch from Illusion Point, shining like a star. It was so similar to Gaia's watch. One to speed up time, another to stop it. The power of time was in my hands, yet I still felt so powerless.

Become a fae or live in my own realm. One was a guarantee with Bash, the other was risky. I could imagine the fae pillaging the mortal realm to find their lost queen, and I shivered.

I would never be safe from them. But if I became a fae . . .

If I became a fae, I could find a way to free the mortal queens forever. I'd give up myself to save the rest of them. And I'd have eternity to do it. Countless years to search until I'd saved them.

I swallowed as I tucked both watches away.

My fingers hovered over the bracelet next. *This gives me power. I will never be weak and mortal again.* It was the one security I had that this fragility was only fleeting.

If I chose this path, tonight I'd feel real power as Bash turned me into his fae queen.

The new plan almost brought me to my knees. I hesitated over my bag as I considered pressing the button on my watch now, if only for the additional minutes to plan what would determine my life. Instinct told me to run as far as I could. But something inside told me I had to save the queens.

I had to stay for them.

I buried my face in a pillow and screamed. Either way, I felt trapped.

The doorknob turned and I pushed my sleeve over the bracelet.

Odette entered and nodded in approval at my attire. "There's the queen we've missed."

"Just need jewelry." My voice was thick as my head still swarmed.

My jewelry box sat on the desk, and I flipped open the small latch to find a gold necklace and two nose rings. I sat and Odette worked her fingers through my hair weaving it together into a braid as I adorned myself.

She made a strange sound and I looked up. "Are you crying?"

"I saw Gaia." Her voice broke. "I saw her body."

I immediately stood and held her as she cried. What had she said to me the last time I saw her? Losing the queens was the worst torture this realm had to offer.

"Soon that will be you," she said, weeping harder. "And I'm going to lose my best friend. Again."

I wiped at her tears. "You'll never lose me," I promised.

She sniffed as I played with the idea of telling her what was about to happen. If I used this bracelet to siphon the ambassador's power, then Bash and I would enact the plan tonight, so there was little chance of things going wrong now. It was cruel to allow her this misplaced sadness when I had a solution, and she'd know later I'd kept it from her.

So I told her.

"I'm becoming a fae tonight. I can't die as a Mortal Queen if I'm not mortal."

As soon as the words left my mouth, I knew they were the right ones. I would stay and find a way to save the mortal girls that came after me. That would be my life's purpose. For Gaia's sake. I would not die, and I would not let any others die after me.

Odette placed her hands over her mouth. "How? You found an ambassador willing to give up their power for you?"

I shook my head. "But I'm going to control one with Lord Winster's help. And Bash is helping me. This bracelet will hold the ambassador's power." I pushed up my sleeve to show her.

Odette went pale.

She didn't clap. She didn't cheer. She only stared at the bracelet.

"Where did you get that?" she asked in a far-off tone.

I replaced my sleeve. "Bash stole it for me. We're giving it back as soon as I'm a fae. Please don't tell. It could cost him his kingdom if the lords knew he took it."

"Take it off now." Her voice was hard and I blinked.

"Why? Don't you want me to become a fae? I'll be like you." She grabbed my arm and began to claw at the bracelet. I yanked my arm away. "What has gotten into you?"

"That's one of the King's Bracelets," she said. "It's a power-stealer for the kings. Thea, it doesn't harness power. It *steals* it. The moment you have power to steal, that bracelet is going to suck it all away from you and put it in Bash. Once you force the ambassador to give you their power, that bracelet will drain you of everything you have and leave you on the verge of death. You won't become a fae if you use that. You'll die."

All the hope I'd felt moments before was stripped from me, leaving behind a heavy confusion. Humiliation.

I staggered. "He tricked me?"

Odette nodded just as the trumpets blasted again.

"Don't use that bracelet," she begged. "It will kill you."

I struggled to breathe. "He wasn't going to make me a fae."

She shook her head.

I struggled for a solution. "Then I will order the ambassador to give me her power without the bracelet. I have control over her."

"A mortal cannot hold the power of a fae. All who have tried have died."

"Then why would Bash suggest it?"

Odette didn't answer. She didn't need to. He'd never intended to make me a fae. He only wanted the power of an ambassador. He needed authority to rule the lands after taking the kingdom from his father, and he thought the ambassador's power would make him strong enough to do so.

He was willing to let me die to do that.

This realm had played many games with me, yet I had begun to grow fond of it in an odd way. My face heated as I realized how foolish I must have appeared, confessing to Bash how I wanted to stay here with him and become a fae. How I loved this realm. Naive, young mortal. He'd played me well. He'd almost gotten me to steal the power of an ambassador for him—and to do so willingly.

While I fawned over him, he must have been laughing at me.

I could cry. I could scream. But the trumpets blasted again.

"You have to go," Odette urged. "It's time to see your realm again. But, Thea, do not use that bracelet."

"I won't," I breathed. "I won't."

She sighed in relief. "We will find another way for you to live."

My eyes went to my bag. I had another way. "I need a moment. You go. I'll be right out."

I watched her leave, closing the door behind her.

If my heart were glass, it would have shattered right there. The worst part was that I'd been warned repeatedly. I'd been told Bash couldn't be trusted, that he was ruin, that he was incapable of love. Yet somehow I believed his pretty words and that he'd fallen for a Mortal Queen. I'd believed, in our short time together, I had changed him and that he was capable of love. I'd looked upon his perfect heart and honestly convinced myself that it would love for me. As if I were special.

Bash would always be the fae whose heart couldn't be cracked. And I'd be nothing but the girl who'd tried for him anyway.

Out of all the tricks in this realm, this one hurt the most. It nearly killed me.

There wasn't time to cry or drown in this pity. Forget about Bash. I'd almost lost sight of my true home. I reached in my bag and pulled out the gold watch. The one to stop time.

I put it on my wrist next to Bash's bracelet. I'd had a plan before Bash convinced me to try his. Today at the ceremony, I'd stop time and escape. I wouldn't be returning to this forsaken realm where queens die and kings lie.

With the watch on my wrist, I was ready to face the fae.

I marched down the stairs and out to the courtyard where the fae cheered and the ambassadors waited beside a chariot. The six kings sat on their thrones, each looking at me with admiration, Bash beaming brightest of all.

My eyes narrowed at him coldly and his smile faltered.

I waded through the crowd to the center where the three fae stood. The silver-haired fae, the silent one, and the black-haired one. Same as last year. The two lanterns Gaia and I had lit were unlit now, waiting for me to return with a new queen.

The ambassadors would be returning with only one.

"Are you ready?" the silver-haired ambassador said.

I scanned the crowds until I found Lord Winster, curling his mustache that had grown back. I held my gaze on him, my eyes asking the question. He nodded.

If things went wrong, I could still control the silver-haired ambassador for the day. That was my only comfort as I climbed aboard the chariot and wished this realm farewell.

"Take me home."

35

THE AMBASSADORS FORMED A
circle around me as the chariot took to the sky, shaking with the
cheers of the fae. As the silver fae and the silent fae watched the
skies, the dark fae leaned closer to me. I put a hand over my wrist
to hide the bulge in the sleeve from the watch and bracelet.

"An hour ago, they cheered only for the fact that we would soon
have a queen again," he said. Even at a distance, where we could
hardly see the palace, we still heard them. "Now they cheer that the
lost one has been returned."

"Will they not mourn for Gaia?" I asked through straight lips.

He straightened. After giving me a look, he shifted outward.
"We have been mourning her for eight months."

His pinched expression almost made me regret my remark, but
I didn't. I'd had enough of this realm. My thumb stroked the watch.
A few more minutes until I saw my brothers again.

The chariot dropped at an alarming rate, and every muscle in
my body tightened. The stars stripped away, dulling in color. The
islands fell back. The air grew colder. In a heartbeat, we had left the
fae realm and now traveled through a void that belonged no more
to one than it did to the other and held nothing of value to make
either side claim it.

I found myself drifting near the silent fae to peer over the edge of the chariot. As my realm appeared, I was overcome with homesickness for the large oceans and the five islands, even with their heat and sand.

The darkness faded, then there it was.

The sparkling, blue ocean with trims of waves cast throughout, beating against the five islands. Ruen sat to the east of the center island, and I absorbed every inch of it. It was my first time seeing the island that should have been my home. Banners hung throughout to welcome the fae, even though we'd never touch down there. The people still crowded the streets with their eyes on the skies. Searching for us.

"Why can't they see us?" I asked.

"Protection enchantment," the dark fae answered.

They didn't need a protection enchantment. The mortals adored the fae and would never hurt them. It was the same thing the fae said about their Mortal Queens, but no fae died in our land.

Then the center island came into view, and nothing else mattered. The musicians were playing their song, and it grated against my ears. Somewhere along the way, I'd become accustomed to the music of the fae realm enough to lose taste for my own. It saddened me. What else had I lost taste for?

My skin heated, and I gasped. I tilted my face up to welcome an old friend that once bothered me, but now shone more beautiful than a fae star. The sun. I hadn't seen the sun in a year. The rays seeped into my cheeks to spread life through my body as if restarting my heart after it had sat still for too long. As the chariot dipped toward the governor's house, dust found its way to our noses and I smiled. I was home.

No one would trick me here. People said what they meant, and they gave friendship freely. No one would fool me into loving them on the five islands.

Yet as we stepped off the chariot and into the miniscule courtyard of the governor's home, I cast one last look to the sky. The fae realm was closed to me now.

"It's time to choose our next queen." The silver fae led us from the chariot and through the fig trees into the governor's empty home. We moved to the back where the mortals chattered anxiously, eyes never leaving the dais for too long.

Words couldn't explain how odd it felt to be on this side.

I wanted to tear away from the fae now, but I forced my steps to come steady and bided my time. First to fulfill my final duties as a Mortal Queen, then to stop time and slip away. As soon as they announced the next queen, I'd be gone. I wouldn't wait around to lie to her about what an honor this was. She'd be lied to enough.

I'm sorry I cannot save you. I can hardly save myself.

The silver fae opened the back doors, and the crowds caught sight of us with a loud cheer. They waved banners, shouted my name, and sped up the music. All the mortals dressed in their finest, cooked their finest food, played their finest music, and it all hit me differently now. I'd seen riches greater than this. I'd seen beauty a thousand times grander than what was before me now. I'd smelled food sweeter than what drifted through the air. And it was hard not to cringe at the music.

I'd lost my taste for it all.

Just as the thought of the deceiving fae realm put a sour taste on my tongue, the mortal realm no longer satisfied me. I'd have to live forever in mediocrity, knowing what I was missing.

At least I'd live.

The three ambassadors kept blank faces as they took their spots in a line before a glass bowl, while I scoured for my brothers.

"Thea!"

My breath caught as Malcom reached his little arms out from Cal's shoulders to wave. They must have come as soon as the sun rose this morning to find a spot at the front of the ceremony, close enough to touch.

I broke an unspoken rule about the decorum of returning queens. I left the ambassadors and fell on my knees on the stage before my brothers. Tears fell down my face.

"Malcom, Cal." I threw my arms around their necks and

squeezed tight. Malcom braved the wrath of the fae by climbing on the stage next to me and onto my lap. He wore a new suit that must have cost a small fortune, and rings on his fingers dug in where he clung to me.

Cal smiled through teary eyes, and then my attention shifted to the figure next to him.

"Father." I had no words beyond that. My father stood next to Cal, eyes moist and mouth trembling.

"You are every bit as beautiful as a queen should be." His grey hair had grown out and drifted along his forehead, and that conniving smile was replaced by one that—dare I think it—could be pride.

"Come, Malcom. The fae are looking at us." Cal reached his arms out for Malcom, who went back to his brother. At their side stood Eliza, dressed in a black slip dress with her hair plaited and lips painted, and her hand wound through Cal's arm. She gave me a smile.

I smiled back. When I left, I'd asked her to look after them. She'd done well.

"I will see you very soon," I promised before standing to retake my place beside the fae who were all casting disapproving glances at me.

The silver fae cleared her throat, but I didn't hear the words she said. I was too busy gazing at my family and touching the watch on my wrist, counting the moments until I could escape and be with them. I'd feel their embrace, hear their laughter, and share my stories of the fae realm as if it hadn't just broken my heart.

The silver fae continued with her speech, saying how honored they were to have a mortal girl to rule over them and how much they loved their queens. It took all my strength not to spit at the words.

Somewhere in the crowd, I spotted Gaia's mother, searching for traces of her daughter among us. I tried to pull my attention back to my own family, but it kept going to her. Eventually, our eyes met.

With a heavy heart, I gave her a smile, as if nothing were wrong at all. She smiled back.

I shifted. It was almost time.

"We are ready to select our next Mortal Queen." The silver fae dipped her hand into the large glass bowl to fish around the names a few times. The crowd hushed, and even my brothers stopped looking at me to look at her.

I reached for my watch. Almost time.

They would get their new queen, then I would be gone.

She selected a name and held it up to the crowd. Then she brought it close to her and opened it slowly. My fingers trembled over the watch.

The silver fae's smile was radiant. "The fae have selected their next Mortal Queen. Eliza Nadine Nadell, will you rule over us?"

No. No, no, no.

While the center lit up with the cheers of the mortals' celebration, Eliza's jaw dropped, and the fae clapped politely. Cal and I looked at each other. There was no joy in his eyes.

It was an honor to be chosen. It was all the girls dreamed of. We wanted it more than anything.

But the charm of it had left Cal. Even the thrill he'd expressed when I'd been selected was absent, and his jaw tightened. He'd given up his sister to the lavish fae realm, but now it asked for too much. Now he'd lose Eliza too. The girl who had been his loyal partner for almost five years. The girl who'd stepped up as a mother for Malcom when I left. The girl who promised me she'd take care of them and had done so faithfully.

It was an honor to be selected. But Cal gripped Eliza with no intention of letting go.

It was my father who forced his hand away. "You have to let her go," he said. Cal desperately reached for her again, but the crowd pulled her away. Eliza was caught between looking at the fae and looking back at my brothers. Little Malcom called her name.

My hand lowered from the watch.

As Eliza came through the sea of people, Cal's focus turned to me. Whether he was mouthing the word, or it got lost in the hum of voices, I couldn't guess. But I could make out what his lips were saying as they spoke of what dwelled in his eyes.

Help.

My brothers were destined to lose every woman in their life—first Mother, then me, then Eliza. And in the fae realm, Eliza had no one to protect her.

With a tight heart, I mouthed back. *Okay.*

Eliza climbed the dais next to me. Her eyes were panicked and her hands fumbled with her dress. The silver fae ignored it all.

"Eliza Nadine Nadell. Will you rule over us?"

"Yes." Her voice was meek, and she cast a look at Cal.

My breathing was strained. We wouldn't be long in this realm. My chances for escape were dwindling.

As the fae placed a crown on Eliza's head, her hand moved slightly to brush against mine. I squeezed it.

If I left, Eliza would surely die. It seemed the fae held one last trick. I had no choice but to stay with her.

Eliza and I stood side by side in the presence of the fae as the realm clapped for us, our chins held high—the two fated Mortal Queens. She had no idea what awaited us. I did. Fear was not a good look on a queen, and neither was rage. Right now, both consumed me.

The silver fae smiled as if she knew what she'd just done to me. "Are you ready?" she asked Eliza.

Eliza looked to me. I strengthened my grip on her hand. "We will go to your home to get your things."

"Your home," she corrected in a small voice. "My things are there."

That was one small solace. I'd see my brothers once more. Already they were peeling through the crowd with Father behind them, sprinting back to our home.

The fae nodded and turned to the governor's house.

Eliza pulled me back.

"I know it's an honor," she whispered. I could hardly hear her over the blast of the mortals behind us, still waving their ribbons and consoling daughters who weren't chosen. Eliza gave them a longing look. "But I don't want to go. I want to stay with Cal and Malcom."

I closed my eyes. "I know. I do too."

My fingers went to my watch again. Could she escape with me? Gaia's watch worked for both of us, so maybe mine could work for two as well. We could freeze time and both run.

But my mind recalled what Odette told me of the eight dark months without their queens, how the fae prowled the realm to find us. We couldn't both hope to escape their clutches, and Cal and Malcom wouldn't be spared from their wrath if they harbored lost queens. We could run, but we could never hope to escape them now.

Truthfully, my plan may never have worked, even when I planned to escape alone.

"We will find a way back to them," I promised her.

Her lips tightened. "Gaia didn't return." Her tone was too sharp to be anything other than accusing.

The ambassadors had realized their queens didn't follow, and they sent a low sound of displeasure that wrapped around us. Eliza trembled.

"We will return," I said with force. I touched her arm. "But now Cal and Malcom are waiting."

She appeared to be collapsing under the weight of the crown, and her breathing came in short gulps until her face was white and her body unstable. She couldn't fall apart on me now. She needed to be strong.

I half dragged her after me. The fae waited until we'd passed to walk behind us through the familiar, dusty streets of the center island. The merriment sounded behind us to cover the silence as Eliza shed a lone tear.

Behold, I thought. *The mighty Mortal Queens.* As we walked in a solemn line, it looked like we marched for a funeral.

And for a fleeting moment, I almost used the watch. I almost ran. But then I heard my brother's voice and remembered all I fought for.

If this was how Dhalia had escaped, I'd lost my chance. I'd need a new way to survive.

Father waited at home with the door open as Malcom huddled behind him. Eliza's breath hitched. "How can I feel such excitement and such fear at the same time?" Her hand clutched the neckline of her shimmering gown to pull it away from her neck where sweat had gathered.

"It's a feeling I know well. Luckily, you have me."

"Is it as wonderful as they say?"

I'd asked Gaia the same question. She'd given me the wrong answer.

"It is," I said. She didn't need the frightening bits yet. Let her feel hope for a little while longer. Hope made the goodbye easier. "It's glorious there with every corner drenched in beauty we could only imagine. The wine is richer, the colors deeper, and their kings more handsome than any of our men. And they will adore you with every fiber of their bodies."

Her smile grew at each word until the fear lived only in her eyes, and even then it was hard to find. As we crossed into my home, the smile fell. She spoke in a soft whisper.

"This realm was beautiful enough for me. I didn't need more."

36

A HUNDRED CHANGED DETAILS MADE

home different. It smelled like primrose, and a beige rug had been rolled across the floor that our feet sank into. Framed art clung to the walls, each piece depicting what mortals guessed the fae realm was like. I could laugh at how wrong they were, but my stomach pinched with the realization that my family had filled their home with this crude art to bring themselves closer to me.

The most obvious change was that Father held on to Malcom, tucking his youngest son's small frame in front of his wide body as if hiding him from the fae. Father's hard gaze slid over the three fae before settling on Eliza.

"Cal is in your room," he said. Eliza nodded and ran up the stairs.

The silver fae scowled and moved as if to go after her, but I held her back. "Give her one minute," I commanded.

The other fae exchanged glances, but the silver fae's eyes glazed over and she stepped back. "Yes, my Queen."

Either she respected my rank, or Lord Winster had truly come through for me.

I knelt for Malcom, and he broke away from Father to wrap his arms around me. I took my first deep breath in ages at his touch and closed my eyes against the world. His curls tickled my neck, and his arms were tight enough to bruise, but I held on fiercely.

The entire splendor of the fae realm couldn't compare to the beauty of this one small child. At only five—no, he'd be six now—Malcom was all that was pure and innocent and good.

I might regret this. One day, this might be an obvious mistake.

But I knew that all too soon the fae would be placing a mask over Eliza's face and earrings in her ears, and we'd be gone.

I need this. It's worth it.

I strained to reach for the watch on my wrist, and before I could give my logical side time to assess the decision, I pressed the button.

Time froze.

The fae were looking to the stairs for their new queen to return, my father was watching me with his blue eyes glistening, and Malcom's arms were still around me. I couldn't give him extra time. To him, this embrace would last no more than a few breaths, but I could take the next precious twelve minutes and hold tight to one of the most important people in my life.

Tears rolled down my cheeks. Those tears turned to uncontrolled weeping.

I cried for my brothers, whom I wouldn't get to see again. I cried for Eliza, who was being stolen away. I cried at the lost relationship with Bash. I cried for Gaia. This year had chipped away so many pieces of my heart. I was as broken as little Antonio with his missing arm. I'd thought myself strong, but as I hugged my brother, I looked over to my father to let his words echo in my ears.

You are not ready for the fae realm.

He'd been right all along, and I'd still never learn how he knew.

His jacket was pressed and his hair combed in a way he'd only ever styled it before Mother went missing. His face was clean, nails trimmed, and he wore a fine watch on his wrist, something that before would have been a token to bet away. Something had changed here since I'd left, something more than I originally thought. From the way Malcom had gripped Father's hand and inched closer to him in the presence of the fae, I could see the bridge between my father and my brothers was not as broken as before. Repairs had been made. As I studied him, my father blinked.

Every muscle tensed in my body, and my arms dropped from Malcom. Father took in air as if he'd been holding his breath.

I gasped at him. "How?" Even the ambassadors were trapped in my frozen time, yet my father straightened his jacket and stretched his legs.

"I've long since guarded myself from fae enchantments. Parlor tricks won't work on me."

The question remained. "But how? You're mortal."

"You're mortal," he reminded me. "Or have you been swept away by the fae realm enough to believe yourself one of them?"

I stood. "You have answers, and I need them quickly."

"Then ask. There is no better time." He added a wink, but my mind was spinning too fast to process humor. The question from so many months ago slipped out.

"How did you know I would be chosen?"

Father's brow raised as if I'd given him an answer and not the other way around. He leaned against the wall and sighed.

"I received a letter explaining you'd be summoned."

"Who summoned me? Don't give me half answers—I need everything you know."

"I do not know who, but upon receiving the letter, your mother went to the fae realm first to prepare the way for you."

I no longer breathed. I did nothing but stare at him and blink. At last, a word tumbled from my trembling lips. "Liar."

He darkened at the accusation. "Never. Though I'm curious to know why you haven't learned that for yourself yet. What purpose does she have for you that she hasn't revealed herself?"

"You said she's gone," I said accusingly. "You spent months looking for her."

"I spent months in the fae realm with her, until she was ready to take it on alone. Then I returned and prepared you for the day you would join her. Training you to wield weapons, asking Cal to teach you chess, and showing you how to survive on your own."

I could hardly stand. All those years of his ruthless training, followed by his distance. It was to make me strong. All those years longing for my mother. She was caring for me.

"Mother is with the fae?"

"She was when I left her," Father replied. "But if she has not shown herself . . ." The possibility hung in the air between us. She could be dead. I bit my lip hard enough to draw bitter blood. He looked at me, sorrowfully. "There are unspoken rules even I don't dare break, one being that the chosen queens cannot know they will be selected. I couldn't tell you, therefore, I couldn't tell you where your mother was."

I glanced at my watch. Five minutes remaining. The other seven had gone by far too quickly. "You could have told me she was alive."

"Alive and choosing not to be with us? That would have been unkind."

But it was true—she was gone for me. My mind was reeling.

Father wandered over to the fae to examine them. "Everything I did was to make you strong to survive their realm."

I decided to ignore his questionable methods. "How did she get there?"

He turned away from the ambassadors. "I took her there."

"How?"

He cocked a brow. "You've been there a year. Are you not smart enough to figure it out?"

I scrambled to come up with a clever reason. They knew I'd be chosen. Father took Mother to the fae realm. He wasn't captive by fae enchantments. An answer came, and while I didn't think it particularly clever, it was the only one I had. Though, I almost didn't dare speak the word out loud.

"You're fae."

"So, you are shrewd after all."

My mind kept working. The ambassadors had been the same ones since Dhalia's time, so Father couldn't have been one of those. Somehow, without their power, he'd found a way from this realm to the fae one. There must be a bridge of sorts, which meant I had hope.

Father watched me think, until my watch ticked. I pulled up my sleeve to see the second hand drift to the two, then the one. One minute remained.

"Time is almost up, child. Any further questions?"

My breathing quickened. I had a million more questions. "How do I survive being a Mortal Queen?"

He assumed his place by the stairs and shifted into the frozen stance. Only his mouth moved. "I spent your childhood teaching you to fight. You are strong enough to find a way."

I knelt at Malcom's side and wrapped my arms around him once again, holding tight, wishing I could press the watch again. The clock ticked thrice more, then life unfroze. I pressed the watch again, but nothing happened. I was out of time.

"One more minute," I begged.

Malcom let out a squeak. "Thea? You're crushing me."

Prying metal bars apart would have been easier than releasing my arms from Malcom and watching him step away.

Eliza came down the stairs with Cal in tow while we all pretended not to notice their red eyes.

The dark-haired fae approached her.

"Choose a mask." He opened his hand to show the five colors— white, gold, silver, black, and red.

She looked at me. "Black, just like Thea."

The fae frowned. I smiled.

"As you wish. We shall have two queens in black masks." He lifted the mask and secured it to her face. Her blonde hair accented against the black in a way my dark hair didn't, and already she was stunning enough to fit in with the fae.

"Now the earrings."

Cal stepped forward. "Do you have to do this?"

The fae growled as if Eliza was his to protect, but Cal didn't back up. Father placed a hand on Cal's shoulders. "It will be over in a moment."

I was trying not to look at him for fear of the fae seeing all I'd learned through my expression. But I was only half here and half in my mind, as if the answers were there if only I looked the right way.

"Our queens are strong," the fae was saying. He took out the earrings. Cal held Eliza's hand just as Malcom had held mine, and she clenched her jaw against the pain. I could almost feel it with each hole he punched into her, but Eliza didn't shed a tear. Her chin only raised.

"And the pension."

She glanced to Cal. I guessed whose name it was she signed. My brothers would be well cared for on two queen's pensions.

"Say your goodbyes. Our realm is hungry for its queens," the silver fae commanded.

Father frowned at this, and Malcom's arms were around me again. Cal pulled Eliza into him and buried his head over her shoulder.

"You be good," I whispered to Malcom. "And I'll be back soon."

"Promise?" he asked.

I brushed his hair away to see his brown eyes. "I promise. Antonio will take good care of me until I return."

He brightened. "Antonio is a good soldier."

"Yes, he is. The very best."

Cal had released Eliza and was wiping his eyes while Eliza opened her arms for Malcom. He embraced her with as much fervor as he'd embraced me, and I heard him say that Antonio would watch us both.

I crossed to Cal. He'd grown in the past year, and my arms fit around him differently. He still smelled of old books.

"Take care of her," he pled in a low voice. "Bring her back to me."

I was grateful he couldn't see my face. "I'll watch over her."

"She was already a queen in my eyes," came his reply. We reluctantly separated and his eyes caught on my wrist where I must not have pulled my sleeve back over the watch. He lifted my hand. "There must be great wealth in the fae realm. It's very pretty."

My hand flew to cover my wrist. The stolen bracelet was visible as well. While Cal harmlessly looked at it, the silver fae stared too. She gave me a knowing look.

I tried to tell myself I didn't care, but now Bash would be in great trouble.

He deserves it, I told myself. But an enemy was no doubt made today.

"My Queens?" The silver ambassador glanced at my wrist once more before she opened the door and stepped out, where the breeze swept against her silky gown. The other two fae followed her.

Father didn't move until they were out of the house, then he relaxed. I expected him to say something more before I left, but he only picked up Malcom and shoved his other hand into his pocket.

"Farewell, my daughters." It rang like a final goodbye.

Eliza paused at the door to look over my family. Our family. The door shut behind us, and her entire body trembled.

Mine did too. My fingers lingered on the doorknob, and I strained for the last sound of their familiar voices and closed my eyes to imprint the memory of their faces.

The silver fae raised a hand, and the chariot appeared in the courtyard just as before, ready to steal us away. My fingers fell from the door.

Eliza's jaw dropped, and she ran a hand along the shining gold chariot that sent flashes of reflected light across her mask. Her eyes were torn between marveling at it and looking back to the house. The three ambassadors mounted, then turned to us. While the other two stood still, the dark fae lowered himself into a bow.

"It is time, my Queens."

"Do people bow to you often?" Eliza asked under her breath while her feet stumbled over the steps. Her crown toppled from her head and clinked against the foot of the chariot.

"There is a lot you'll have to get used to," I replied, picking up the crown and handing it back to her. She held it close, staring at the hundreds of tiny jewels across the band with her lips parted and her eyes wide.

For the next year, it would be me and her against the fae realm. "I hope you're ready."

She blinked her eyes dry, raised the crown, and placed it on her head. "I'm ready."

ACKNOWLEDGMENTS

It's hard to believe this book is done! This was the sort of story that stole my attention away from everything else and demanded to be written, even though I was halfway through a different project. Huge thanks to my husband, who reads sci-fi but listened to my relentless tale about seven fae kings and a girl who must trick them all. I wouldn't be where I am without your support. For my kids, you are too young to read this right now, but old enough to understand that I write stories and to excitedly tell people about my books. Thank you for your never-ending enthusiasm. I hope one day you love these books as much as I do, for everything I do is for you.

My wonderful publishers, Enclave Publishing—you take my messy, raw stories and turn them into something readable. I'm forever grateful for the care you put into each of your books, and that you allow me to write for you. Everyone on the Enclave team and the Oasis Audio team is delightful, and I can't thank you enough. Trissina, you are time and time again a valuable friend to me when I feel overwhelmed with social media and need help. You are caring and informative as you guide me through the process, and I would be very lost without you. To each of my editors: Steve, Lisa, Sara, Jodi—my readers and I are all grateful for you, because you are the only reason these sentences are coherent.

To my family, who reads all the messy drafts of ideas I send them, and to my in-laws, who don't read but support me with all their hearts.

Thank you so much to my friends across all platforms who cheer me on every step of the way. You are an endless well of encouragement for me, and I'm grateful for each of you.

Most importantly, thank you to God who gave me this desire to write and who guides me on which stories to pursue. I put my trust in you, and you have my heart.

ABOUT THE AUTHOR

Victoria McCombs is the author of The Storyteller's Series and The Royal Rose Chronicles with hopefully many more books to come. She survives on hazelnut coffee, 20-minute naps, and a healthy fear of her deadlines, all while raising three wildlings with her husband in Omaha, Nebraska.

BEWARE THE WATERS.

THE DANGEROUS DEEP BRINGS RUIN TO ALL.

THE ROYAL ROSE CHRONICLES

Oathbound

Silver Bounty

Savage Bred

Available Now!

www.enclavepublishing.com

IF YOU ENJOY

THE FAE DYNASTY

YOU MIGHT LIKE THESE OTHER FANTASY SERIES:

www.enclavepublishing.com